DIVINE ENDORSEMENT

PART ONE OF THE JOHN HARROD TRILOGY

ANDREW J. WEIS

DIVINE ENDORSEMENT

Printed and bound in the United States of America.
Published by Arlington Gate Books LLC

ISBN-13: 978-0-9993956-0-8

With the exception of Raymond Collishaw and William Bishop, the characters in this book are fictitious. All events in this book, including those involving the individuals above, are fictitious. Any similarity to real persons, living or dead, is coincidental and not intended by the author.

Cover Art by David Provolo.
Visit www.AJWeis.com.

CHAPTER 1

ONE WIN. I only wanted one win that mattered in my lackluster life. If I won today, I could at least feel like my college wrestling career was worth all the pain and heartache I suffered through over the last four years. Then, I could face the world after graduation with confidence, and discover what my purpose in life was without the distraction of homework assignments and exhaustive workouts in an overheated gym. Only one more match stood in my way.

My career-long rival, Anderson, loosened up across the mat from me. I eyed him with an intensity and confidence I hadn't felt in weeks. When I turned to the stands to look for my sweetheart, Mary, my eyes locked on those of a strange old man sitting in the bleachers. The old man stared coldly back at me with a focused air of urgency. Among the hundreds in attendance for the NCAA Division I Wrestling Finals, he got in my head faster than Anderson pinned me the last time we wrestled.

I always came up short against the two-time heavyweight champion, but I felt today was my day. Nobody can win all the time, not even him. He cornered the market on wrestling glory and treated me as nothing more than an inconvenience to him. That old man in the bleachers was the perfect distraction I didn't need at this point.

Next to the old man sat my girlfriend Mary, my petite lovely with wavy brown hair that gently cascaded over her shoulders. My parents, who managed to attend this last meet, sat next to her. I felt relieved they were all here. My mom watched with a bouncing knee but managed to shoot a nervous smile my way.

I spied Anderson while I strapped on my headgear. He was an undefeated, egotistical thug with Olympic aspirations and he kicked my ass twelve times over the last four years. Just when I thought I had him, he came up with something that knocked me flat, the tricky bastard. The crowd grew more excited as my match neared, and he sought to close out his college career by pinning me in record time.

I glanced over at Mary and noticed the old man was gone. There was no way he got out of there during the three seconds I looked away. Anderson eyed me angrily, the way he did every time we squared up. I never forgot the awesome failure I felt when he pinned me in the first thirty seconds of the first period the last time we met. If anything, I wanted him to go to Olympic training with the knowledge that he got beat by an average guy like me.

My best friend Dave Sowell, a Texas transplant from cattle country, helped me train for this match with the hope that I'd go out on a high note.

"Don't take his crap, John," Dave said. His chestnut-colored, Longhorn mustache barely stirred as he spoke.

I nodded, hopped up off the metal folding chair, and jogged in place to get my blood flowing. I shook out my arms and hands to shave off some nervous energy, but today I couldn't shake them enough. The cheers from the bleachers echoed off the painted cinder block walls and funneled into my aching ears.

As the seconds leading up to my match passed, I thought of the old man again. I looked at Anderson, then for the old man. Why was I so concerned about him when I had a big match in a few seconds? The judge blew his whistle, and I dashed onto the mat to square off against my adversary. The split second after the whistle chirped, I tackled Anderson for a quick takedown and scored two points. He squirmed on the mat as I struggled to keep him under control. How a guy his size could be so nimble amazed me. Before I knew it, he was on his feet for an escape and got himself one point.

We grappled again. He spun me down to the mat and knotted my arms. The gym lights above me sent a familiar wave of failure through my mind. While I struggled like a fly in a spider web, my eyes squeezed shut, and like it had many times before, the whistle blew. The referee's brash slap on the mat was the final nail in the coffin that was my wrestling career.

I remained on my back for a moment, absorbed my humiliating defeat, and slapped the mat in utter disgust. I shook Anderson's hand then the referee raised his massive arm once again. Damn it.

I plopped onto a brown metal folding chair beside my teammates, and clutched my head. The magnitude of another failure rested comfortably on my shoulders and it never felt heavier.

"John, I know losing sucks, but don't worry about it. It's over now," Dave said in his thick Texas accent and patted my shoulder.

My wrestling career was over. I'd miss the competitions, the workouts, but not the sour tinge of sweat that rooted in my nostrils for the last eight years. I didn't close out my season on the high note I wanted, and I couldn't get over it.

While I wallowed in a heavy dose of self-pity, I trailed Dave, Mary, and my parents as we left the University of Chicago gym and climbed into my dad's Cadillac Fleetwood to go back to my apartment near

Wrigley Field. The car's fan blasted hot air throughout the freeze that gripped the interior but did nothing to warm my spirit. During the ride home, I fielded the usual consolations.

"Don't feel too badly, son," Dad said. "Anderson's a three-time national champ and an Olympic favorite. You have to give him some credit."

"I thought I had him figured out this time," I said. I looked toward the Chicago River at the broken ice sheets caused by a passing barge. "I guess I'm not that good."

I gazed at my 1986 NCAA heavyweight class second place plaque. It'd look great next to my junior league third place bowling trophy.

"John, you're plenty good," Mary said and squeezed my hand. "Give yourself some credit. You'll get your chance one day. Then everyone will see the great guy I see. God has a plan for everyone."

I appreciated Mary's spiritual positivity, but so far, God didn't have much laid out for me other than the rough path of disappointment and unachieved glory I knew all too well thus far in my life.

"Judging from my lack of success, I can already see the kind of plan He has for me. Nobody remembers the also-rans," I said while I stared out the window and my warm breath fogged the car window.

"Everything will turn out fine for you. You'll see," Mary said with her sweet smile that hooked my heart for three years running.

Dad parked the car in front of my apartment building, and we headed inside. I led us inside the apartment Dave and I shared for the last two years, dropped my sports bag on the floor, and shook off my black leather World War Two-style bomber jacket. I hung our coats on a row of coat hooks on the wall beside the door.

I brushed by Mary and caught a waft of lilac from her hair. Warm memories of the first day I met her sophomore year filled my mind. I remembered how my face flushed when she smiled at me that first time. I knew then that she was the girl for me.

"Well, I'm glad we got to see your last wrestling match, son," Dad said as he gripped his brown leather fur-lined gloves.

"I wish the result were different, but thanks for coming out," I said. "At least you got to see me win a couple prelim matches yesterday, so the trip wasn't a total waste."

"Come on, John enough of the sad sack stuff. I'm proud of you."

"We both are," Mom said. She reached up to my head and pulled it down toward her to kiss me.

"Thanks," I said. "I did everything I could but still got my butt handed to me on a platter."

"You'll do great things with your life, John. This is just wrestling, so keep it in perspective. You'll find your purpose." Mom caressed my cheek with her soft, warm hand. She had an alleviating touch that always made me feel like a five-year-old boy.

"Sure you will, Son. Listen, you mother and I have a dinner date to get to. Don't beat yourself up over this. You have the rest of your senior year to think about what you want to do with your life," Dad said and adjusted his red plaid alpaca scarf.

"You don't need to be sad," Mom said with a proud smile. "You'll be fine."

"Okay, thanks for coming out. I appreciate it," I said.

"You have nowhere to go but up," she said.

After my parents had left, the thoughts of the old man returned.

"Hey, Mary, at the meet, did you notice the old man sitting next to you?" I asked.

"Old man?" she asked quizzically.

"Yeah. Right before my match started, I spotted an old guy in the bleachers. He just sat there staring at me. He totally broke my concentration."

"You're not blaming an old man for losing, are you?"

"Of course not. Do you remember what he looked like?"

"No, I don't. Sorry, John."

I threw my hands up and felt my mouth hang open in disbelief.

"How could you miss him? He sat right next to you," I said. "I know I didn't imagine him."

"I guess I was too busy watching you that I didn't notice him," Mary said.

"Maybe so."

I replayed the moment I first saw the old man. She said she didn't remember him, but I recalled that she slid away from him a little as if he sat too close to her. I didn't want to make a big deal over some old guy who sat next to my girl, so I let it go.

"Mary, you want to go to Sluggers with us?" Dave asked.

"That's a good idea," I said. "You can help celebrate the end of my wrestling life."

"Sorry, but you'll have to go without me again," she said.

"You have to go this time. It's always where—"

"The action is," she said like she had many times before. "We have midterms next week, you know," she said.

She glided her arms around my waist, and a big smile crossed her wondrous face. I kissed her twice and slid my hands over her shoulders.

"You two need some quiet time?" Dave asked with a smug grin.

"I'm leaving," she said with a smile. "Call me when you get back, okay?"

"Sure thing, baby," I said.

Mary grabbed her coat and left. A wave of concern washed over me as I again thought of the strange old man.

"What's wrong, boy?" Dave said.

"I don't know. I'm still bummed about the meet, I guess," I said.

"Sluggers will fix that. You can't stay in moping all night. Clean up, and we'll head over."

Dave had a point, so I grabbed my gym bag and headed for the bathroom.

Sluggers on a Saturday night was always fun, even when I felt down. We bought a bucket of beers, went upstairs to the batting cages, and discussed our approaching plans for the summer.

"You're not going back to Texas after the bike trip?" I asked.

"I thought about it a lot, but I like it here. My Pop wasn't happy because I won't be around to help with ranching, but he has plenty of help already. I told him I'd come down for a visit after we get back. Besides, he was thrilled when I told him I got accepted to grad school."

Upon first meeting Dave, I never pictured him, a ranch hand, as a genius electrical engineer. He breezed through the coursework seemingly without much effort, but I knew he studied his butt off. If I didn't know he was from Texas, I would've sworn he was a biker. Oddly enough, he didn't like motorcycles or tattoos.

"That's great," I said. "I guess we know what you'll be doing next year."

"What about you? What are you going to do after we get back from France?" Dave asked. The metallic clink of aluminum bats on baseballs pierced the Phil Collins music that blared through the bar's speakers.

He had to ask. My grades as a computer programmer were average, but making a career of it didn't interest me anymore. Once on track to play college football, a lame knee injury right out of high school branded me damaged goods. Wrestling proved to be a suitable alternative, except for my misfortune of being in the same weight class as Anderson.

"I'm not sure," I said. "I thought about going to graduate school to learn more about business. Programming doesn't seem sexy anymore."

"Have you given any more thought to pro wrestling? You're as big as Lou Ferrigno."

"The spotlight isn't for me," I said then noticed I was subconsciously gripping my bicep.

I loved weightlifting. Over the last few years, I've trained like a bodybuilder, a powerlifter, and used every other workout combination in between. Being able to lift heavy weights was the only thing I did with confidence. No referee could stop me with his annoying whistle. Besides, I loved feeling strong.

"You don't know for sure," Dave said. "It could be good for you."

"I don't think so," I said.

"All right, if fame isn't for you, how about quantum physics?"

"How the hell am I going to make a living at that?" I bellowed. "I'd need a doctorate first, and I don't have the smarts or the energy to study another five years."

Dave removed a worn, red batting glove from his back pocket and shoved his hand into it.

"You got a thing for time travel," Dave said. "You're good at math. There has to be some kind of job out there for you. Maybe you can find a way to travel faster than light."

"Wow, I thought I was a dreamer. Anyway, time travel is fantasy, but it'd be sweet to be able to go to different times as an observer."

The idea of going to different times and places captivated me. Who didn't daydream about visiting old relatives, making untold fortunes, or walking the grounds of the 1934 Century of Progress Exposition like my grandparents once did?

"All the scientists think it's possible," Dave said.

"I've read the theories, but that's all they are, theories. People will never be able to go back in time, not with machines anyway."

"I guess you're right."

I thought about the prospect of going back in time in less scientific terms. "Suppose traveling back in time is more intangible than physical. What do you pass through if you go through time? Air and space?" I explained.

"Maybe."

"To travel through time, you'd have to know what you're moving through. Nobody knows what the parts are that comprise time. Therefore, how could anyone build a machine to go through it?"

I never bought the idea that a machine could transport a person to a place in a different time. What could a machine do to manipulate something people can't see but only sense?

"It beats the heck out of me," he said as he selected a bat.

"That's why I don't think a machine could work. Maybe there's another way nobody thought of."

"Well, if you do go back in time, don't mess up my life."

Most people fantasized about going back in time to make a fortune through stock picks or buying oil land before anyone knew there was oil there, but not me. The nostalgic perspective of the past enamored me the most. I wanted to observe or maybe live the way people did back then, preferably in the 1930s.

"I'll try not to. Anyway, are you up for drunken batting?" I asked.

"You like to live dangerously," Dave said and chugged his beer.

"Is there any other way?" I asked and smiled. We clinked our beer bottles together and drank. Dave lifted the gate latch and entered the cage.

With my last year of college coming to a grateful end, thoughts of our trip to bicycle across France came into focus. The trip provided a nice diversion until I'd have to decide what I'd do with my life.

Despite growing up in the Texas backcountry, Dave took a liking to the city. Like others our age, he fell in love with the summertime vibe of Cubs baseball. At Sluggers, folks loved to trash talk the White Sox and defended the poor Cubs at every turn.

On a clear Saturday morning, my mom stopped by to pick me up to go grocery shopping at Jewel. We pulled into the parking lot and cruised up and down a couple aisles searching for a parking space. Whenever I entered a parking lot, I usually drove straight to the back of the lot and parked in the first open spot I saw. My mom always had good luck and today wasn't any different as she found a parking space near the store's entrance. The parking lot still had remnants of small, dirty-snow mountain ranges at the back of the lot where the plows piled the snow high a month before. Fifty-degree temperatures melted the snow hills and captured the pollution from passing cars. Those first warm days of spring never made me feel more alive.

"There's a spot near the front. Must be your lucky day, Mom," I said.

"I usually don't care where I park, but I always take the first open spot I see," she said.

We carefully stepped around puddles as we walked toward the store entrance when a blue sedan turned down our aisle. The passenger leaned out, aimed a gun at us, and opened fire. I didn't remember hearing anything only that I felt my eyes bulge wide open as I swarmed my mom and covered her on the ground.

My eyes followed the car as it continued down the aisle. I blinked a couple times, bewildered by what I saw. Inside the car, an odd flash of light like a giant strobe light went off. The car rolled forward, bumped off a parked car, and rolled onto a snowbank. I sprinted to the assailant's car. I pounded on the window but saw there was nobody inside. I ran back to my mom, who lay on the ground motionless.

My heart thumped viciously within my chest as I wrapped her in my arms. With short, panicked breaths, I gazed at her. Her eyes were half-open, devoid of their usual sparkle. I lifted her head and saw a thin stream of blood flow down her cheek. Then a wave of anguish flooded my eyes.

The warm spring breeze swayed the budding branches of the stately oak and maple trees of Rosehill Cemetery. I stared at Mom's grave situated beneath a trio of towering maple trees. Puffy cumulus clouds floated overhead while the pastor delivered the eulogy. The crisp, dry air ravaged my body with goosebumps. I squeezed Mary's hand as my heart tightened with the realization that I'd never see my mom again.

I thought of the countless times my mom helped me when I was a kid. Her softness soothed my soul, and her calm voice took the sting out of the many injuries I incurred as a child. When a car ran through a stop sign and clobbered me when I was seven years old, Mom taught me how to deal with pain. When two older boys used me as their personal punching bag during junior high, Mom taught me how to fight back.

Once I reached high school, I woke up to the ways of my world. I joined the wrestling team where I built my physical strength and much-needed confidence. I grew strong fast and tolerated less from the bully community. Eventually, I earned a reputation for protecting weaker kids, which I embraced. In time, I even won over some of the bullies of my youth.

I attributed everything I learned about the streets to my mom. Her common sense approach to life taught me valuable lessons, most of which I remembered to this day. Tears continued to stream from my eyes all morning. With my mind in a fog, I realized that despite my mom teaching me to look out for others, I failed to look out for her. Then, a tsunami of guilt gripped my heart.

As I wallowed in pitiful nostalgia, the distinct sound of a single-engine plane reached my ears. I looked at the clear skies, but I didn't see any planes making such a sound. The engine abruptly stopped and started again. Nobody around me seemed to notice it. I returned my gaze to my mother's eternal bed as the sound of that plane finally faded away. A bounty of colorful flowers and white lilies adorned her casket. God, I missed her.

After the funeral, we went back to my parents' house in Lincoln Park. I hung Mary's coat on the coatrack stand. My younger twin brothers sullenly climbed up the stairs to their room, while Dave, Mary, and Dad went into the dining room. I moved a small vase of flowers from the center of the mahogany table and put it on the placemat where my mom always sat. I worried about Dad and how he would handle the house with Mom gone. He had a strong personality that served him well as an executive at the phone company, but like the rest of us, he'd have to learn to navigate his way through life without her.

Dad grabbed a six-pack of beer from the refrigerator. He set it on the table, went to the foyer closet, and returned with a small wooden box. We each took a bottle and with labored breaths, we drank to Mom's memory.

"I loved your mother and she loved you boys with all of her heart," he said with a fractured voice. "After she visited Grandpa Devers in Colorado a couple weeks ago, she came back with some things that may interest you, John, considering your upcoming bike trip."

Dave took a swig and silently observed with sadness in his eyes. If I were in his shoes, I probably wouldn't know what to say if his mother had died.

"I don't think I ever met Grandpa Devers. He had a strange first name," I said and reached for the charred lockbox.

"You never knew him. Harrison was his first name."

"What was he like?"

"He was a troubled man. She said he had a lifelong nightmare, whatever that meant."

Inside the box were brittle, delicate papers. A quick volley of mortar explosions unleashed in my mind. I shook my head, and the sounds stopped.

"John?" Mary murmured with a look of concern.

"Sorry," I said. "I thought I heard something. Did you read these, Dad?" I gingerly handled the fragile browned papers.

"I tried but didn't get far."

"This letter looks like it might've been military. It says of Discharge November 12, 1917. Was Grandpa Devers in the army?"

Dad stared as he pondered the question, then he dabbed his eyes with a handkerchief.

"I believe he was in the British Army. Can you make out any words?"

I picked up a section of the paper and it crumbled in my hand.

"I can only make out parts of sentences," I said. "This one has some pieces of sentences. This date looks like 7 September 1917. Engaged in affairs . . . willingness to consort with . . . unexpected disappearance. I can't make sense of this."

"It almost reads like an apology," Dad said.

"It could be a confession too," I said.

"What would he have to confess about?"

"Can we ask him? Is he still alive?"

"He is, but he has advanced Alzheimer's. I remember when he was first diagnosed around Christmas in 1976. The news hit your mother hard because she was so close to him. The last I heard he doesn't recognize anyone anymore," Dad said.

"That's a shame. I guess we'll never know the truth."

Dad excused himself and dragged his heavy heart upstairs to his room. Dave gave me a hug and left to return to our apartment. I spent the rest of the night with Mary, reminiscing about my mom and rereading the strange letters left in her wake. While I pieced together the handwritten sentences, I heard that single-engine plane again.

I stepped onto the deck to look for the plane when it abruptly stopped. My mind suddenly flooded with horrific war-like images as I gazed up at the passing clouds that reflected the dull orange glow of the city lights.

When the sound of an unexpected explosion went off in my mind, I grabbed my head, dropped to the floor, and let out a bloodcurdling scream. As quickly as the sounds plundered my mind, they ceased. While I violently twisted on the deck, I jolted at the touch on my shoulder. My eyes bulged to see who was there.

"John, what's the matter?" Mary asked in an alarmed tone. Apparently, my display alarmed the crap out of her.

"Mary! Did you hear that?" I said between sharp breaths.

"No, John. Come inside." She helped me up to my feet as much as her diminutive stature would allow.

She walked me back inside where we sat at a table in the kitchen. I grabbed my beer bottle and aggressively gulped the remaining contents until it was empty.

"I don't know what's going on with me. Mary?" I said as she seemed to zone out uncharacteristically. Her half-opened eyes made me think she was having a stroke.

Mary's trance-like expression scared me until I saw her lips move. I caressed her shoulder, and she slowly turned her head toward me. Her eyes blinked rapidly and her breathes shortened. I gently shook her and she looked at me.

"Mary? What is it?" I asked softly. "What's wrong?"

Mary's chin quivered, and then she erupted in tears. I pulled her close to me and struggled to understand what happened to her.

"I'm sorry, John," she said as she trembled. "It was strange, like a ghost spoke to me."

"A ghost?"

"Yes, but it wasn't. I don't know what it was."

"It's a bad time for all of us, Mary. We'll get through this somehow."

I held Mary close as tears streamed down my cheeks. I didn't know what I'd do without her.

A month after Mom's funeral, Dave and I focused on our long awaited bike trip across France. The reality that someone murdered my mom still hadn't sunk in. The police didn't have any leads. What did she do to anyone? How did the gunman disappear in a flash of light like that?

The unexplained sounds of war continued to haunt me, but my alcoholic stupors suppressed them, at least temporarily. Dave didn't interfere at first. Soon, my studies suffered. One Saturday afternoon while I recovered from what I declared to be my last jackhammer hangover, we finalized our trip.

"The more I look at this map, the more I think Paris," Dave said as he pulled the tab on his can of Coke and released a hiss of carbonation. "We should find some action there. What do you think?"

"Paris sounds as good a place as any," I said between skull-bashing throbs. I strained with all my might to focus on the map. I hoped that once I sobered, Paris might sound exciting. "Where do we go from there? Even though we'll have about two months to bike anywhere we want, we can still only go maybe seventy miles a day. That doesn't consider hills, extended stays, weather, injuries, or breakdowns. We're not conditioned for this so we might crap out early."

My head spun wildly while I considered what I'd just said. An internal rush to throw up surfaced, but I focused enough to fight it off.

"You look like hell, John. Your flattop grew out, and you haven't shaved in days. You're as pale as a baby's butt in winter."

"Don't worry, I'm done boozing," I said.

"You better be. You better hit the gym again too. You're looking soft when you need to be strong."

I knew what he meant, but there was something strange about the way he said *need* that hit me funny. I quickly forgot about it and studied the atlas. We decided to begin in Paris. From there, we'd continue along the River Marne, with stops at Sezanne, Chalons En Champagne, and undetermined points east.

"How far is all that?" I asked. I placed Dave's sweating Coke against my burning forehead. After a moment of relief from the battle raging inside my skull, I guzzled the contents. The bubbly sweetness stung my throat as I gulped it, and my eyes squeezed shut as I took the burn knowing relief would soon follow.

"About 200 miles. Maybe we should scout some more before going any further. This way leads through some hilly country. I hope we don't bust our butts on the first day but whatever. Is this a go?" he asked and rested his feet on the coffee table. He then tried to sip from his emptied Coke can then set it down on the table.

My breaths came steadily while I successfully kept my innards from initiating any surprise attacks. My mom taught me that time had special healing powers. I felt I'd be better able to negotiate living without my mom in my life after I returned from the trip. I'd love to find the sonofabitch who killed her. Then maybe my healing could begin.

"It's a go. I think this trip is exactly what I need," I said.

Once graduation passed, Dave and I finally headed to Paris. We spent a couple days in the City of Light checking out the usual tourist attractions. Afterward, we set out on our bike ride along the road to Sezanne. I looked toward the early afternoon sun, partially obstructed by massive cumulus billows. The sunbeams stretched beyond the clouds to the far reaches of the horizon. While Pink Floyd's *Dark Side of the Moon* oozed from my Sony Walkman tape player, the roaring sounds of the mysterious single engine plane rudely bashed my serenity. In a frustrated fit of impatience, I yanked off my headset.

"Hey, Dave! Do you hear that?" I shouted.

"Hear what?" he shouted back.

"That plane."

"Are you hearing that thing again?"

"Yeah!"

The bikes squealed to a stop on the gravelly shoulder. Dave turned to me with an impatient look. The engine sound lingered longer than it usually did, and sounded more real.

"Are they the same as before or different?" he asked with a sharp tone. He seemed to lose his patience with me, and I didn't want to ruin our trip with this living aggravation that took root in my subconscious.

"Different. I can still hear the damn thing!" I covered my ears to break the sound from my mind but wasn't successful.

"Here, take a swallow," he said and handed me his water bottle. "There's no plane, no nothing. It's all in your head."

Instantly the sound of the plane stopped, then I handed the bottle back to him.

"What the hell is wrong with me?" I pleaded.

"It's probably fallout from your mom dying. It might be like shell shock."

"Why the hell would I hear sounds of war?"

Dave started to speak but stopped himself. He didn't have an answer either.

"How much longer will this last?" I asked.

"I don't know, John. It could be hours, maybe never, but don't worry. Losing your mom is a huge blow. Time will help you deal with it."

The mysterious origins of that plane irritated me to no end. Despite Dave's support, the sounds became more frequent, intense, and I grew more weary. Was some power singling me out for a special insanity? Completing the trip was one goal, but getting through this day posed a greater challenge than I expected. We looked forward to this trip for a long time. However, I wondered how Mary and I would handle the realities of life once they hit us. Either way, she was my girl, and we were ready to face life's challenges together.

After riding for an hour along the busy road, Dave stopped in front of a sign with two arrows that pointed north to Reims and east to Sezanne.

"Sezanne is that way," Dave said as he pointed down the road.

The rather flat terrain gave way to gentle hills. The gear we stored in our bike trailers didn't drag nearly as much as I expected. However, I didn't expect the easy ride would last for long.

Dave crooned some country western tune, something I'd expect to hear on that Texas ranch of his. Since I grew up in Chicago, I couldn't imagine riding on horseback in the middle of the country chasing an errant calf. In a feeble effort to distract myself, I tried to sing along. Maybe it would take my mind off that damned plane.

Another sign for Sezanne appeared which showed we had another five kilometers to go. Without traffic, the sounds of bike chains and road noise filled my ears. The sky above in all its vastness was my only refuge from my torments. I absorbed the vibrant blue and warm summer breeze. I yearned for peaceful times like those people experienced during the years before the atomic bomb. Subconsciously, I kept an open eye, or rather an ear, for that haunting plane, but it hadn't returned.

Like any American who never visited France, I imagined the buildings all fronted cobblestone streets. Excitement mounted as we approached our first stop, the village of Sezanne.

Surprisingly, the village was disappointingly modern, as even McDonald's had set up shop. We pedaled our way through town and stopped in front of a small cafe. The main street merged with another and formed a sharp 'V,' with the cafe wedged in the apex. Dozens of cars passed by and some of them honked at pedestrians who darted across the street, not much different from any street in Chicago.

A large, bright yellow canopy covered an adjoining patio crowded with small tables draped with flapping, white tablecloths. We found a bike rack and locked our bikes among a tangled bunch of others before we ventured inside the cafe. The savory aroma of baking bread sent my stomach on a grumbling crusade. We bought sandwiches, bottles of water, and a six-pack of beer for later consumption by the campfire.

The cafe bustled with activity while I scanned the covered patio for an open table.

"There's one, Dave," I said.

My Chicago accent alerted the clientele to the presence of Americans as heads turned our way with annoyed, yet curious expressions. With a smile, I respectfully recoiled to the table.

A young Frenchman with combed-back black hair, breezy white shirt, and tan slacks, stared at me with disgust until I sat down. I dubbed him, Pierre. I nodded at Pierre, yet he still leered at me in the same way Anderson did.

Pierre eventually left the café, but not before giving me a repulsed look. Oddly enough, I expected to get a look like that from a Frenchman at some point on our trip. Back home we heard that French people were rude but giving dirty looks was universal in nature. Some people were more obvious about it than others.

"What's with Pierre?" I asked.

Dave watched as the man in question walked across the street, got into a little black Fiat Uno, fired up its little league engine, then drove east.

"I don't know. What'd he do?" Dave asked.

"He gave me a nasty look."

Dave chuckled.

"Were you afraid he was going to kick your ass?" Dave asked.

"Yeah, right. I just don't want any trouble on this trip."

"Well, he's gone so don't worry about him. I'm going to get the map."

I absorbed the view of the merging streets with its traffic and pedestrians who strolled along the sidewalks. The awning trapped the dry northerly breeze wonderfully while puffy clouds floated across the bright blue sky.

Dave returned with the road map and unfolded it.

"How much longer do we have until we get to the campground?" I asked.

Dave placed his thumb on the map scale to determine a rough distance to our stop for the night. "I'd say another three hours at most."

"Great. That'll give us enough daylight to set up camp and knock down some cold ones," I said.

"You read my mind. I think at the next stop I'll get me a new gel seat," Dave said while he rubbed his butt.

"Gel seat? What's the matter? Are you going wussy on the first day of the trip?"

"That's Mister Wussy to you."

We continued riding east to our next stop, Chalons en Champagne. My legs felt the burn of over-exertion as we rode up gentle hills. There wasn't any way we could do seventy miles a day. I figured we'd improvise going forward. The landscape grew denser with trees as we approached Chalons.

We rounded a sharp turn and spotted a sign. An arrow that pointed west read 'Foret de Vertus 3 km'. Another arrow pointed east that read, 'Chalons En Champagne, River Marne 9 km.'

"The campground is about five miles west of here," Dave said, while he studied the map. "The town of Chalons is east of us."

We pedaled for another hour and met the little black Fiat Uno on the side of the road with its hood up. Dave and I stopped riding to offer some help. That was our nature. Maybe we were too trusting, but considering our physical sizes, we didn't feel too threatened. Pierre stepped away from the car then drew a gun on us. Maybe he did want to kick my ass. A burly man sporting a red beret and a thickly stubbled face stepped out of the car and revealed a large revolver.

"Go there," Pierre said in a thick French accent. He pointed toward the forest with his gun.

We reluctantly headed into a patch of field in front of the woods, with Pierre shoving us occasionally so we'd pick up our pace. Chills ran down my spine, but if the right moment surfaced, I'd let them have it big time.

"What do you want?" I asked with my hands raised.

Pierre only waved his gun toward the forest.

My mouth dried up, and a lump grew in my throat. I never had a gun pointed at me before. I've handled many types of guns when I was younger. Over time, I became proficient with high-powered rifles. I went on many pheasant hunting trips as well as numerous target shooting outings with my Dad and Grandpa Ray. However, being at the other end of the barrel reminded me of what my dad always said, 'you can only think clearly when you're calm.'

"You think they want money?" I asked in a whisper.

"Not sure, but I wish I had my gun," Dave said with steely eyes.

"Once we hit the woods, we'll make a run for it. I ain't playing *Deliverance* with these clowns. I doubt they're good shots anyway, especially with handguns and all these trees around."

"I'm in," Dave said with gritted teeth.

We stepped up our pace, and once we reached the tree line, we bolted in zigzag fashion into the woods. I never ran so fast, and despite the danger behind us, we put a sizeable distance between Pierre and us. Gunshots popped behind us but quickly became more distant.

We stopped to catch our breath behind a dead tree near a stream. I slowly peeked around the trunk at the forest behind us.

"Did we lose them?" Dave asked as he caught his breath.

"I don't see them," I said.

"Shit, I'll bet they took our bikes. The French are bike-happy."

"They didn't look like bike riders to me."

"Why don't we cross the stream and then backtrack to the road? Maybe we can find a cop or a ride back to town," Dave said.

"Works for me," I said.

More gunshots flushed us from our makeshift refuge and we darted across the stream. After running for another twenty minutes, the sound of the shots faded once again.

"I think we lost them this time," I said as I caught my breath. Dave scanned the woods behind us. Ahead of us, daylight grew brighter. That had to be an open field or a cliff.

"It looks like we're running out of forest. Want to head back?" Dave asked while he tied his shoe.

"No. Let's keep going. I want to see what's there."

"All right."

Before we resumed our escape, I spotted several unusual grid-like growth patterns on the forest floor. Dave crouched for a closer look then yanked away the overgrowth of weeds. A well-rotted, wooden skeleton about ten feet long and six feet wide emerged. Close by rested several other sections of overgrown frame members.

"John, what is this?" Dave asked.

I studied the relics as well.

"I don't know," I said.

"I think it's a wreck." Dave searched a few feet farther. He found larger pieces and the rusting hulk of an engine.

The odd rectangular shape consisted of warped, rusted metal strips. Tattered remnants of olive green canvas with burned edges hung rotted and drooped earthward.

"I think this was an airplane," I said.

As I continued to pull off the overgrowth, I uncovered a section of the wreck that was once a fuselage. There, I noticed a faded portion of a bullseye marking. The imprint had a red center, a white inner band, and a blue outer band.

Deep thunder rumbled overhead then rain started to fall. I didn't think much of it when a flash of lightning nearby nearly gave me a heart attack. Still, the wreck intrigued me.

"This is a British marking. Probably from World War One," I said.

"How can you tell?"

"It had some kind of fabric covering. The frame is wood, and the engine looks too big to belong to a truck. I can't believe it's been here all this time. There's something written on the side, *aby*. The rest is gone."

I ran my hand along the remains of the vintage aircraft. The roar of the single-engine plane stormed into my mind like never before. Unable to remove my hand from the wreckage, I felt the fury of distant spirits calling my soul. Then, an agonizing scream raged through my head.

Visions appeared before me of aerial dog fighting, bombs exploding, and soldiers attacking. The appearance of a magnificent tree guarded by angels sent my mind into a panic. The image crashed from my consciousness when gunshots chipped at nearby trees. I almost crapped my pants.

"Shit, our friends are back! Come on!" I yelled. We raced for the open field.

We hurdled over a fallen rotted tree, then I stopped dead in my tracks when a circular ring that looked similar to rippling water rings on a stone-struck pond suddenly appeared in front of us. My heart beat wildly as the gunshots rang louder, closer to us. I slowly tried to touch the oddity that rippled in front of us when Dave shoved me into it. I closed my eyes and a dead silence overcame me.

CHAPTER 2

WE TUMBLED ACROSS the tall, dewy grass. The stiffly-pointed tips of the grass blades pricked my face and brushed across my leather jacket without notice. Funny, I wasn't wearing boots or a jacket before. Falling back on years of wrestling drills, we instinctively rolled onto all fours. We then raised our heads enough to see back into the forest.

"Pierre still coming?" Dave asked under rapid breaths.

"I don't see anyone," I said as a gallon of adrenaline immersed my pounding heart.

The old wrecked plane in the woods was gone. The meadow grasses waved gently in the warm breeze. The foliage of autumn had turned to bright gold and with each gust, a steady shower of leaves floated to the forest floor.

"John, this place gives me the creeps," Dave said. "The leaves were green when we left."

My neck hairs stood firm with my eyes opened wide as I scanned our immediate vicinity. Dave looked toward the spot where we emerged from the woods. I noticed our clothes were different, but thanks to the shock of our sudden change in environment, the realization hadn't triggered the part of my brain that controlled speech.

We listened to the distant drone of propeller-driven aircraft and the soft rhythmic popping noises of faraway machine gun fire. The ground around us flinched with dozens of rapid thuds. I looked up, my mouth fell open, and my eyes nearly burst from their sockets.

"Look out!" I shouted. We dashed into the forest right as a huge German biplane bomber crashed where we stood moments ago. A thunderous explosion followed as the fuselage drove into the ground like a massive wooden nail, and its wings crushed into crumpled knots.

One of the German aviators screamed while flames engulfed him. His arms flailed as he tried to free himself from the inferno, but within moments, the fire consumed him.

"Holy crap," I said.

Two French biplanes swooped down, buzzed the wreck, and departed for the sky.

"John, what the hell's going on here?" Dave asked in near hysterics.

"I don't know. Planes like those don't exist anymore," I said.

We watched in stunned silence, confounded at our circumstances. My tongue felt like a slab of dry, gritty meat while I tried to comprehend these most spectacular events. I breathed heavily as if I just sprinted a mile, and I tried like crazy to make sense of our situation.

"What happened to our clothes?" I asked.

We looked over our strange military uniforms. The tight-fitting tan slacks tucked into my dark leather knee-high boots felt stiff. Starchy, white long sleeve shirts and brown leather flyer's jackets completed our attire.

"Dave, this is weird. Our clothes are different, but our watches and fanny bags are still here."

"What do we do?" Dave demanded.

I rubbed my velvet-like scalp in desperation to come up with a plan. Only in my wildest dreams did I imagine myself going back in time. However, I struggled with the one conclusion my heart knew to be true, but my brain denied.

"Say something," Dave bellowed.

"Hold your horses," I said. "First, we were at the plane wreck when Pierre started shooting at us. Then, we ran to the field, jumped over a log that isn't there now, and fell on the grass. Then a big ass biplane nearly crashed on us."

"Don't forget about the ripple thing."

"Yeah. Before we ran, I heard that plane engine in my head again. Only this time I heard sounds of war, and saw a huge tree surrounded by angels with swords. Then we ran into that watery ring-like thing."

"Wait a second. You saw angels?" Dave asked in disbelief.

Dave looked at the burning German plane, the last of it collapsing to the ground in a whoosh of flaming embers.

"I know there aren't any planes like that back home," Dave said. "Call me crazy, but I think we went back in time."

"Hold on, let me work this out a little," I said.

"Work it out all you want, but there ain't no denying it."

While Dave observed the planes soaring above, I mentally walked through our steps and waved my fingers like a drunk symphony conductor.

"Got any ideas?" Dave asked while machine gun fire continued unabated. The occasional stray bullet struck the ground nearby. I didn't want an errant slug to take either of us down, so we crouched behind larger trees for protection.

"I know some time travel theories, but none of them describe what we experienced," I said. "I think Pierre had something to do with it. I'd venture to say he drove us here. That ring we went through must've been the vehicle. It didn't change our bodies, only what we had on them."

"A magical water ring changed our clothes to fit the time period? That's mighty convenient."

I rubbed my chin while I thought things over. Then, I looked at Dave through calculating eyes.

"Since my mom died, I've heard plane engines," I said. "Now I'm hearing men shouting, gunfire, seeing weird trees and angels. Nobody else hears or sees anything but me. If I throw in my Great-grandfather Devers's letters, then maybe all of that caused us to go back in time. Right now, my mind has never been so clear."

"If that ring did kick us back in time, then why do we still have our watches and fanny bags?"

My red fanny bag stood out like goose crap on a black Ferrari. I had to do something with it before someone spotted it.

"I don't know," I said. "Our gym shoes changed to leather boots. Our clothes changed to button-down shirts. Maybe the ring couldn't translate them. We're here now, so we have to deal with it."

"Deal with it? Deal with this, bud. We're here in army clothes in a place dodging bullets and crashing planes, and all you can say is deal with it? That's bullshit, John!"

"What the hell do you want from me?"

"An answer," he replied tersely. "Look, maybe we should try going back through that ring now?"

The water-like ring that transported us here wasn't in the woods anymore.

"I don't see it, but we can give it a try. Maybe it'll appear if we get closer to it."

We ran into the woods where we first emerged. Nothing happened.

"Well that was a waste," I said. "Judging from those planes and our uniforms, I'd say we're in World War One. I believe our location is the same as it was before because the field looks the same. If that water ring thing was a time door of some kind, it's gone now."

"Wonderful. So, what are we supposed to do here?" Dave asked.

"Hell if I know. Maybe if we figure that out, we'll find a way home."

"Okay, John. Time travel was your baby for as long as I've known you, so what do we do? Where do we go?"

Dave crossed his arms and waited for me to lead the way. I turned my wrist and checked the time.

"If the time is right, it's 9:48 in the morning," I said. "Since digital watches don't exist yet, we better put them away. No need to draw unnecessary attention."

We put our watches in our pockets and stuffed our fanny bags under our brown leather aviator coats.

On the other side of the field, the sound of German voices grew louder as a string of German soldiers approached. One of them yelled in our direction, then they started shooting at us.

Once again, we dashed into the forest. During our run to safety, British biplanes dropped from the sky and sprayed the Germans with machine gun fire. With the Germans busy, we slipped into the relative safety of the forest.

Dave and I marched on despite what unknowns lay ahead. In the late afternoon as the sun dropped behind the western hills, we encountered a heavily traveled dirt road. The ground trembled, and I saw a long convoy of military vehicles emerge from around a bend down the road.

We ducked behind some evergreen bushes while the parade of military vehicles rolled passed us.

"Those are Allied troops," I whispered.

"Then we're safe. What're we waiting for?" Dave asked.

"We need an explanation for what we're doing out here in pilot uniforms."

The convoy rumbled along for a good half hour. The last truck, an ambulance, stopped alongside the road as steam violently hissed out of the engine's radiator.

The ambulance driver, a robust woman of convincing means with a Red Cross band wrapped around her coat sleeve, went to the back of the truck and hoisted a sizable steel water jug.

Without warning, the arch in my right foot suddenly cramped. I cringed at the horribly inconvenient pain and clenched my jaw to keep quiet while I shifted position. I didn't notice a dead branch when my knee drove into it causing a loud snap. The driver calmly set down the water jug and went behind the truck. She then aimed her sidearm in our direction.

"All right whoever you are, show yourself!" she yelled in a Brooklyn accent. She then fired a warning shot near our position.

"What do we do?" Dave asked.

"Not get killed. Come on," I said.

I slowly stood with my hands raised. I pressed my foot down a few times to kill the cramp still seizing my foot.

"Don't shoot. We're not Germans," I said.

I spotted her shaky revolver with the hammer cocked. She moved from around the truck, the gun still pointed at my chest. I hoped she wasn't an easily excited person.

"Easy, we're on your side," I said.

"You both pilots?" she demanded.

"They shot us down. We've been wandering for hours. Where are you headed?"

"Chalons aerodrome. Where'd you fly out of?"

Dave couldn't come up with an answer any quicker than I could, so I improvised.

"Chalons. We, uh, left Chalons this morning."

She lowered her gun. Dave and I dropped our hands.

"Are you hurt?" She asked.

"No, disoriented. Can give us a lift?" I asked.

"Sure. Fill the radiator, and we'll get a move on," she said as she holstered her gun.

The bumpy ride on the worn dirt roads played hell with my back. The driver wasn't overly chatty, which suited us fine. Her tired face indicated to me that she didn't seem too interested in us, at least not yet.

The countryside fell into darkness, and the long convoy pulled to the side of the road for the night. A distant town marked by a few flickering lights lay about a mile down the road.

"Why are we stopping?" I asked.

"We can't see the road," she said. "Say, where are you doughboys from?"

"Texas," Dave said.

"Chicago," I said. "Going by your accent, I'd guess you're from Brooklyn."

"Nothing gets by you, huh, Chicago?" she asked and smacked my arm.

"Well, you can call me John. What's your name?"

"Helen. We'll hit Chalons tomorrow morning sometime."

A dripping sound caught Helen's ear. She frowned as she lifted the hood and looked at the engine. I looked under the truck and saw a small puddle had formed beneath the oil pan. She kicked the truck so violently that her hat tumbled off her head. She scooped up her hat then swatted it against her pants.

"That darned hose keeps coming off," she said. "Engine Block told me he fixed that. I have to get me a screwdriver."

Helen marched along the convoy to hit up anyone that might have a screwdriver. The dim light from a distant farmhouse was the only light in the growing darkness. Dave removed a folded newspaper from the truck cab.

"John, look at this," Dave said excitedly.

"I can't read French," I said.

"Read the date, genius."

I read the top of the well-weathered paper and couldn't believe it.

"August 29, 1917?" I asked.

Helen came back with a screwdriver then shuffled under the truck.

"That no good mechanic did a number on me this time. Boy, when I see him, am I going to give him what for," Helen said like a mother waiting to punish her son because he was late getting home.

The slip of her screwdriver followed by colorful profanity, highlighted Helen's frustration with her mechanical skills. Helen scooted out from under the truck, and I helped her to her feet.

"Have you heard of a guy named Colonel Devers?" I asked. "I found out he's somewhere in this area."

"Don't sound familiar. Who is he?" Helen asked.

"My grandfather. My family asked me to look him up once I got here."

Helen wiped her oily hands on her pants and shook her head.

"We can check at Chalons. Until then, get some rest. Who knows when the Huns will want to revisit us?"

Before I could ask another question, she climbed into the back of the truck and plopped onto a stretcher. Minutes later, snoring permeated the olive-colored canvas of the truck covering. Dave and I went to the front of the truck.

"What are we going to do when we get to Chalons?" Dave asked in a soft voice.

"Find the base commander," I said.

"What will we tell him?"

"I don't know, Dave. We'll feel the place out. There has to be a reason for us being here."

"And all we have to do is find out why. Perfect," Dave said and stuck his hands to his hips.

We took a couple blankets from the back of the ambulance to cover us while we slept on the front bench seat. As my eyes struggled to stay open, I looked ahead at the convoy. I couldn't believe we were here during the time of the Great War, but why were we here?

The crisp early morning air swarmed my body with goose bumps. My eyes flickered open thanks to a paranoid fear of hypothermia, so I instinctively wrapped the scratchy wool blanket tightly around me. The first rays of sunlight warmed my face when the rattling of a distant machine gun and an airplane engine rudely snapped me out of the sublime moment when I reached deep sleep.

"Dave!" I shouted. He didn't stir. The plane roared down, and the machine gun bullets struck closer to us. I dragged Dave out of the truck then to the ground with me as he finally opened his eyes after plopping on the dirt road.

"What the hell?" Dave muttered.

Bullets plinked invisibly off the truck as the plane zoomed a hundred feet over our heads. The convoy rolled away while I scrambled around the truck to wake up Helen.

"Helen! Wake up," I shouted.

"What the hell's going on, another raid?" Helen groaned.

"Yeah, let's go!"

"Get ready to crank. I'll get us out of here," Helen said as she marched into the truck cab with her jaw protruded.

I went to the front of the truck, grabbed the crank handle, and gave it a hard turn. The engine started, and Helen floored the gas pedal. We quickly caught up with the convoy within minutes.

Enemy fighters continued to assault us. A pair of bombers forced us to stop when their payloads destroyed several of our lead trucks.

"This ain't good," I said.

"John, look up there." Dave pointed to the sky.

A squad of Allied fighters shot down two enemy bombers and several fighters. With the air threat taken off our shoulders, we picked up as many soldiers our truck could carry. Without a moment of lost time, we followed the surviving vehicles to Chalons.

While the convoy limped into the Chalons air base, Helen got out of line and parked beside a large fuel tank. Crewmen scurried in every direction, unloaded trucks, and figured what would go where. Dave and I watched the activity around us.

"Helen, where would we find the man in charge?" I asked.

"He moves around a lot, but he might be in the Command Center, right over there." Helen pointed to a building that resembled a summer cabin I once stayed in during a family vacation in Wisconsin. A look of anger washed over her as she spied the hangar.

"Hey, Engine Block, can you take another look?" she yelled.

The mechanic groaned upon seeing Helen. Maybe he'll fix the truck right this time.

"Old Faithful here sprung another leak," she bellowed, then kicked the truck bumper.

The mechanic grumbled as he crawled underneath the simple truck. From the looks of it, I'd guess the engine didn't have more than a hundred parts.

"Did you make it a point to hit every rock along the way?" the mechanic bickered.

"Don't give me any guff, axel-brain. Just fix it," she said. She crossed her arms and leaned against the front fender.

"Thanks for the lift, Helen," I said.

Helen nodded. "Good luck, Chicago. See you around," she said.

I surveyed the busy air base while we walked toward the Command Center. We didn't want to fight in any war any time soon, but I figured that fantasy would die fast. I noted how unusually clean the air seemed. The smog of the cities wouldn't choke the skies for years to come. A northerly breeze wafted through the trees and carried with it a rich pine scent.

Near the base entrance sat several large hangars where crewmen serviced all the planes. The canvas-covered mess hall reminded me of the one shown in the *M.A.S.H.* television show. The shower tent looked crude and had an adjoining galvanized tank mounted on a platform a dozen feet off the ground. The tank supplied water for the showers and for the camp in general. Behind the mess hall, stood a collection of sprouting olive-drab teepee-like tents planted in four endless rows.

"Since we can't exactly show them our driver's licenses, we'll say our equipment along with our orders got lost in the raid. Until we know anything for sure, let me do the talking, okay?" I asked.

"You're the boss," Dave said.

"We can say we're from Chicago. Seeing how we're in pilot uniforms, we'll tell them we're trainees. I don't know what our insignia means, so I can't say what rank we are. Try to remember anything you can from history classes. It'll come in handy."

"I sucked at history," Dave said with disappointment. "Maybe they'll reject us and put us on a boat back home."

"In wartime, they'll take anyone who can carry a gun. We're stuck until we can find a way out of here. We'll have to keep our fanny bags hidden until we can hide them somewhere."

I grew more nervous as we neared the Command Center. The sign above the door confirmed that we were at the right place. A loud argument resonated from inside, with erratic footsteps on a wood plank floor. We stood outside the door and listened to what went on inside. Whoever they were, they were pissed.

CHAPTER 3

DAVE AND I listened intently to the lively conversation that went on inside the Command Center. Whatever was happening in there, it was rough going.

"Doesn't sound good," I said while I leaned against the door. "I can hear three, maybe four guys in there. They mentioned a French guy named Turel a couple times."

"Must be the resident slacker," Dave said.

"I don't know, maybe."

"Let's wait until things cool down before we go in."

A few minutes later, the bickering stopped, and I cautiously opened the creaky plank door. Inside, four men stood around a large makeshift rectangular table that overflowed with wrinkled, marked-up maps.

A scrawny, pencil neck of a man with black, slick-backed hair, and a thin-line mustache leaned on the table while he studied one of the maps. We hadn't even met and already I couldn't stand him.

The officer assessed us from head to toe as he slithered toward us. He stood inches from my face while he looked me dead in the eye. If it were another time, I would've shoved him across the room.

"We weren't expecting new pilots," the scrawny officer said.

He persisted with a cold stare. His yellowish, crusted teeth and raunchy tea breath raped my senses.

"We're Americans, sir," I said with confidence. "If we're interrupting, we'll wait outside."

A stocky man with distinguished admiral-like looks ambled from behind the table toward the three of us. He rolled a cigar between his thumb and finger and leered at the officer.

"Captain Edmund," the stocky man said. His mustache covered most of his mouth. I barely saw his lips move when he spoke. He motioned to the runt in my face to step aside. "I apologize for the captain's rude behavior. I'm Colonel James Marcus, the base commander. You've just met Captain Edmund, who will now remove himself to reflect on his poor manners."

Marcus eyed Edmund like a cop who stumbled upon a criminal caught in the act of a crime.

"Clear out!" Marcus boomed. In a huff, Edmund left and shut the door behind him.

A quiet moment afforded me the chance to work up a plan while my eyes glanced at the seeming new construction of the Command Center. The room smelled of fresh cut lumber and reminded me of the moments as a kid when my dad cut plywood with his circular saw. I loved that smell.

"Yes, Lieutenants?" Marcus asked, with a shade more civility than Edmund. That answered the question of our rank.

"Sir, we arrived with the convoy. We lost our gear when our transport was attacked earlier this morning."

Luckily, I didn't have to lie, at least not at the moment. I figured nobody would waste time researching our origins with the war raging all around us. Out of habit, I did the one thing a soldier should never do in the presence of a superior officer.

"Did I say at ease, Lieutenant?" Marcus declared.

"What?" I said.

"Where did you serve your basic training, at a school playground?"

I ripped my hand out of my pocket and snapped to attention.

"Sorry," I said.

"Sorry, what?" he boomed back.

"Sorry, sir."

Marcus nodded and grew impatient. The more I studied Marcus's face, the more familiar it became. I sucked at remembering names, but damn if I hadn't seen him somewhere before.

"Then you two men are lucky to be alive. You have something for me, Lieutenant?" Marcus asked.

In my pocket, I found a folded paper. I struggled to remove it and, after doing so, dropped it. Marcus picked it up and resumed looking at me.

He unfolded the paper and read. His brow lifted slightly and after he finished, he stood silent for a moment, then let out a sigh of relief.

"What are your names? Who is Harrod?" Marcus asked as he folded the paper and slid it into his breast coat pocket. He swung his hands behind his back and awaited my answer.

"I'm John Harrod, Lieutenant John Harrod, sir," I said.

Marcus raised his eyebrows then turned to Dave.

"Lieutenant David Levi Sowell, sir," Dave saluted.

The colonel squinted at Dave as if struck by his accent.

"From where do you hail, Sowell?"

"Dumas, Texas, sir!" Dave spoke boldly, like a spunky recruit. It wasn't the place or the time for laughter, but I successfully fought back the urge to and followed Dave's manner.

"I see. Odd grooming habit you have. What of it?" Marcus inquired.

"Sir?" Dave asked.

"Your facial hair."

"You mean my Longhorn?" Dave asked and quickly smoothed it out.

"Longhorn. That's what they're calling the Handlebar in America, hmm? Very well."

Marcus's war-torn countenance reflected a man who knew how to pick his battles. Luckily, we weren't one of them.

"Allow me to introduce my staff," Marcus continued. "There on the right is Colonel Francis Eldridge. On the left is Colonel Joseph Weatherby."

Dave and I saluted them, though awkwardly.

Eldridge, a ringer for former Chicago Bear, Dick Butkus, sported an aggressive militaristic determination while he nodded and returned his attention to the map table.

Weatherby, a pasty-skinned recluse by comparison to Eldridge, appeared more like a distinguished gentleman than a war leader. Tall, but not bony like Edmund, his thick graying hair curled from under his officer's hat. He was the oldest of the bunch and probably should've retired long ago.

"Men, don't trouble yourselves concerning your billet," Marcus said as he led us to the door. "I'll make the necessary arrangements to gain you a new allotment."

We followed Colonel Marcus through the Command Center door. Captain Edmund stood near the mess tent while he smoked a cigarette. I nodded at Edmund who gave me a hostile gaze in return.

"Many of the tents are vacant," Marcus said. "Find one without billeting as it likely isn't occupied. You'll meet the other pilots later. In the meantime, familiarize yourselves with the camp. Learn where everything is. I'll check your progress in due time. Dismissed. Captain Edmund, inside!"

Edmund flicked away his cigarette. He nearly clipped my shoulder as he passed me, ballsy for a little guy. Marcus followed Edmund inside and closed the door.

CHAPTER 4

WHILE MARCUS WORKED over Edmund inside the Command Center, I struggled with the idea that I'd seen Marcus somewhere before. Unfortunately, he had one of those faces that you'd see almost anywhere. Perhaps the shock of being in a different time played tricks on my jumbled mind.

"How do you think we did?" Dave asked with hopeful optimism.

"Not sure. I don't think we're in any trouble for now," I said.

"What was the paper you gave to Marcus?"

"I didn't know it was there until I put my stupid hand in my pocket."

"Anyhow, I think Marcus is cool. Eldridge seemed like a ball buster."

I spotted a crewman jogging with a rattling toolbox that looked rather heavy. He turned his ankle on a rock and fell face first on the ground. The tools crashed out of the metal box and tumbled out. He gathered the scattered tools while uttering some standard profanity suitable for the moment.

"What do you think they expect from us?" Dave asked.

"Since we're at an airfield, I'd say they expect us to be pilots," I said.

"Whoa. Flying might be okay, but what about getting shot at?"

"They have to train us first. Maybe we won't even make the cut. Might be kind of cool, though," I said.

I watched a biplane takeoff then bank hard to the left once it cleared the trees. Flying must be as exciting as it looked.

"We're standing here in army uniforms on some airfield in God-knows-where, and you're happy about flying? I don't know about you, but I want to get back home."

"Hey, I'm as baffled about this as you. Until we find a way out of here, we have to lay low. There's something off about that Edmund guy. Something about him bugs me. Anyway, it might help us to get familiar with the place. Maybe it'll lead to the reason why we're here."

Dave stretched and flexed his arms. The soft cotton fibers of his shirt strained under the stress.

"I suppose," Dave said.

"Anyway, I've been thinking about how we got here," I said. "Maybe the sound of that plane I heard was like a heads-up of things to come. Then finding the wreck triggered the ring window, or whatever it was, to open."

"Screw the time travel theories. We're in over our heads enough, John."

"Okay, how you do suggest we get back home?"

The weight of responsibility rested on my shoulders like a two-hundred-pound barbell I couldn't lift.

"I don't know." Dave sighed. "I guess we could only go back the same way we came."

"Until the magic ring appears again, we do what we have to do to survive."

"What if we have to kill people? I mean, we may be bruisers, but we never killed anyone."

I wiped off the sweat dripping down my face then scratched at the patch of whiskers on my cheek that could never grow a decent beard.

"I've never killed anyone either, but if I have to, I'll start with Edmund. Come on, we're not getting anywhere arguing," I said.

The vast airfield stretched for about half of a mile to the tree line. Takeoffs and landings by the world's first flying war machines cut several parallel paths in the grass like wagon ruts on the American Prairie.

Under the warmth of midday, I wriggled out of my flight jacket. I balled up my fanny pack and stuffed it down one of the sleeves. My shirt revealed nasty sweat marks all over my body. I ran my sleeve across my drenched face. We then headed for the tents to search for a vacancy.

Near the far end of the first row, we found a tent with an open view of the airfield. We ventured inside and sat on a cot. We then heard the distant drone of single-engine airplanes.

"Do you hear that?" Dave asked.

Thank God, he had. I thought my demons paid me another unwelcomed visit.

"That's what I've been hearing all these months. It sounds like a bunch of them," I said.

I pushed aside the tent flap and watched several squadrons of Sopwith Camels approach for landing. The bee hive-like drone was incredible. They came in wobbly, like bumblebees on dandelions. Once the planes touched the ground, the pilots steered them toward the hangars.

The aircraft's simple wood-frame construction wrapped in a canvas-like material stiffened with a coat of varnish made them nimble flyers but not bulletproof. They looked fresh from the factory with the British bullseye markings painted on the fuselage and wings.

"Twenty-seven planes," I said. "I wonder how many they started with."

"Easy with the optimism there, John," Dave said.

"Right. Look over there, Marcus is heading for the small hangar."

Colonel Marcus and two other pilots walked toward us. We went toward Marcus to meet them halfway. The remaining pilots mingled near their planes and lit cigarettes. Smoking was pandemic here.

As Marcus and the war-gritty pilots approached, we saluted them. The pilots returned slow, unenthusiastic acknowledgments. Maybe they didn't like our sweat marks.

"Lieutenant Harrod, Lieutenant Sowell, these are your squadron leaders," Marcus said. "This is Colonel William Bishop. There, is Major Raymond Collishaw. These men will teach you the proper techniques to survive in the air. Learn quickly. Most new pilots survive a dozen days, so keep your wits."

With what little I knew of World War One, I recalled that Ray Collishaw and Billy Bishop were two of the best air aces of the war.

"Harrod, you'll fly with Major Collishaw. Sowell, you with Colonel Bishop," Marcus continued. "They have an insurmountable store of fighting experience, so be sure to pay close attention. What you learn from them may save your life someday. Don't hesitate with any inquiries. Collishaw and Bishop, I need a report on today's run before chow."

"Yes, sir," Collishaw said.

Ray Collishaw, a lively take-charge guy with a boyish face, veiled the seasoned flyer he became over the years. A minor scar around one eye didn't detract from his clean-cut appearance. Even though he was a few inches shorter than me, he was slimmer than I'd imagined.

"Colonel Marcus mentioned you two are Americans," Collishaw said.

"That's right, we got here this morning," I said. "I remember a lot about you. I read how you soloed in a day and painted your plane black to scare the Red Baron. You named your squadron the Black Flight if I'm not mistaken. Neat stuff, uh, sir."

Dave swatted my arm. I jerked my head at his judgmental scowl.

"Yes, well, you're best served if you learn quickly," Collishaw said. "Not to be rude, but I need to get some sleep while I have the chance. We get little rest around here. Suppose we begin training before chow?"

"That's fine," Dave interjected. "We'd like to look around a bit before we go up, so you boys go ahead. We'll catch up later."

Collishaw nodded.

"Say, you must be from Texas," Billy said with a faint lisp. He wiped off his flight cap and unleashed his wavy, sandy hair in the breeze. His dusty little mustache had resembled mine before I gave up on growing one since the stupid thing wouldn't grow even.

"That's right. Dumas, Texas," Dave said.

"I knew a chap from a place called El Paso. He died a while ago from cholera. How about you, Harrod? Where's home?"

"Chicago."

"Meatpacker, eh? That's splendid," Bishop said. "We need to report, so we'll see you after a couple of hours."

Collishaw and Bishop went down the grassy aisle to their tent and stole occasional glances at us while they walked away.

"Meatpacker?" I asked. "Is he trying to be funny? Anyway, why'd you hit me?"

"You were like a star-struck teenage girl," Dave said. "You can't shoot your mouth off like that, or you'll get us in a heap of trouble. Besides, they don't know us, so why are you taking this so personally?"

"I guess you're right. Sorry," I said.

Dave shook his head. My face flushed with a dose of guilt while I absorbed Dave's disapproval.

"Anyway, you heard of those guys?" Dave asked to help break up the awkward silence.

"They were the best fighter pilots for the Allies. I'm not sure why they're both here. They usually spread the best pilots around to train new pilots in other units. As real as all this seems, we still have 1986 American mindsets in 1917 France. Any slip of the tongue can send trouble our way like I just learned."

"We'll just have to keep you away from the famous ones. Tell me, John, did you get hard talking to him?"

His emerging grin lightened a tense moment, and Dave's timing was spot on as usual.

"Jam it, Tex. I'll bet Billy got his ass beat a lot when he was a kid," I said.

"With his lisp, I don't doubt it," Dave said.

"Well, I guess we're in the club. Now, all we have to figure out is why we're here. I'm afraid that'll be tough with guys like Edmund around."

"He might be a slippery one."

"If he tries anything, I'll flatten him," I said.

Dave often told me my bark was worse than my bite. As we walked toward the fighter planes by Hangar A, I had a feeling that I'd see how much of a bite I really had.

CHAPTER 5

THE TIME FOR flight training arrived, so Dave and I headed for the maintenance hangars. In my time, the Great War was over for many decades. I couldn't think of anyone who mentioned a word about it anymore. I always found it captivating in that it was the first hostility in human history that transitioned from horses to machines.

Two pilots smoked cigarettes while they leaned against one of many Sopwith Camels lined up in front of Hangar A, the main maintenance hangar for the fighter planes. Hangar B, the big hangar, serviced the bombers. The ground crew toiled endlessly maintaining the battle-scarred planes inside. Crewmen carried out readiness checks after every mission. The heat of the midday sun only intensified the sweltering work conditions as evidenced by the sweat that trailed down my back as we approached the pilots.

"Hello, there!" I bellowed.

The pilots glanced at each other, then at us.

"You blokes must be Americans," one said and cracked a forced grin.

"Yeah, we're Americans," Dave answered with a slight grin.

"I'm Lieutenant Robert Miller. This here is Lieutenant James Shubert. I don't recollect seeing you men about this morning. Did you manage to duck the shout at sunrise?"

Miller, a pockmark-faced lad about my age, wore circles under his eyes that reflected a tired, starved man who obediently moved from one mission to the next. He combed back the top of his pomade-packed black hair. The sides of his head were nearly smooth-shaven. He returned his comb to his pants pocket and looked us over.

"We got here a little while ago," I said. "I'm Lieutenant John Harrod, and this is Lieutenant Dave Sowell."

"We arrived yesterday," Shubert said in a frothy English accent. "Not many escape dawn patrol. That's bloody lucky for you blokes."

Shubert, a balding thirty-something of an Englishman with bushy eyebrows, never made eye contact with us. I figured the war made him into the social flat-liner he appeared to be. Hollow-eyed and thin-lipped, he must've been through some unimaginable crap to mold him like that. Regardless, I felt exhausted after listening to him speak.

"First mission was this morning," Shubert said. "We tallied four Gothas and six Fokkers."

"Six what?" Dave asked.

I'm glad I wasn't the only one having trouble understanding Shubert.

"Fokkers. German fighters."

"Got it. What are Gothas?"

Shubert's jaw dropped as he looked at Miller in disbelief.

"You sots are new. I suppose we'll have to take you lads by the hand and wipe your noses before we begin, eh?" Miller asked, with a nonthreatening grin.

As hard as I tried, it was tough not to look at Miller's brown-stained teeth. His breath was brutal, so I took a casual step upwind.

"Thank you for offering, but we'll take care of our own noses," I said with a smile.

"Gothas are German bombers. Never seen one?" Miller asked.

"We saw a couple yesterday when our convoy was attacked," I said. "One almost crashed on us. I didn't realize that's what they're called."

Even though we must've appeared like idiots, I sensed a mild buddy-like camaraderie with Miller and Shubert. "When is dinner around here?" I asked.

"Dinner? Expecting linens and caviar, are you? Chow's in about three or four hours," Shubert said. He spied his watch with a wide yawn. "See you chaps after."

"Seems like Shubert's done this a few times," I said.

"That he has. After a time, you'll understand his meaning. However, a word to the wise, every time you take to the skies, if you see a kraut, kill him. That's what you do up there," Miller stated. "If you have doubts about killing, you won't survive your first dogfight. See you at chow." Miller then trotted to catch up to Shubert.

I quickly realized our cold, stark reality. There wasn't any glamor here or heroes parading around.

"They make sense," I said.

"Maybe, but, man, they're a pair, huh?" Dave asked.

"Miller seemed okay, but I'm not sure about his partner, Mr. Giggles."

"Something messed up Shubert. A guy like that could snap at any time."

"Killers with a conscience don't last long up there," I said.

Two Sopwith Camels revved their engines and took off down the airfield. The smoky, oily exhaust blew our way. I fanned it away from my face and watched as they went airborne within one hundred yards of starting.

"So what do you know about flying?" Dave asked.

"Nothing. Check it out," I said.

Dave climbed onto the wing to view the cockpit.

"There's nothing here," Dave said in disbelief. "There's nothing but a stick, a metal bar on the floor, some dials, and a machine gun."

"Maybe handling one of these planes is a lot like those computer games we play. Think of it as a big joystick. The plane goes where you move the stick."

"How fast can they go?" he asked.

"Not sure. Manned flight is new. The Wright brothers did their first flight only fourteen years ago. Remember when we saw those planes land earlier today?"

"Yeah."

"Their top speed isn't much more than that," I said.

"You know, I'm almost burning a fire about this, but a bullet could easily pop through this thing," Dave said. He tapped at the stiff covering. "It almost feels like fiberglass."

I slid my hands along the fuselage.

"This won't protect us from anything. Not to worry, just dodge the bullets whenever possible."

"I'll try to remember that. No wonder guys don't last long in these tubs," Dave said.

"The German planes are built the same way. The Sopwith Camel had an edge in its design, which enabled it to make sharper turns," I said. I walked around the wing for a closer look at the engine.

Dave reached into his pocket and palmed his watch with the LCD display.

"Hey, man. Keep that thing under cover, will you?" I said. I jerked my head around to see if anyone saw him.

Dave casually stashed his watch into his pocket.

"Sorry," Dave said. "It's almost three o'clock. Those guys should be here any minute. Speak of the devil, here they come," he said.

Bishop and Collishaw approached from the row of tents, each carrying their flight cap and goggles. The brilliant afternoon sun shone on their tanned war-seasoned faces. Their stride reflected a confidence about their purpose, a comfort where they knew they were going to be fine up in the skies. My purpose was still unknown to me, but my instincts didn't think it had much to do with flying. Collishaw shielded his eyes from the sun.

"Lieutenant Harrod?" Collishaw asked.

"Yeah," I said.

"Chow will be in a couple hours, so let's get started."

"Sure. Uh, but you should know that neither of us has flown a plane before."

"That's fine, Harrod. Marcus asked that we train you and Sowell personally."

"He did?"

I felt honored, but it struck me as a little cockeyed. Why would Marcus go to the extent of assigning the best pilots to train Dave and I of all people?

"John, you come with me," Ray said. "We'll use one of those trainers in front of Hangar B. We'll see you chaps at chow later then review your first outing."

"All right, Ray," Billy said and escorted Dave to their plane.

Collishaw and I walked toward the trainer plane. My stomach nerves acted up as the reality of flying an aircraft sunk in. However, a conflicting feeling of restrained excitement fell over me at the same time. Collishaw appeared more reserved than Bishop, and that put me at ease.

"Have you ever been in an airplane?" Ray asked.

"No, sir, I haven't," I lied, but I couldn't tell him I once flew in a Boeing 747 to California.

"First, call me Collie. Most of us pilots prefer it that way, except for the base commander, Colonel Marcus."

Collie? I'd think of Lassie if I called him that. I liked big dogs, but not long-haired breeds.

"Would you mind if I called you Ray instead?" I asked.

"If you prefer."

"Okay. How long have you been in the war, Ray?"

"About a year. You arrived yesterday, right?"

"No, this morning."

"From where did you say you came?"

"Chicago."

"No, from where were you deployed?"

"Oh, uh, Paris."

I felt like I stood on a frozen lake and cracks in the ice resonated beneath me.

"The convoy took a beating, but we made it," I said.

"Here we are," Ray said and put on his flight jacket.

Ray handed me a pair of goggles, a flight cap, and a white silk scarf. I scanned the insides of Hangar B. Several crewmen serviced four huge biplane bombers lined up side by side. Perhaps after I'm done with this time travel crap, I could work on airplanes. That could be cool.

"This is a Sopwith Camel," Ray said. "This particular plane has been adapted with an extra seat for training purposes. They have a top speed of 112 miles an hour with a range of about 350 miles. You'll need to keep focus, as these planes are wily in inexperienced hands. You can climb to about 19,000 feet, any farther, you'll black out. There are two belt-fed thirty-caliber machine guns. There, on the panel, is the altimeter, fuel gauge, and speed indicators. The box underneath contains rounds for the guns. Questions?"

"Not so far," I said enthusiastically.

"You're one big fella," Ray said and sized me up with a smile. "I trust you can squeeze your way into the cockpit. If you can't fit here, we'll have to train you on a bomber."

"That would be cool."

"Cool? Absolutely, it gets quite cold up there."

"No, I mean, well, let's see if I can fit in there."

I climbed into the cockpit. While I situated myself, my shoulders felt like they might spill over the sides.

"It feels a little snug in here, but I can move around okay." I wriggled on the wicker seat in a vain attempt to gain some extra room.

"Fine. The main controls are the rudder, elevator, and ailerons. Approach the rudder bar as you would the rudder on a boat. Press the right side of the bar with your right foot, the plane moves right. The same goes for the left. The stick controls the elevator. To go up, pull back. To go down, push forward. The ailerons control banking. Move the stick to starboard."

"Starboard?" I asked.

"That's the right side, port is the left side."

"Got it."

I moved the stick and watched as the rudder moved with me. I felt the tension on the cable want to return to the center position, an excellent safety feature to restore my center while in the air.

"I recommend you get used to the movements in both inclines and declines. Those can unsettle you quickly, especially when you're in a dogfight. To increase speed, pull back on the throttle. Move it forward to slow. Good?"

"I'm still good."

"To start the engine, flip that switch into the up position."

"Okay," I responded.

"Now, when we get going, all I want you to do is hold the stick. Don't move it. Feel the way the airplane responds to the movements. It'll be noisy up there, so you'll have great difficulty hearing anything other than the engine."

"Okay. Once we're in the air, how will I know what to do if I can't hear you?"

Ray tapped me on the head twice.

"I'll tap you on your head then I'll motion what we'll do next by moving the stick. Follow my lead. After that, we'll land. Landings are tricky, so I'll do them the first couple of times. Do you have any questions?"

My eyes wandered toward the airfield and watched a wobbly French fighter plane, a Spad, come in for a landing. The Spad bounced hard and startled us as the plane somersaulted forward. Several crewmen rushed over to get the pilot and his instructor out of the crash. The instructor yanked off his cap, threw it away, and verbally ripped into the trainee. At least nobody was hurt.

"That's how you don't land," Ray said and thumbed at the Spad.

"Ray, to be honest, I'm nervous. What if I forget everything you just told me? Can you give me the *Reader's Digest* version of what we just talked about?"

"The what version?" he asked curiously.

"I mean, sum up what's going to happen here."

Ray positioned his goggles over his eyes. "You know what we're doing, so you tell me."

My heart squeezed, and as I did on numerous tests in my academic career, I blanked. I calmed down and took a breath. My mind frantically searched for the learning track Ray took me down. Then in a spark of clarity, it came back to me.

"I'll basically shadow you, right? You'll tap, I'll look and follow the plane's movements," I said.

"Good enough. Let's go," Ray said as he climbed into the seat behind me.

I breathed a sigh of relief. Sometimes I can't stand myself. With a scrambled, attention deficit-plagued mind like mine, it was no wonder I didn't have a purpose in my life. Adrenaline surged through my body as I pulled down my goggles.

"What's *Reader's Digest*?" Ray asked.

I strapped on my flight cap. I wondered if *Reader's Digest* even existed yet. The discomfort of being in a different time period made me feel a little awkward not to mention prone to making stupid mistakes.

"It's, uh, an expression we have back home." I perked up my head. The plane's upward angle prevented a straightaway view. "Hey, Ray, I can't see anything in front of me."

"Look over the sides if you want a better view. Flying also requires some common sense. Okay, all set!"

"Contact!" the crewman said.

I looked over the port side and watched the crewman grip the propeller blade.

"That's you, John!" Ray rapped me on the head. "Set the switch, the choke, then throttle the engine after it starts."

"All right," I said. I set the choke and the switch. "Contact!"

The crewman pulled down on the propeller. The engine coughed, and in a momentary plume of white smoke, roared to life. The oily stench of exhaust blew away as I engaged the throttle and pushed in the choke. The engine vibrations lessened after increasing the RPMs. The engine took on a smooth roar then grew louder as I opened the throttle. The plane slowly inched forward, and my heart raced.

I pulled the throttle all the way out. The plane lurched forward and gained speed as we sped toward the open airfield. We jostled in the cockpit as we accelerated down the uneven field. Then, the plane's tail lifted slightly, and I saw as the forest approached rapidly.

While my hands loosely gripped the stick, I felt it move back. As the stick moved back, the plane left the ground, and cleared the treetops at the southern edge of the airfield. I felt like I rose to heaven while I sat mesmerized by the clouds and the spinning propeller in front of me.

The late afternoon sky with its massive, textured cumulus clouds provided a serene, peaceful backdrop. We cruised across the sky with minimal turbulence when a vision of a wide sea suddenly appeared before me. I knew we were far from the Atlantic Ocean, so I attributed my vision to yet another of my crazy daydreams until we flew over what looked like an angel nestled in the clouds. His eyes followed mine as we approached a place similar to a Caribbean island where turquoise waters gently kissed the white sandy beaches.

The shore gave way to a lush garden where a single magnificent tree with a massive mushroom-like crown stood boldly near the center of the garden. The sweet scent of cherry blossoms and visual serenity made me forget my place. What was this about?

My daydream vanished in the clouds in front of me when I felt the stick move to starboard. I raised my hand to gauge the wind. The cold, cutting breeze stung my cheeks, yet the sun felt warm.

I felt the stick move to port. The plane banked to the left. The motion felt more like a stationary pivot, something of an illusion because the ground was so far below.

The engine strained in inclines and screamed in dives. Banking during a decline was as unsettling as Ray had cautioned. During dives, the G-forces flattened my stomach as we pulled out of it.

Ray tapped my head twice. I took a firm hold of the stick and was in control. How liberating! My senses absorbed everything about the flight. The sensation of the cold racing wind in my face and the first sight of the Eiffel Tower on the horizon permeated my soul. With an iron grip, I felt how the plane responded to my cautious movements. My hands started to cramp, so I relaxed my grip, which became more sensitive to the plane's movements.

We flew around the Eiffel Tower several times then followed the Seine River. I steered the plane toward the blues and purples that ushered in the heavenly beauty of nightfall and slowly consumed the western sky.

While we weaved around the clouds, I flew as though I'd done this my whole life. The fun abstained when I felt a sudden tap on my head. The stick moved to the right and we followed the river back to Paris and then for Chalons.

Soon Chalons came into view. As we descended, the grassy airfield grew closer and wider. We bounced off the ground several times before we touched down for good. I released the throttle, and the plane quickly slowed to a crawl. The cool wind of flight yielded to the warm heat of the airfield. I unhooked my safety harness, pulled off my goggles, and rested them on my flight cap across my forehead.

"That was great, man! When can we go up again?" I asked.

Ray shrugged out of his jacket. He removed his cap and ran his fingers through his hair.

"You were a natural up there, John. However, you still have much to learn. If every day progresses like this, I'm confident you'll solo quickly."

My confidence soared with Ray's assessment of my ability. There were many more planes parked about the airfield now than before we took off.

"Where did all those planes come from?" I asked. "Is this place always so busy?"

Men gathered in small groups around Hangar A.

"Not normally. I'll find Colonel Marcus to see what's developing. Find Dave and Billy. I'll catch up directly," Ray said.

While I searched for Dave, I felt the eyes of the pilots follow me as I weaved through the groups of men. With my flight jacket draped over my arm, my physical grandeur may well intimidate people of this time. Keeping with our rule, I only nodded when I made eye contact and I spoke to no one.

I walked through the crowd from Hangar B to Hangar A. There, I found Dave and Billy sharing a laugh beside their plane.

"Hey, Dave, how'd you do?" I asked.

"That was one wild ride. How'd it go with you?" Dave asked with enthusiasm.

"Great. Ray thinks I'll solo soon."

"Terrific," Billy said, as he untied his scarf. "The sooner you solo, the better."

"I can't believe we're going to be fighter pilots," I said with an excited smile.

"Fighter pilots?" Billy laughed. "You aren't going to be fighter pilots. Marcus ordered us to train you as recon scouts. You can shoot down balloons if you see any, but if you meet any fighters, turn tail and get out of there."

It took a second to sink in, but I felt relieved.

"You mean to say we aren't going to be fighters?" Dave asked.

"Your flying ability's best suited for scouting assignments. The better the photos you get, the better our chances of gaining on the Germans."

"I suppose we wouldn't make great fighter pilots on our first day any easier than making trail boss on our first drive," Dave said.

"Well spoken," Billy said.

I saw Ray weaving his way through a thicket of pilots toward us. Ray clutched his flight cap as if he were afraid to lose it.

"Something is in the works. Marcus was busy with Eldridge, so I didn't have a chance to inquire. However, Marcus mentioned there would be an announcement either tonight or tomorrow. In the meantime, if you want to eat, the mess tent is next to Hangar A."

"All right, chow time. Are you guys going?" Dave asked.

Thanks to today's excitement, I realized that I hadn't eaten a bite, and my hunger pangs swung into high gear.

"Not now. We have to see if we're on dawn patrol. We'll meet you later," Ray said.

The sun set fast, and darkness descended on the airfield. Dave and I shuffled forward in a long line of personnel to enter the mess tent. The delicious smell of cooking food, regardless of quality, was inviting. We followed a line past the food table where cooks slopped potatoes, beans, and bread. The only drink available was tea, but I wasn't about to complain. I wanted to talk about what I saw in the clouds, but with so many men around, I kept quiet.

We left the mess tent with full trays and found a place to sit in the cool night air. Dave saw Robert Miller and James Shubert sitting about ten yards away from us, so we went to join them.

"How was your first time up?" Robert asked. He then took a big bite out of a potato.

"Exciting," I replied.

"Humph. That feeling will pass when you encounter your first Kraut. You know that new pilots only last a couple of weeks?"

"Hey, you were new once."

Robert raised his eyebrows while he scraped his plate. He ate as if he hadn't eaten in days. He sat quietly for a moment then released a gurgling belch, short of having to chew his food again. James never flinched at Robert's manners. Having finished his meal as well, James stood and left without saying a word. Robert watched as James returned to the mess tent.

"What's with him?" I asked.

"Shubes has it bad. His wife and baby were killed during the fighting at Ypres."

Dave set his plate on his lap. At times, when I felt moments of fitting in with the group, reality blindsided me to the fact that we had no business being here. Dying here wouldn't help anyone with anything either.

"He lost his whole family?" Dave asked. "Does he have any other kin?"

"Nobody," Robert said and gulped his tea. "Nobody I know of anyway. He was orphaned, grew up in a boarding home. With no other family, he once told me he hasn't anything left to live for. That's why he named his plane the way he did."

"Like what?" I asked.

"It says *Nobody's Baby* on the fuselage. Since he lost his family, he's scored nineteen kills. He made ace in one day. I've seen him bag a Hun and shoot at him all the way to the ground. He wants them to suffer."

I sipped my tea from the tin cup.

"God, this stuff is strong," I said. The scalding tea scorched my tongue. The sides of my mouth tightened from the bitterness.

"Have you two been flying together all this time?" Dave asked.

"We've been together in this war since flight school." Robert watched Shubert head toward the tents. "Excuse me, boys. I don't like to leave him alone too long. See you after."

Robert jogged up to James and followed him into their tent.

Shubert's loss reminded me of my mom. What James went through was anyone's guess, but I had an idea. My heart felt heavy, and I empathized with him.

"No wonder Shubert's messed up," I said.

"He may have issues, but he seems better mannered than Miller. I've seen pigs eat more civil-like," Dave said.

After eating, Dave and I set our tins onto a pile in the mess tent. We continued to our tent past the dozens of planes that occupied several neat rows.

Dave and I stepped into our tent where we found two footlockers stacked between the cots. We yanked off our boots and rubbed our feet on the cool grass.

"This must be the billet stuff Marcus mentioned. I don't want to deal with this now," Dave said and yawned.

"Why don't we bury our fanny packs in that trunk? It makes me nervous carrying them around," I said.

Dave nodded. We buried our fanny packs in the trunk under all the stuff they gave us.

"All right. You know, something weird happened when I was flying," Dave said, as he pulled off his boots.

"Like what?"

"When I was up there in the clouds, I could swear I saw massive mountains with towering trees swarming with colorful exotic birds. The air smelled like cherries. It was the most beautiful thing I ever saw," Dave said.

The hairs on my neck shot up as chills swarmed my body.

"I saw that too," I said. "I also saw a colorful sea, a lush garden and, get this, an angel."

"An angel? You saw an angel?" Dave asked.

"No, yes, I don't know, but it sure looked like one."

"Did it have wings, white robes, and stuff like that?"

I thought for a moment but couldn't recall any specific details.

"I don't think so. It was more ghost-like than a man standing there in the air."

"You didn't see an angel, John. With all the clouds up there, you probably thought you saw one."

Marcus entered our tent and tucked the flap behind him. His intense gaze, one I hadn't seen so far, alarmed me.

"The angel was real," Marcus said in a soft voice.

CHAPTER 6

I DIDN'T BELIEVE a word Marcus said, yet a crushing wave of goose bumps flared over me again. Angels? I never believed that angels existed but thought of them more as confidence boosters perpetuated by grandmothers and religious leaders around the world. My mind told me I saw an angel in the clouds, but with my imagination, I saw all kinds of things in all sorts of places. I carefully looked at Marcus then suddenly made a realization.

"You were at the wrestling meet," I said as I pointed at him. "You were in the bleachers next to Mary."

"Yes, John, that was me. There wasn't time to take a cautious approach, so I windowed to you to get your attention. We've been following you closely."

"Windowed? What are you talking about?"

"Time windows. You recall those men who forced you into the forest that first day?"

"You mean, Pierre? You knew them too?"

"I only know that they forced you here. You passed through a time window en route to your arrival here."

"So we really did time travel?" I asked.

"Yes, you did. Only angels from Hali can window or permit others to move from one time period to another. It's a divine endorsement granted to you for your assignment."

I looked about the tent and at Dave. My mouth gaped open, while I tried to comprehend what Marcus said.

"Wait. What assignment? What the hell is this?"

"You need to find your Great-grandfather Harrison Devers. There's an evil angel after him. The angel is here, in this war someplace."

"I must find him? Look, I don't know what you're talking about, but so far, you sound like a nut case. All I want to do is get our asses back home."

"If you find Devers, you'll be returned home."

Dave stood then shook his head.

"Wait a second," Dave declared. "We travel through time with divine whatever, and then you come along and tell John he has to find his own great-grandfather, and once he does, we can go home? You're screwing with us. If you're saying we saw real angels, then it stands to reason that you're an angel as well," Dave said with a sarcastic chuckle.

"I'm as human as you are. Others permit my passage through time just like they had with you."

"Why is an evil angel after my great-grandfather? Doesn't Devers have a guardian angel or something?"

"Devers had a guardian, but he was removed to make Devers harder to find."

"What does Devers have that this evil angel wants so badly?" I asked.

Angels. Seriously, what's the point of believing in beings you can never see, touch, or feel? Then, after we die, we see mobs of them? What a great fairy tale.

"Devers is in possession of the last page of the *Book of Ancients*. It's a divine text that describes how to create, maintain, and destroy humankind."

"You mean the *Bible*?" Dave asked.

"It's much greater than the *Bible*," Marcus said.

I laughed in disbelief. I figured Marcus was nothing more than a delusional, shell-shocked army dude.

"Okay, I'll play. If Devers has the last page, where's the rest of this magic book?" I asked.

"It's in a divine purgatory," Marcus said. "It can't be read or its directive executed without the last page. If that evil angel gets the last page, the book will assemble in his hands, at which point, they can do as they please."

"Sounds like an angel problem best handled by other angels. Why use humans?"

"Evil angels are all around. They appear as people looking to trap you, trick you, and kill you when they no longer need you. If angels fought instead of you, then all humankind will be lost since the creator doesn't want humanity to fall under evil control. Evil is intent on recreating humanity in its own corrupt image."

"How do I find Devers?"

"You must search by following a natural course of events. That's the safest way. I won't lie, an arduous journey awaits you two."

Of course. Why on Earth would I expect an easy path?

"I don't believe this. Can I get help from anyone?" I asked.

"You mustn't tell anyone where you're from. You must be cautious of what you do and avoid mistakes that can expose you, excepting the few verbal miscues you've already uttered."

"If you brought us here, why'd you plant us under a crashing bomber? Our death would've ruined everything for you, wouldn't it?"

Marcus nodded.

"Yes. You weren't supposed to emerge there. Those persons that forced you into the time window got to you before we could. You were expected to enter the time window at the campgrounds you planned to stay at on that first night."

"This nightmare keeps getting better," Dave said.

"Your course is now established," Marcus said.

"So the one who finds Devers first wins?" I asked.

"Correct."

"Marcus, you tie my hands, blindfold me, then tell me to keep quiet. How in hell can I find him under these conditions? Look, I'm not your man. I can't even win wrestling matches let alone waltz through a war looking for a relative I never met. You have to send us back home and tap some other guy to do your dirty work."

Marcus worked his mustache. He stepped around our tent and occasionally stole glances at me.

"I'm serious," I said and grabbed Marcus's coat. "Send us home. Now!"

Marcus swatted my hand off him.

"I must go now," Marcus said. "Only when opportunities are ideal may we speak of this matter further. You must observe strict silence regarding what I've told you. Talk of this to no one else. Find Colonel Devers. Your lives depend on it. Good luck."

After Marcus left the tent, my head spun. I struggled to believe anything he said. The angel part scared me to death more than anything. How could I find Devers without anyone helping me?

I never believed in angels. Marcus told me they were with me the whole time. How come nobody else saw them? Did I piss off one so bad that it let me get my ass kicked throughout my life as a twisted form of divine payback? If that weren't enough, why'd they send me back in time to save an old relative I never met and who doesn't even know I exist? This whole thing sucked.

CHAPTER 7

THE OPEN SPACES around the Chalons air base buzzed with activity. I wondered what we'd have to endure to succeed at finding Devers, not that I believed any of Marcus's story anyway. Even if Marcus told the truth, with all the flying we'd have to do, I wouldn't have time to do any searching. Maybe if we checked local towns under the guise of a missing person search, we'd stand a better chance at finding him. Until then, we'd have to play soldier boys.

We continued our training for two intense weeks. We knew our planes inside and out. We spent most of our daylight hours in the air and evenings shooting the bull with the other pilots.

We met Ray and Billy at the mess tent every morning at six. They made it their mission to burn the procedures for handling the cameras while we flew our planes into our memories. The cameras, about the size of a microwave oven, fit alongside the fuselage next to the cockpit. A small hole cut through the wing gave an unobstructed view below.

Once we arrived at the target, we pressed a plunger to take the picture. To reload, we removed the exposed plate then replaced it with a fresh one. Operating the camera one-handed was tricky, not to mention what we'd do if German fighters spotted us snooping on them.

Today started out like every other day. The bugler showed no mercy for anyone. I groaned as Dave arose from his creaky cot.

"This is getting downright silly. John, are you up yet?" Dave asked. Then I felt a sock land on my face.

"Yeah, I'm up," I said and kicked off my scratchy, woolen blanket.

I got off the cot, pushed aside the tent flap, and stepped outside. Dave followed me.

"I'm going batty," I said. "This early morning crap is for the birds. I don't know how regular army guys do it," I said.

I closed my eyes while I stretched. Every muscle in my body made me yearn for the gym, so I cranked out a dozen push-ups on the wet grass. Damn, I got weak fast. I swung my arms in circles, but loosening up physically wasn't helping my mind to loosen up along with it.

"Marcus wanted us here to find Devers, then tells us not to look for him. That's bullshit," I said.

"What about the letters he gave your mom?" Dave asked.

"Only bits of the letters survived, but one of them had a November 1917 discharge date."

"That's not that far from now," Dave said, as he stroked his mustache and sniffled.

Dave stretched his back as he limbered up for another day. He locked his legs, bent over, and tugged at the glistening, dewy, grass.

"Until we find him, or someone who knows him, we have to keep low profiles," I said.

"Sure, but the longer we're here, the easier it'll be to slip up," Dave said, as he wiped his hands dry on his pants.

I didn't know what more to say, so I decided to act on something I could change.

"Anyway, I need a shower," I said.

"Good idea. I'm smellier than a wet dog."

We went back inside our tent, and I cracked open my footlocker. Inside were undershirts, trousers, a shaving kit, towels, gloves, a blanket, food rations, a 45-caliber revolver, and a bar of soap.

Dave strapped on his revolver. He cracked his knuckles and prepared for gunplay. He twirled the gun, flipped it up, and spun it methodically. I grabbed some clothes, soap, and a towel.

"Come on, Doc Holliday, you can play later," I said.

"Just don't want to lose my timing." Dave twirled the revolver into his holster.

I dreaded the showers. Everyone here called it the bath shed. It had a thick wood plank floor, and a box-like surround wrapped in canvas. Who knows what crawled on the floors of this place? The water was usually the same, arctic cold. After a few showers, I was ready to join a polar bear club. On several occasions, the water was lukewarm, thanks to the sun.

Straight razor shaving was an interesting experience. With no electric shavers or twin blades, there wasn't any other option. I figured out which way to angle the blade, but not before suffering through a few nicks.

On our way back to the tent, we eyed the fighter planes parked along the western tree line of the airfield when Dave's towel slid off his shoulder. We paused after he picked it up.

I looked at Hangar A and spotted Captain Edmund tracking us. He flicked away his cigarette and shoved his hands into his pockets. He studied us for another moment before he walked toward the mess tent.

"What's the matter?" Dave asked and threw his towel over his shoulder.

"I just caught Captain Edmund checking on us. We haven't seen much of him the last few days. Now that creep is everywhere."

"I don't know what his problem is, but maybe he's one of those angels following us to see if we'll find your grandpa," Dave said.

"Edmund's too stupid to be any angel."

I felt as though we stood out in the crowd and one mistake would send us before a firing squad. Everyone else on the base had jobs to do, yet I had no idea what Edmund did here or why. We arrived at our tent, where inside we found Ray and Billy.

"Okay, men, it's a quarter past six. Are you ready for another go around?" Ray asked with a grin.

"I'm ready," I said. I smiled at their period terminology. Another go around sounded like a dance routine.

Dave was less enthusiastic.

"You ready, Dave? You look a might pale," Billy said.

"I'm okay, just didn't sleep well last night," Dave said.

Billy smiled as he eyed Dave.

"Buck up there, Texas. The cold morning air will freshen that mug of yours," Billy said.

"I'm sure it will," Dave said and yawned.

Ray and I climbed into our plane. We followed the same preflight procedure as always. I then gave the word.

"Contact!" I shouted.

As I fed the engine more power, the plane rolled, and we headed for the skies. Once in the air, Ray tapped me on the head like before. Flying became routine. I even learned an Immelmann turn, which was a fancy vertical U-turn with a half twist. In quick order, I found a groove in my flying ability. The plane became an extension of me and I didn't have to look at the controls anymore to make sure I moved them in the right direction.

As we approached the base, Ray shadowed the stick for the landing but allowed me to do most of it on my own. Ray discussed my progress while the ground crew refueled our plane. After establishing a new course of instruction, we went up again. I flew three more times, improving another notch with each outing.

The late afternoon sun began its descent as we returned from our fourth outing of the day. Ray and Billy held a private discussion then turned to Dave and me.

"How do you two feel up there?" Billy asked as he unbuttoned his coat.

"Like riding my horse back home," Dave said with confidence.

"How about you, John?" Ray asked as he wiped off his flight cap.

"I feel good up there too."

"Now, once the planes are refueled, you men will go up again, this time alone. You're ready," Ray said then removed his jacket.

"You mean solo?" I asked.

Doing anything on my own for the first time sent my bowels into nervous overdrive. The biggest problem with flying solo was the thought of coming down without help, and there weren't any bathrooms in the clouds in case my stomach nerves took over.

"Your efforts have been your own the last few days. You men are ready," Ray said then draped his coat over his arm.

"I don't rightly agree," Dave said.

Billy stepped in.

"What's not to know, Dave? You won't be doing anything you haven't already done. I've been letting you do almost everything for the past week."

"No, you haven't. I felt you tapping my head the whole time," Dave said.

"Right, but that's all I did. You did everything else. Keep your wits and don't panic."

Angry shouts caught our ears from Hangar A. We turned toward the commotion and watched as a pilot and his trainee got into a shoving match. They wrestled around for a few minutes before a large mechanic intervened and broke them up. It was the same pilot and trainee we saw scrapping after their plane did a cartwheel a couple of weeks ago. I hoped neither of them was in our squadron.

"I guess we're as ready as we'll ever be," I said. Dave nodded then spied the activity in Hangar A.

"Yeah, let's saddle up. Let the beginners duke it out," Dave gave me a high five, a departure from his usual cowpoke self.

Ray and Billy watched us then swapped curious grins.

"You Americans have the strangest manner," Ray said, as he scratched his head, which was something of a nervous tic of his that I noticed.

"I guess that's what makes us Americans," I said.

"You won't get an argument from me," Ray said. "Billy and I will bring Colonel Marcus up to date on your progress. Good luck, men."

"Okay, Ray."

With the fuel tanks topped off, the ground crew stood ready to start the engines. We climbed into our planes once more. Before starting our planes, Billy directed us to fly toward Paris where we'd avoid any possible enemy encounters.

Dave and I relished our solo over Paris. My heart soared from the freedom I felt moving the plane where I wanted. While I snaked the plane through the clouds, I wondered what it would be like to be in a real dogfight. I didn't give a dime's thought about dying, as I never felt so invincible.

As we soared over the Seine near the Eiffel Tower, Dave engaged me in a mock dogfight. Down below, a long military convoy followed the main road on the eastern outskirts of Paris. They headed toward Chalons but could've been going anywhere. Dust cloud plumes trailed the procession, which looked a mile long by my estimate.

I looked over at Dave and watched as he ran his finger across his throat then pointed at his instrument panel. My fuel gauge needle was low as well, so I gave him a thumbs-up. In return, he gave me the middle finger and a smile. Funny guy, that Dave Sowell.

As we approached the Chalons airfield, my stomach grew queasy. My heart raced and I tightened my grip on the stick. When I remembered what Ray taught me, I took a breath and loosened my grip. The wings wobbled slightly as the ground seemed to reach up and grab me. The plane bounced roughly, but once I felt the tail drag, I killed the engine and coasted the plane short of striking Hangar A. Ray and Billy ran up to us.

"Harrod, next time cut your engine sooner after landing," Ray said sternly.

"Okay, Ray," I said.

"How did you men fare?"

"Aside from a rough landing, it went well."

I removed my flight cap then ran my sleeve across my forehead. The heat of the airfield amplified my adrenaline rush, all the while sweat poured over my face.

"I felt solid up there too," Dave said.

"Excellent," Ray said. "Colonel Marcus ordered a survey of an area southeast of here. Ray and I will fly escort while you two work the cameras."

"We have a mission already?" I asked.

"There's no time to waste."

Nervous pressure showed me different faces. Sometimes it made me run to the bathroom. In worse times, it didn't give me time to worry.

"That might explain the tanks and soldiers southeast of Paris we saw heading this way," I said.

"Sounds like reinforcements," Ray said. "Colonel Marcus will brief everyone after we get the pictures back."

"When do we go up?" Dave asked.

"Get some chow first, then we'll go," Billy said, looking at his watch. "We'll have time before sunset."

Dave seemed torqued up about flirting with death. However, my stomach applauded Billy's idea more.

CHAPTER 8

MY MIND WAS fearful at the thought of flying near an active front where mortar barrages and gunfire occurred every day like the tides. They said the mission would be simple. Despite the assurances, I wondered when I'd get a chance to find Devers then get the hell out of here. I wasn't any good to anyone if I got my ass blown out of the sky. After we had killed fifteen minutes in the mess tent, we headed for our planes.

I strapped on my flight cap and saw Captain Edmund near the Command Center. He puffed away on his favorite coffin nail then scribbled on a small notebook. That little bug crawled under my skin and only fueled my fire by taking notes. He tucked his little notebook into his front trouser pocket then casually scanned the base.

"Edmund's spying on us," I said to Ray as he and Billy strapped on their flight caps.

They turned their heads in Captain Edmund's direction while they shrugged into their flight jackets. Edmund sauntered away from the camp then headed into the woods. Ray and Billy didn't seem to care what Edmund was up to.

"I know they're under duress to make gains in the east, so get the best photos you can," Ray said.

"Didn't you hear me?" I asked.

"I did."

"It doesn't bother you that Edmund keeps giving me mean looks? Now I bust him taking notes. What's his story?" I planted my hands on my hips.

"He has no bearing on our assignment, so I find his behavior trivial at best. Have you angered him?"

"We've never spoken for any length of time. On our first day here, we walked into the Command Center, and he got in my face about something. Colonel Marcus got him out of the way."

"Marcus is keen on you two. From my witness, Captain Edmund and Colonel Marcus aren't on good terms. I've seen this more so this week."

I buttoned my jacket and saw Marcus in front of the Command Center. It seemed like everyone respected Marcus. He stood with a commanding posture then flicked ash off his cigar while he viewed the bustling camp. He nodded at me then walked toward the hangars.

Dave and I climbed into our planes as did Ray and Billy. The four of us took off in pairs, one behind the other.

We flew in tight formation under bright blue skies absent of German fighters. About fifty miles southeast of Chalons, our target approached. Ray pointed at the ground. Our instructions were to take pictures of a five-mile stretch of enemy territory then return. The mission sounded easy, but I hated the idea of flirting with any German fighters we might encounter.

My heart pounded like a war drum while adrenaline raced through my body like a cheetah in full stride. Between each photograph I took,

I scanned the skies for enemy planes. The paranoia at one point caused me to fumble one of the picture plates. It flopped overboard and I watched helplessly as it fell toward the ground. I regrouped my plates and prepared for the next shot.

We circled the target several times to be certain we'd covered all the necessary ground and captured the required images. Ray had made one last pass before we returned to Chalons.

Our foray into enemy territory went unnoticed. Engrossed with the constant buzz of the engine, I gazed out at the late afternoon sun, whose warmth put me at ease. The sensation of floating high above the clouds temporarily freed me from my fears and anxiety.

The rattling of Ray's machine gun shattered my daydream. I looked at Ray who pointed down to the Chalons airfield. I looked over the side and saw that Dave and Billy had landed. We circled again, dropped down, then landed.

Billy supervised while Dave and I stacked our photo plates into neat piles.

"Boy, that's a lot of plates," Dave said, thrilled at our first successful mission. "I hope they turn out good."

"Me too, brother," I said.

"As do I," Marcus said and made me jump. I had no clue he was behind us, and his announcement startled me. "Our goals depend on them."

"We just got back, sir," Dave answered.

"I can see that. Any enemy encounters?"

Dave knocked over his stack of plates then rushed to organize them.

"Not as far as I could tell, sir," Dave said.

"That's correct, sir," Ray confirmed. "Other than clear skies and forest, the flight was uneventful."

Marcus cracked a slight grin. "Good, very good. Harrod, you and Sowell take those plates to the Command Center for development."

"Yes, sir," I replied then saluted.

"Briefing will be after chow in front of Hangar B."

We scooped up the plates, and then headed to the Command Center, while Ray and Billy retreated to their tent.

After we dropped off the photo plates, we headed to our tent and a well-deserved shower. As we approached the rows of tents, Captain Edmund appeared down the aisle. A large man, nearly as tall as I but obviously not a musclehead like me accompanied him. He wore a menacing scowl as if he'd been the loser in a knife fight. His dark red beret seemed typical, but I was curious why a civilian was on the base.

"Looks like Edmund brought his bitch," Dave said.

"I'm way ahead of you," I said.

My eyes fixed on Edmund. We stayed to the right, but Edmund and his friend stayed on a collision course with us. The big man continued toward me, then threw his shoulder into my chest. I barely moved, but I wasn't about to let it slide as an accident.

"You got a problem, pal?" I asked. The short hairs on my neck flared high as I shoved the aggressor and watched him stumble onto his butt.

"Yes, you!" he said then scrambled to his feet.

He threw a weak right cross at me. I caught his fist in mid-throw with my left hand and squeezed his knuckles with all my strength. The result of years of heavy deadlifting clamped down hard, and his knuckles crumpled under my grip.

My vision inexplicably faded to white as an astounding internal strength grew within me. I marveled at the purity of my strength then felt as though I hadn't exerted any real effort. My opponent emitted an increasingly louder groan and a look of surprise washed over his face.

I shook my head, kicked him in the groin, and slugged him square on the nose. He groaned his way into a fetal position with bulging eyes. I then turned to Captain Edmund.

"Edmund, if you got a problem with me, take it up with Colonel Marcus. If that's not good enough, maybe we should settle this now." I said and took a slow step toward him.

Edmund swallowed hard. He took quick, troubled looks at his partner who cringed in pain on the damp grass. I wiped my nose, lowered my head, and stood ready. I sensed an odd, sinister presence about him as if a greater power pulled his strings. I felt my back muscles flare out while I waited for Edmund's first volley.

"Hey, come on now, Edmund," Dave said. "If you got a problem, let's go to Colonel Marcus and clear this up right now. I guarantee you don't want to tangle with John." Dave nodded toward the poor soul rocking back and forth on the ground.

Edmund stared at Dave for a moment then returned his hostile gaze at me.

"You're nothing but trouble," Edmund said. "The moment you walked in on our meeting, I knew you'd be nothing but a headache to me."

"What the hell are you talking about?" I demanded.

Edmund didn't answer, but the anger in his eyes intensified.

"Just stay out of my way, or I swear you'll regret ever coming here."

"Tell you what," I said and stood inches from Edmund's quivering face. "You leave us alone. In return, I'll forget about the damage I thought about doing to your head."

I gave Edmund a steely, soul-piercing glare. His brow furrowed as he shifted his hands in his jacket pockets as if he held something to his belly. We stepped away from Edmund then continued to our tent.

"That bumstead is going to have one banger of a headache for a while," Dave said. "I wonder if you broke any of his fingers."

"My dad always told me not to let my temper get the best of me." I turned to look at my groaning opponent. "Edmund's such a prick. I was so close to kicking his ass."

"If you didn't, I would've. In all the time I've known you, I've never seen you rear up and take somebody down like that."

"It felt weird. It was as though my body was taken over."

"Probably adrenaline," Dave said.

"It wasn't that. My vision went almost all white, as though I looked through another set of eyes. I don't know. It was freaky."

Even though my vision went white, I could still see, so I thought. The strength that coursed through me didn't feel like my own.

Several other pilots observed my skirmish with Edmund and his gorilla. When I looked back at them, they turned away as if they hadn't noticed.

"We can't mess with people like this, John. Marcus said not to draw attention."

"What was I supposed to do? Let the guy take a free shot at me?" I said defensively and stopped walking.

"A nice shove might've done the job. You didn't have to call him out like that. I think your ego got the best of you. You could've let it go, but you went after him like some high schooler, beating your chest with pride."

Dave was right, but fighting my natural instinct to protect was hard to compromise.

"As long as jerks like Edmund are running around, I ain't taking any flak from any of them. It's easy for Marcus to tell us to be good sheep, but that kind of thinking isn't practical. That guy provoked me so I say we do whatever we have to do to find Devers so we can go home."

"So what Marcus said doesn't mean anything to you anymore? You're fine with changing the rules to suit our situation? That's mighty convenient for you, John."

I shook out of my jacket then toyed with a rock on the ground.

"Since that joker back there took a swing at me, we're no longer bystanders. If we have to kill people to get to Devers, then I guess that's what we'll have to do."

Dave reluctantly agreed. Something had to give one way or the other and soon. We entered our tent, but I still fumed. I tossed my jacket onto my footlocker then I plopped down onto my cot.

"Boy, my dogs are burning," Dave said and slid off his boots. He rubbed his foot then shook his head with a frown. "These cowhides got nothing on my snakeskin boots."

I pulled off my knee-high boots then slid my feet along the cool, damp grass.

"I hope we don't run into any more trouble with Edmund. He's no good," Dave said.

"Maybe he got the message to leave us alone," I said.

"Or, maybe he's pissed off more than ever and went to enlist other dopes to come after you."

"Doubtful. He only got a taste of me. I'm ready to Hulk-Hogan anybody who screws with us now."

Dave set his boots beside his footlocker then spotted a shirtsleeve that hung out of it. He opened the lid, searched through it furiously, and let the lid drop shut.

"Crap," Dave said in disgust.

"What's wrong?" I asked.

"Our fanny bags are missing."

"What? Damn it! I'll bet Edmund and his goon took them. I thought Edmund looked like he was holding."

"What do we do now? We can't call him out because we'd expose our hand."

"Edmund wouldn't know what to do with any of our stuff so we might be okay. Besides, we have Marcus on our side to back us up. If Edmund calls us out, we'll say it was Marcus's idea since he knows our story."

"That ain't cool seeing he clued us in on why we're here."

"Big deal. Remember, they forced us here," I said.

Chow time was a couple of hours away. Dave lay on his cot with his mouth open and snored his way to more restful environs. I went toward the tent opening then looked out over the sea of grass that served as the airfield. My thoughts kept steering toward Devers's letters and the evil angel who Marcus said hunted him. In my heart, I felt a chilling suspicion that Devers was here, if not in name, then in body.

A gentle breeze wafted into the tent then riddled my body with goose bumps. I wondered how the following days would play out. Would there ever be a chance for me to search for Devers?

Marcus and Eldridge were planning something big. The war would eventually end about a year from now, then I recalled from history class about an event called a big push. Since it was now September 1917, the big push must be coming soon.

I looked back at Dave, who snored softer. It must be nice to sleep that soundly. I returned to my cot and put my socks back on. I folded the pillow in half and rested my head on my laced fingers. The flapping roof of the tent, like a good dose of Valium, relaxed my fatigued soul and infused me with peace.

A trumpet blared from the mess tent. We sprung up off our cots and tried to catch our breath.

"I hate that damn thing. Every day that bugler ruins good sack time," Dave said. "It damn near gave me a heart attack."

"That's the military for you," I replied in mid-yawn.

I dug my watch out of my pocket and checked the time.

"Wow. We got a couple hours of sleep," I said then returned my watch to my pocket.

"Come on, let's go eat."

We joined the many men who made their way to the mess tent. We picked up the requisite tin tray, but this time the cook slopped on beef stew with mashed potatoes.

"Must be a special occasion," I said.

"Maybe it has something to do with that announcement Ray mentioned."

"Maybe this is our last supper."

We grouped by our usual tree then speculated on what the big announcement might be, but nobody knew anything specific.

A repeated whistle blast pierced the crowd chatter. All eyes turned toward the source. Marcus, Edmund, Eldridge, Weatherby, and several other officers stood at the front of the mess tent. An aide tied a large map onto the side of the tent in plain view of all of us seated on the ground.

"Men, I have important news," Marcus said as he held a thin, wooden pointer. "Over the past several weeks, Allied high command has tried locating a point of entry vulnerable to attack and permit penetration into German territory. Tomorrow afternoon, five divisions will congregate at locations northwest of Chalons. They will stretch fifty miles to the southeast section of our base."

Marcus traced the lines he described using his pointer. "Our established front, the Gate, is roughly ten miles due east and is the focus of our efforts. Tank and infantry battalions will be stationed along this artery, increasing in strength to this point," Marcus said and struck the map with the pointer. The popping sound rolled across the large crowd of several hundred. The position Marcus indicated was near the sectors Dave and I photographed earlier.

"Due to lacking gains on this front," Marcus continued, "General Haig has granted me the authority to assemble airplane squadrons and tank battalions for a special offensive into Germany. We've named this effort the Chalons Offensive.

"Tomorrow, Colonel Eldridge's division will plunge deep into German territory through a weakly fortified location. Getting as many men as possible quickly into German territory is paramount.

"Colonel Weatherby's command is now completing deep mining efforts under a frontal ridge similar to that used at Messines. The mined line runs parallel two hundred yards in front of the Gate for nearly a mile. The principal role of the Gate is to trap as many German troops as possible as the rapid advance of Colonel Eldridge pushes them from the south. We expect resistance to be minimal provided our advance is expedient."

Captain Edmund sat expressionless with his arms crossed. He sucked away on his cigarette and paid little attention to Marcus. When Edmund's eyes met mine, his expression turned to that of defiance, the jerk.

"Air support from Chalons is vital to the success of this offensive," Marcus resumed. "This will be the largest drive thus far in the war. One tank battalion will remain at Chalons. Another battalion will stage at the Gate. The remaining three tank squadrons are in transit to Colonel Eldridge's position near Colmar. I want all flight commanders to report to the mess tent at twenty-two hundred for a final briefing. That's all, men. Dismissed."

Marcus retreated and directed Edmund to remove the map, which he did reluctantly.

"What part will we play?" Dave asked.

"Marcus will want more pictures, probably deeper into Germany this time."

"Great."

"Come on."

Dave and I headed to our tent. I stuck to my reasoning that, to stay alive, we had to act. If history changed because of our actions, we'd have to deal with the results when the time came. In the distance, the echoes of mortar fire resonated across the countryside like a distant thunderstorm.

"John, I've been thinking," Dave said as he pushed the tent flap aside. "With Marcus telling us about angels, how are we supposed to find Devers with him being the target? Following a natural course hasn't done jack for us so far."

"We obviously can't rush things," I said. "Since we've been here a while now, we know the people a little better and that Edmund has it in for us."

"What if Edmund is the evil angel who is after Devers?"

That thought never occurred to me. How would I spot an evil angel if I encountered one? If evil angels couldn't be nice, then spotting them would be easy, so I thought.

"If Edmund is an evil angel, then he could be waiting for us to lead him to Devers," Dave said.

"That could explain the note-taking."

"If Marcus is Edmund's boss, then who is Marcus's boss?" Dave continued. "That'd mean Marcus might be evil as well. Damn. The more we think about this crap, the more we paralyze ourselves."

"I say we have to trust Marcus regardless," I said. "We need that foundation. Anyway, I believe that Devers's letters have a big part in all this. Even though my parents said he wasn't in the war, I think he was. I believe he's here somewhere."

Dave rolled his eyes then took a deep breath.

"Well, that makes our job much easier. Thanks for the wrinkle," Dave said.

"Don't get huffy. It's only a hunch," I said.

"Okay, if your grandfather's here, it could take forever to find him."

"He's close by. He has to be, or we wouldn't be here."

I pulled off my shirt then dug into my footlocker for a clean one.

"I'll have to do wash again tomorrow. I'm running out of shirts. There's no sense time traveling stinking like an ox," I said.

"Dude, you have to keep quiet about that. These walls ain't made of brick you know," Dave said.

Suddenly, the tent wall shook as though someone tripped over one of the tie-downs.

Dave darted outside to see who was there. I saw a man duck into the woods then melt into the darkness.

"Who was it? Did you see him?" I asked.

"I couldn't see his face," Dave said.

"If that was Edmund, we might've screwed ourselves."

"We can't let him go."

"Let's bird dog him," I said.

Dave and I pulled on our boots, threw on our jackets, and ran into the woods after the eavesdropper. I didn't know if we could find him, but sitting on our asses was more than I could take at this point. It was time to hunt Devers.

CHAPTER 9

WITH NOTHING MORE than a partial moon to light our way through the forest, we caught up with the running soldier. We stayed a safe distance behind him while we followed him through the damp, chilly woods to points unknown.

After a thirty-minute jaunt, we stopped and listened to the distant mortar fire. The soldier stopped about fifty yards in front of us. I watched his breath rapidly shoot from his mouth then realized that if I could see his breath, he could see mine, so we squatted beside a tree.

We continued following the soldier's dash through the forest. A short while later we arrived at a dilapidated one-room log cabin. The man went inside and closed the squeaky-hinged door. We sneaked up to a cracked-open window, close enough to see them and hear what they said.

I inched my eyes closer to the window opening, peered through the breaks of a tattered makeshift curtain, and saw Edmund standing before a large French dude seated at a worn table. I observed the Frenchman with thick stubble on his face, while he sat spellbound, staring at a candle flame as it flapped with each of his breaths. His scarred, filthy hand reached for a wine bottle, and raised it to his lips. He gulped from the bottle but didn't seem to care that wine streamed out of the corner of his mouth and onto his crackled black leather jacket.

He emptied the bottle then stood with an unsteady head. He staggered to a closet and threw open the door. Edmund watched with a disgusted look on his face. While the Frenchman returned to the table with another wine bottle, Edmund removed something from under his coat.

"Turel, I found something," Edmund said while holding my red fanny pack.

"Dave, that's the Turel guy we overheard the colonels argue about in the Command Center," I whispered.

"Great. What are they talking about?" Dave asked.

I shrugged and turned back toward the window.

"I waited hours," Turel said in a thick, slurred voice. "Where were you, Edmund? Where's Jean?" Turel's head wobbled as he stared back at Edmund. Turel's thick-whiskered face barely disguised a sneer.

"Jean was unsuccessful in his efforts against John. That isn't as important as what I've found. Look at this."

Edmund set my fanny pack on the table. That sonofabitch went through my stuff. Turel fiddled with the strange little bag with the plastic nylon belt.

"What is that?" Turel asked.

"A gunny sack. I think it ties around your waist, like a belt. The objects inside are most curious."

Turel pulled the zipper and found my wallet. He removed several cards, one of them my driver's license. Damn it.

"Who is John Harrod?" Turel asked.

"The American Jean faltered against. They claim to be pilots. I'm not sure I believe that as I just overheard a curious conversation. One of them mentioned something about time travel."

Turel tilted the license then marveled at the hologram that danced before his eyes.

"Strange. This says *Driver's License*. Who is George Ryan Secretary Of State? What is Illinois?"

"Illinois is a state in America."

Dave and I took a few steps away from the house.

"They know we ain't from here," I whispered.

Dave nodded then gently nudged me back to the window. I pursed my lips as I leaned closer to the window to listen more.

"Date of birth, 1964?" Turel asked with a confused look.

Turel slammed the desk and snatched the wine bottle.

"What else is there?" Turel bellowed.

Edmund removed my Sony Walkman tape player from the pack.

Turel shook his head. As he inspected the player, he grew curious while he gazed at the oddity. He set down the player then picked up the wine bottle. He put the bottle to his lips and then froze.

"Does Marcus know these men?" Turel asked with a sinister lilt.

"Yes. He sent them on a reconnaissance mission earlier today. He seems enamored with them."

Turel walked about the room. Dave and I retreated from the window to keep Turel from spotting us.

"This American, or one of them, is likely the Interceptor. The Escort must be near."

"You had me force them through the time window to scare up the last page, but nothing happened. You said nobody would find us here, and you'd be able to build your armies with Marcus's help," Edmund said. "Now the Americans are right on our laps."

Turel slapped Edmund, but Edmund persisted. I gave Edmund credit. He didn't take crap from anyone including the big guys. While Edmund rubbed his cheek, his eyes intensified as he studied Turel.

"We've given you all the information your German friends wanted," Edmund said.

"What more did Marcus say?" Turel demanded.

"He's determined a point to enter Germany."

"He'll come from the north?" Turel asked through gritted teeth.

Edmund shook his head.

"I tell German contact that you'll come from the North," Turel said.

"No, South," Edmund said. Sweat trickled down his forehead. The soft candlelight reflected off each drop like tiny gold beads. "There's a small position in the west at a point called the Gate. The colonels might be having second thoughts about our arrangement with the Germans. Inform your contacts to head west instead of north."

"Don't tell colonels about these things." Turel stood and shook the tape player, then slammed it down on the fanny pack.

Turel towered over Edmund as he placed his filthy hands on Edmund's shoulders.

"The colonels have new loyalties in the Americans," Turel said. "They know more than they will tell. They betray us!"

Turel grabbed the wine bottle from the table and hurled it against the wall. Glass and wine sprayed all around.

"What should we do about them?" Edmund asked.

"I go to see our German friends at Colmar. I explain that Marcus will wait for Germans to advance. Once the Germans handle Gate, they crush Marcus. You don't get payment now. I don't pay men who double-cross me."

"Then what are you going to do?"

"Kill the colonels."

Turel fell onto the chair and his head wobbled. He lifted his chin and stared at the items on the table. He cracked an evil grin before downing another bottle of wine. I had no idea how he stayed awake after slugging down all that wine.

"There's more," Edmund said softly.

"You anger me, Edmund," Turel said with impatience.

"The Americans know about it."

"About what?"

"Hali."

Turel raised his head then looked at Edmund angrily. I didn't like the idea that they had me made, but everything Marcus told me about my angelic involvement began to gel.

"What have they said?" Turel asked.

"Both John and Dave have seen the tree."

"That's how we start with you. Now you want us to change our plan to save the colonels when you and I both know they need to die."

"I won't stand for your insults," Edmund declared. Turel smiled at him.

"You speak like this when I first take you from the Alamo."

"Speaking of which, I demand that you let my family be. I've done everything you asked."

"You demand nothing. You have a new history. Here you will stay," Turel said then tapped on the table with a collapsing finger. "Not everything about the *Book of Ancients* is known. Maybe John goes mad or dies, like his predecessors. Our success in this war, by killing more people than history recorded, will mean more souls and a larger army for us."

"What if John prevails?" Edmund asked softly.

"They don't know who I am or that we forced them into the time window to bring them here. Someone else got in our way. They brought them to Marcus. Perhaps it was another archangel or more likely an Escort. Now that John and Dave are here, we must be vigilant. If John or Dave is the Interceptor, they'll lead us to the last page. Stay close to them, but don't give them a reason to be suspicious of you. Now leave before you anger me further."

We shuffled behind the house then ducked behind a large pine tree. I watched Edmund hang his head as he started walking back the way we came.

I approached the window once more to look inside. In amazement, I watched Turel take my fanny pack, walk into a familiar watery-looking ring, and vanish.

"Dave, Turel can open time windows. He's a time traveler. He just mentioned something about Edmund and the Alamo," I said. "What are we going to tell Marcus?"

The revelation that Turel could time travel added another weight to my already overloaded shoulders. He seemed fluid in opening time windows, and he knew about the last page. He might be a pawn in this nightmare like me, perhaps under the same pressure to succeed. Maybe he was the evil angel after Devers. Either way, the race was on.

"What can we say? He's in on the scam," I said.

"So, what's Marcus after by hooking up with those two mugs?"

"I think the colonels are selling secrets to the Germans with the help of a time traveler," I said, and then it hit me. "Hey, since the colonels know the country so well, let's let them lead us to Devers. All we have to do is stay close to them. That way, we can follow their lead without drawing attention."

"That'll be hard to do with Marcus putting us up in airplanes all the time," Dave said.

"True," I said with disappointment. "Maybe we should talk to Marcus about this," I said. "It feels like we're in the middle of a much bigger war here than he first led us to believe. Besides, what kind of army is Turel trying to build by winning rigged battles here?"

"I don't know, but I don't want to think about it," Dave said. "Who the hell's going to help us stop what that drunk Turel is cooking up?"

"Beats me, but I do have one question," I said.

"What's that?"

"What's an Interceptor?"

CHAPTER 10

AFTER OUR LATE night excursion, all I could think about was the trouble I was in. Since Colonel Marcus announced his intentions of a major drive into enemy territory, I had to find an opportunity to talk to him about what we witnessed with Edmund at Turel's cabin. I felt disgustingly overwhelmed.

Dave awoke and swung his feet to the ground. He looked about the tent then shook his head. He yawned wide while he removed his shirt. Years ago, while on his parent's ranch, a thunderstorm spooked a horse Dave rode upon. The horse threw Dave then dragged him across open country, which resulted in scars that crisscrossed his back like a city map. He was fortunate to have survived. He stepped to the tent opening where the morning air breathed easier.

"After what we saw last night, I feel like we're getting screwed on both ends," Dave said.

"I know the feeling. I'm curious as hell to see what Marcus thinks of what we found out last night at the cabin," I said and dug through my footlocker for a pair of socks.

"Here comes Ray. Better keep quiet."

"Good morning, men. I need to talk to you," Ray said in a serious tone.

Dave motioned Ray to come inside.

I shook out my shirt and drove my arms through each sleeve while Ray sat on my footlocker.

"Some of the men said you had a scrap with Captain Edmund yesterday." Ray's voice faded as he observed the scars on Dave's back.

"The guy walked into me on purpose and threw a punch. Am I in trouble?" I asked.

"I believe Colonel Marcus isn't abreast of the incident. He would've approached you by now if he knew about it."

"That's good," I said.

"Your problem may be with Captain Edmund. I always thought him to be a strange specimen, but this is out of character even for him."

"Why doesn't Marcus transfer him out of here?" I asked.

"That I don't know. Is there anything, no matter how trivial, that might've provoked this action from him?"

I picked up my shaving razor and honed it on a leather strop. I decided to go with the discussion as if I never heard Edmund and Turel's talk of sabotage.

"We don't know Edmund," I said. "How could we be any threat to him?"

"Whatever he's doing, he gained himself support," Ray said. "Tread lightly around him."

Dave nodded then pointed at me like a stern grade school teacher.

"See that? He thinks the way I do on this, Hoss," Dave said. "Let's stay out of Edmund's way and stick to business."

"Okay, but if he starts anything, I'll finish it," I said.

"I ask nothing more," Ray said. "Dave, what is 'Hoss'?"

"Oh, uh, that's our ranch head back home, Hoss Cartwright. He's a good man."

I quickly brushed on some shaving cream to cover the growing smile on my face. With a sharp razor against my neck, I stifled any chance for laughter. Dave's comedic timing sometimes caught me off guard. Consequently, I'd erupt in laughter at the worst times.

"Yes, now, as you recall at yesterday's briefing with Colonel Marcus, the offensive will begin shortly," Ray said. "Today, we will survey deeper into Germany. If possible, we'll perform three sorties. The ground troops will be in position by tomorrow morning. When the offensive begins, fighting will be nominal. Shortly after, we anticipate the Germans will attack with vigor. Hopefully, they'll be weakened by our efforts."

Dave removed his silk scarf from his coat pocket then tried smoothing it out.

"So, when do we get a move on?" Dave asked.

"Do what you need but be ready in an hour," Ray said.

"We'll meet you guys by the planes," I said.

"Very well," Ray said then left our tent.

As Dave and I entered the mess tent, Edmund came out and shot us an inhospitable gaze. I swallowed my pride and fought back the desire to kick him around like a soccer ball. Like a good boy, I walked by him without making any contact and picked up a tin plate.

"Pass me one of those buns, please," Dave said.

"One brick coming up," I said.

I reached into a wooden barrel containing dozens of miniature bread loaves then handed one to Dave. Devoid of anything that could've added needed flavor, they fought off hunger for a long time. We poured ourselves some black coffee. Without the luxury of cream or sugar, I started liking coffee straight up.

"We have to meet Ray soon, so let's hurry up," I said.

"Right," Dave said with a wad of bread packed in the side of his mouth.

We finished eating then went to our planes near Hangar A. I looked about the grounds, but Ray and Billy weren't in sight.

"Are you lads looking for someone?" a voice asked from the plane next to mine. Shubert stepped around his plane and fiddled with his flight cap.

"Yeah, Ray and Billy," I said.

"Right. I'm flying with you chaps today," Shubert said with a deadpanned expression. "Command got nervous about sending two inexperienced recon scouts, so they asked me to join you. Did you chaps solo yet?"

"Yesterday morning. We did our first recon too," I said.

Shubert nodded then climbed into his plane without any further acknowledgement. He turned his attention to his cockpit and threw a switch. "Contact!" he shouted. The crewman flipped the propeller, and the engine coughed to life.

I looked at the *Nobody's Baby* moniker painted on the fuselage. I thought of the moment when I first saw the remains of this plane and wondered how it would eventually become a wreck in the forest.

Billy hustled over then hopped into his plane. Ray shouted over Shubert's engine for us to get into our planes. As I climbed in, I found several photo plates on the seat. Within minutes, we were all in the air and on our way to the front.

The views of the countryside were expansive and picturesque. The quaint villages exuded great character. I wondered what it was like to live in these little towns in 1917 without any of the modern inventions of my time. I recalled how small the town of Sezanne appeared on the first day of our bike trip. Most of the cobblestone streets of 1917 would eventually give way to the asphalt roads of 1986.

Everything on the ground seemed so peaceful from the air. The war seemed far away, but our immediate reality dictated otherwise.

While the leaders gained altitude, Dave and I took photos of the ground below. Once we went through all of our photo plates, we headed back to base. The uneventful mission lasted about three hours.

When Chalons came into view, I thought about my personal safety. Other than the machine guns mounted on the nose of the plane, all I had for self-defense was a sidearm. Personally, I'd feel more comfortable if I had a rifle with me. I landed and coasted beside Hangar A. Dave killed his engine as he parked his plane next to mine.

All about the camp, hundreds of ground troops labored at digging a trench as well as setting up machine gun nests along the eastern edge of the airfield.

"Hey, if we got shot down, I don't think a little handgun would be enough protection, you know?" I said then loosened my scarf.

"There ain't room for anything more with the photo plates on board," Dave said.

"I think I could get a rifle and a knife to fit somehow."

Dave tucked his flight cap into his coat and brushed back his wavy brown hair.

"I don't know about you, but I'm concentrating on flying, not crashing," Dave said.

"I'll be back in a minute," I said.

I started for our tent when Ray, Billy, and James blocked my path.

"Harrod, one moment, please," Ray said. "While the planes are being refueled, grab a quick bite, then come right back. We have two more sorties to get in before the day is over. We need to check in with Colonel Marcus, so we'll take those plates in for you."

"All right, Ray. You need anything, Dave?" I asked.

"No, I'm good."

I ran the entire way to our tent, and quickly realized I needed to get back in shape. I huffed like mad then, as I entered our tent, my heart froze. Someone scattered the contents of our footlockers all over the place. Near the back wall of the tent, a time window rippled open. It was identical to the one we saw when we first arrived as well as the one we saw last night at the cabin.

A large man burst through the time window then shoved me across my footlocker. My boot clipped a corner, and I landed on my back. I got a good look at the intruder's scarred face and his evil bloodshot eyes. I shot to my feet then prepared to tear him up.

I charged the man, and we wrestled around. He seemed to toy with me, but when he effortlessly stood me up with his iron grip, he pulled me closer to his face.

"You look too weak to be an Interceptor. Who are you?" he asked. Like a thunderbolt, he head-butted me. I blinked then fell back onto the ground and blacked out.

I opened my eyes and sat up. Stars speckled my field of vision. I didn't know how long I was out, but I figured it was only a few minutes. The invader was gone, but I'll never forget his face. It was the time traveler with Edmund in the cabin, Turel. Since he was gone, I had to get my mind back on business.

I sifted through the mess. After several moments, I managed to recover a bayonet, a rifle, and four boxes of bullets. There wasn't anything of value here, so what was he looking for if he left our guns? Whoever Turel was, he didn't need weapons.

I left my tent and tried to fight off a growing headache as I approached my plane. I set everything on the ground beside the fuselage. After taking a few deep breaths, I gently rubbed my forehead.

I wedged the rifle snugly beside the wicker seat. I carefully scanned the cockpit for a place to put the bayonet. I pulled the backrest forward then put the bayonet across the back of the seat, where it fit nicely. I opened a box of bullets then poured as many as I could into a small map pouch attached to the right side of the cockpit. I put the rest of the rounds in my coat pocket. I outfitted Dave's plane the same way.

My stomach rumbling prompted me to run to the mess tent for any food scraps. Hundreds of new soldiers milled about the tent rows like ants invading a picnic. I weaved my way through the crowd then caught Dave as he emerged from the mess tent entrance.

"You don't have time to eat in there," Dave said. "Some small-timer made a trade with a local and scored a bunch of apples. Here, I got you a couple."

"Thanks, man. Hey, that dude we saw last night at the cabin was in our tent. We got into a fight," I said.

"What?"

"It was Turel. I don't care what you guys say, this changes everything."

"Hold on, John. We still have to be careful. I don't care if you want to kill Turel or not, we lay low like Ray said. It's safer to follow the colonels' lead like you said."

"I don't know how, but Turel knows we stand out. He called me an Interceptor too, whatever that is," I said.

"We've heard that word before. What's it mean? What does he think you're intercepting?" Dave asked.

We tried hard to stay out of the spotlight, but after Edmund showed Turel our wallets and my tape player, laying low now was impossible.

"I don't know. He knocked me out, and then he bolted," I said. "I think he might be that bad angel Marcus told us about."

"Well, that would change everything for us," Dave said.

"We can't tell Marcus about this because he might think we're on to his involvement with the Germans."

"Whoa, I didn't expect to be stuck between those guys. It might be every man for himself if we're not careful."

"I think it already is."

A sudden trembling sensation permeated the soles of my boots. My legs quivered as the waves radiated up my leg. Out of the southwest portion of the airfield filed two columns of clanking, squealing, iron-grinding tanks. Everyone watched as the lumbering behemoths crawled out of the woods.

The tank engines formed a line, shut off their engines, and went silent. Then, the occupants emerged through their hatches. Three men headed for the Command Center, while the remaining men smoked cigarettes beside their tanks. They relaxed quietly as they watched aircraft take off and land. I took the last bite from my apple then tossed it on the ground.

"You don't see that every day," I said.

"Not any day," Dave said.

We arrived at Dave's plane where I showed him how I rigged his weapons.

"Check it out," I said. Dave continued eating his apple and nodded as he chewed. "I put your rifle beside the seat. The ammo is in the side pocket. The bayonet is behind the backrest."

"Good work," Dave said with a wad of apple bulging his cheek. He studied my handiwork then nodded with approval.

"You guys ready to go back up again?" Billy asked from behind us.

"Oddball tanks they got here," Dave said.

"Yes, I suppose they are a bit odd," Billy said and eyed Dave curiously.

"Those tanks belong to the first squad. Four other tank squads will be here soon while the remaining squads are en route to Colmar. We may meet some resistance this time since we'll be over an active sector. If you need to engage the enemy, do so. We'll cover you as best we can.

Also, if you see any balloons, knock them down. A quick burst will finish them. If you survive a crash, keep a bearing to the northwest."

"Man, suddenly I don't like this," I said.

"Relax, John. We have the best with us. You watch my back, and I'll watch yours," Dave said.

"Right," I said nervously. "Ray, any chance I can talk to Marcus before we head out? It's important."

"We can talk to him when we get back. He ordered us to go immediately."

Not the answer I wanted, but I couldn't make waves now.

We climbed into our planes and took off. Low-level scattered clouds filled the sky, which meant we'd be flying closer to enemy ground fire.

Our mission continued for over sixty uneventful minutes when a loud, deep buzzing noise suddenly exploded out of the clouds fifty feet above our heads. Two German Gotha bombers roared by and headed toward Chalons. Ray and Billy dropped out of formation and chased after them. Shubert took over the lead of our squad. Once over our target, Shubert waved his arm over his head, the signal for us to get busy with our photographs.

I took pictures frantically. The experience of my near miss with the German bombers replayed in my mind. The deep roar of the bomber's engines and its massive condor-like wings cast a brief, eerie shadow as it passed over my head. Seeing them in action so close to us was an ominous yet exhilarating thrill.

During the picture-taking, every minute felt borrowed. After going through my photo plates, I noticed several German fighters to my right. My heart pounded wildly. I shouted as loudly as I could at Dave, but he couldn't hear me.

One German plane, an Albatros, attacked Dave. I maneuvered my plane into position behind the Albatros. I sighted it then squeezed the trigger. My amateur shooting skills luckily clipped the Albatros's fuselage. The sulfur dust of the gunpowder smoldered in my nose while it slammed my face like a sandblaster.

My inexperience with the machine gun caused little damage to my opponent. The quick succession of bullets vibrated my hand like a jackhammer. My feeble efforts successfully got the Albatros off Dave and onto me. I pulled back on the stick sharply, climbing as fast as I could, yet the Albatros stuck to me like Velcro.

There were far more German planes than we expected. A pair of French squadrons joined the fray. James shot down two German fighters when I drew the Albatros from Dave. Ray and Billy couldn't have returned at a better time to help finish off the rest of the German squad except for one red Fokker triplane that tailed Dave. Dave did all he could to elude his pursuer, but seconds later, his plane billowed smoke and spiraled to the ground.

CHAPTER 11

MY HEART CRANKED faster than my plane's pistons as I traced the smoke trail left by Dave's plane. I followed the intensifying billow, did a low flyby, and saw his plane consumed by fire. I banked my plane hard for a clear view below. The cockpit looked empty and I didn't see his body nearby.

The idea of navigating 1917 without Dave terrified me, but since I was in no position to cry about it now, I had to make sure I got my ass back to base so I could live to find him.

I climbed to about 2,000 feet and headed north. About two miles from Dave's wreck, two observation balloons loomed in the distance. I took heed of Billy's advice and fired a machine gun burst into the first balloon, which ignited the hydrogen instantly. The German observers in the basket quickly bailed out. Their parachutes opened, and they narrowly escaped incineration. I veered to port and sideswiped the fireball. The radiant heat warmed my face briefly.

Immediately beyond the smoke, the second balloon came into view. I fired upon balloon number two then it fell rapidly to earth in a black, smoky blaze. The observer inside bailed, but his parachute didn't open in time.

I felt a moment of ease but suddenly realized I was alone. My nerves sprang up as a strafe of bullets from German ground troops punctured the underside of my fuselage. Fortunately, their aim was off enough to avoid striking my legs. When I realized I was at about 500 feet, I pulled hard on the stick and launched the plane skyward.

I circled back to Dave's wreckage to look for any new signs of him. His plane continued to burn, and I dove for another look. I zipped past the wreckage but still didn't notice him anywhere.

I eyed my fuel gauge then reluctantly maneuvered my plane northwest to Chalons. Leaving Dave behind was the most horrific thing I'd ever done and a profound sense of failure chewed at my heart. The prospect of going back home without him wasn't acceptable. I had to get him back.

If Dave wasn't dead, he was still in enemy territory. I felt furious and guilt-ridden. I had to find him, but I couldn't do it alone. However, unlike my search for Devers, I had a starting point to look for Dave.

In the distance, three biplanes soared through the clouds. There I found Ray, Billy, and James, then I assumed my place among them.

We landed at Chalons late in the afternoon. We parked our planes between the mess tent and Hangar A. After I climbed out of my plane, I marched toward Ray.

"They got Dave, Ray. They shot him down!" I said. I felt like a distraught mother whose kid got away from her at a shopping mall.

"I know, John. I saw. Did you see him?" Ray asked calmly.

"I got close to the plane but didn't see him in the cockpit."

"He must've made it out. If his pursuer didn't return to finish him, there's a good chance he survived despite the significant, yet unexpected, German presence in that sector."

"If he ain't hurt, he can take care of himself," I said, recalling Dave was no pushover when it came to one-on-one confrontations.

Dave learned to use a revolver while on his family's ranch and in judo he was nearly unstoppable. However, there wouldn't be a referee to ensure a clean fight here.

"When can we go after him? I can't leave him there."

Ray's youthful face didn't seem too fazed at the possibility of Dave's death.

"We have one last sortie, and it was to be the most important of the three. If we get spotted, we might compromise our location. With the offensive to commence tomorrow morning, I'm confident we can't risk searching for Lieutenant Sowell at this time."

My eyes swept the airfield in widespread frustration. I couldn't believe my ears.

"My mom taught me to watch out for myself as well as those weaker than me and to never leave a friend to defend himself. So can we look for Dave as soon as the planes are ready? We can fly straight to where Dave went down. I can even take more pictures on the way. What do you say?"

"It's worth a try," Ray said to Billy. "There's still plenty of daylight."

"All right, Collie. Let's go," Billy said then strapped on his flight cap.

Shouting in the distance sidetracked our impromptu rescue mission. We took off our flight caps to hear the repeated message.

"All squad leaders report to Command for immediate instruction!"

Ray watched as my frustration grew after listening to the call.

"That means us, John. We'll see what's doing and meet you here, all right?"

"Sure, whatever," I said as I put my cap back on.

"I mean it, John. That's an order," Ray said.

"What? Do you think I'm stupid enough to go up there alone?"

"From what you said about your mother, I believe you might. Stay here!"

Ray sounded like my dad, at which point I realized I had behaved like an idiot.

"I'd be lying if I said I wasn't considering it, but I'll wait," I said.

"Good," Ray said.

Ray, Billy, and James went to the Command Center.

"Sonofabitch," I said then pounded the fuselage with both fists. I watched Ray and Billy walk away then I decided to go with them. I wanted to hear the big news as well.

While in the Command Center, Ray and Billy went through their debriefing routine with Marcus, while I hung back and observed them. They went to the map table and showed Marcus where we encountered the Germans. I leaned beside the door and stared at Marcus. While Ray spoke, Marcus occasionally stole a glance at me then he suddenly seemed impatient with Ray's summary.

"Very well," Marcus said. "In the meantime, we can afford a quick search for Lieutenant Sowell, but you'll need to return before sunset. If you encounter any Germans, you must return immediately."

Ray turned to me. "Is that satisfactory, John?" Ray asked in an annoyed tone.

"It'll do," I said then looked back at Marcus.

"Good. Let's get going then," Billy said and started for the door.

"Harrod, a word, if you don't mind," Marcus said. Ray and Billy paused, eyed each other, then left the Command Center.

Marcus stared at me as if he wanted to make me go to him. I was too pissed for formalities.

"Do you have something you wish to say?" Marcus asked. "I can understand you being upset with your partner in enemy hands."

"Bullshit," I snapped. I marched closer to Marcus and stood inches from his face. "There's more going on than Dave getting shot down."

"Then speak."

I hated condescension, but since Marcus brought us here, I felt he owed it to me to offer up more information than he had thus far.

"I got jumped in my tent this morning by some French guy named Turel."

"Turel came to you?" Marcus asked with a raised brow.

"Yeah. Do you know him? I think he's a time traveler," I said as I planted my hands on my hips. "He tore up our tent, kicked my ass, and left in one of those time windows."

"That's unusual for him to intercede without knowing your complete status. This only means the Escort must be here as well," Marcus said as he stepped around the map table. His brow furrowed, as he seemed to go deep in thought.

"Do you know who Turel is?" I asked.

"Yes. Where did you see him?"

"Other than in our tent, Dave and I saw him at a cabin in the woods, and he was drunk as hell. Is Turel a time traveler or what?"

"Turel's a fallen angel working for Lucifer. However, it seems even Turel's succumbed to human vices, in this case, alcohol."

"A fallen angel?" I asked in disbelief.

This was perfect. Not only is an evil angel after my grandfather, but he was also a drunken angel too.

"John, nothing for you has changed. You must still find Devers and locate the last page as soon as possible for you to return home. Time is of the essence."

I shook my head. An angry grin cracked my face as I thought of that condition which Marcus kept shoving down my throat. I felt I got nowhere in my unwanted assignment.

"There's more, Colonel. It seems Turel's working closely with Edmund. Edmund was in that cabin talking with Turel about meeting Germans."

"There has been recent speculation that Edmund held secret meetings," Marcus said. "Your witness to that meeting confirms that suspicion."

Marcus leaned on the table and lowered his head.

"What's wrong?" I asked.

"A disturbing thought entered my mind. If Dave's alive, it's possible Turel has him in his custody."

I grabbed my head in frustration then looked into Marcus's eyes.

"Then I have to find Dave," I said. "I'm the one that has to find Devers anyway, but maybe I can get Turel to help us without him knowing it."

Marcus took a deep breath then gently shook his head.

"Pursuing a fallen angel isn't without its risks."

"What kind of risks?"

"Death. Avoid Turel at all costs and find Lieutenant Sowell."

CHAPTER 12

RAY LED ROBERT, James, Billy, and me to Dave's crash site. I feared Dave was either dead or captured. The thought of going home without him sickened me. How would I explain what happened if I came home alone, let alone tell his family he died in a World War One dogfight?

About two miles from Dave's crash site, Ray and I descended to 200 feet and searched for any sign of Dave in the surrounding countryside. Robert, James, and Billy flew cover at around 1,000 feet. While we cruised the crash site, we swerved around trees, in the hopes we'd catch sight of our fallen brother.

We closely surveyed Dave's crash site from the air. His plane rested in the southwest portion of a clover leaf-shaped field bounded by tall trees. I made eye contact with Ray, pointed to myself, then to the ground. Ray shook his head, but I landed on a grassy patch near the wreck anyway. I was sure I'd get a nice beating from Ray, but I had to know for sure what became of Dave. Ray circled with the others above while I checked things out.

While the propeller chopped at the air with enough RPMs to keep running and not roll forward, I climbed out of the plane. Only a charred skeleton remained of Dave's biplane. All the weapons I tied in it were gone. I dashed around the immediate crash site for any signs of him but instead found the remains of several German soldiers. Near a cluster of small trees rested the bodies of two civilians. A shootout was evident, but I couldn't tell who won.

Gunshots suddenly popped from the woods, chipped off pieces of bark, and deflected off my face.

As I raced back to my plane, I saw Ray lead the charge toward a grove near my position. I climbed in and throttled the engine. I spun the plane around and sped along the grass.

While eluding gunfire, I pulled back on the stick at the last second and my wheels clipped the treetops of the forest edge. I found Ray, and I veered to join him and the others.

As we flew back to Chalons, Ray gave me an angry eye, so I at least had that beating to look forward to, but I didn't care. It would be worth it.

The sun fell below the horizon as Chalons appeared ahead. During the whole flight back, I worried about Dave and his well-being. I recalled the many memories I had of him and the number of good times we had together. Then, machine gun fire from behind snapped my thoughts to the present. Out of instinct, I looked behind me and saw the white flashes of a machine gun from a plane on my tail. Three Fokkers had quietly followed us back to Chalons.

Our squad scattered to pursue their target of choice. Despite our skillful maneuvering, the Fokkers dogged us closely. A quick burst of bullets ripped through my plane's tail. While in a cloud, I jerked back on the stick and flipped over. I swooped out of the cloud and found myself behind my foe, who didn't chase me into the cloud.

My heart pounded while I struggled to get the Fokker in my sights, a task akin to threading a needle while riding a roller coaster. I hoped for the best when I squeezed the trigger every time he graced the crosshairs of my gun sight. Finally, I struck the Fokker. His plane spun downward and out of control, his fate sealed. Above me, I saw my squad members dispensing with the enemy while men on the ground scrambled for cover to dodge any errant bullets.

Billy and Ray continued after one fighter while James and Robert hounded another. Ray fired and the Fokker's engine caught fire. Moments later the pilot bailed out. Billy dove toward the parachute and fired. The pilot's body jerked about as white-hot bits of thirty-caliber death ripped through his defenseless body.

James aggressively chased his foe but nearly clipped Robert's wings in the process. Robert pulled away, allowing James to finish the kill. Fortunately, none of the three German fighters survived to tell of the Chalons air base.

After landing, I coasted toward the other fighters by Hanger A. I took a breath then pulled off my flight cap. I was glad we got rid of the enemy fighters and the win felt good. Ray rushed up to my plane and shattered my moment of reflection. He scared the crap out of me while he lit into me like a drill sergeant on a new recruit.

"What the bloody hell were you doing back there?" Ray shouted. "I ordered you not to land!"

"How could I assess anything from 200 feet in the air? Besides, you guys were with me. I had to see for myself what happened to Dave."

Furious, Ray looked about my plane then noticed Billy, James, and Robert had gathered nearby. Ray slammed his fist against the fuselage.

"Get your ass out of that plane," Ray shouted. "Feel free to tell us what you discovered, if you think us worthy of the consideration."

Sheepishly, I climbed out and stood before everyone as if testifying before a jury. Although the words didn't hurt, I went against his order, which got under his skin. I knew I screwed up, but I at least knew Dave wasn't there.

"I think Dave's alive," I said.

"How do you know?" Robert asked.

"I checked out his plane and the crash site. The weapons I put in his cockpit were gone, but there were several dead German soldiers and two civilians. I don't think they took Dave prisoner because nobody touched the German bodies."

"What do you mean by civilians?" Billy asked.

"Both of them had burgundy hats, I mean berets. Maybe they were National Guard."

"What in blazes is the National Guard, meatpacker? Speak English."

"Focus, Billy!" I snapped back. "There ain't time for a witch hunt. If you're trying to be funny with that meatpacker crap, I ain't laughing."

"Chicago is the meat packing center of the world. You don't see my humor regarding the stockyards? Come on, it's your home. If, of course, that's where you're from."

"What are you talking about? Chicago hasn't been a meat packing city for over thirty—"

"Thirty what?" Billy asked and stepped closer to me.

I stopped dead in my tracks. In my time, the stockyards were a distant memory but in 1917, it was a thriving place. I restrained my anger then regrouped my thoughts in record time.

"Look. There was a, uh, bad virus going around, so they closed the stockyards for a month. Anyway, I'd appreciate it if you'd quit calling me that name. I don't like it."

"When was this?" Billy demanded.

"This, uh, past summer. Why?"

"No reason." Billy nodded then stepped back.

The others stared at me awestruck as if I had apples dropping out of my ears. Something told me in the back of my mind that I seriously screwed up somehow, but I didn't have time to sweat over it.

"Anyway, there were dead militia guys near Dave's plane," I continued. "They didn't look like regular army soldiers, but more like ordinary people, civilians."

"Sounds like French Underground," Miller said.

"Did any of them have their weapons?" Ray asked.

I thought for a moment then shook my head.

"I didn't see any. Germans wouldn't take French weapons and leave their dead to rot in the sun, would they?" I asked.

"No," Billy said. He removed his flight cap while his eyes remained fixed on me.

"If that's the case, then I'd say Dave got picked up by the Underground or at least got away on his own."

"Probably so," Ray said. "Any civilian or French Underground member in that sector would help him. With the offensive beginning tomorrow, we might be able to pick up his trail. We best report."

While Ray, Billy, Robert, and James went to the Command Center, I headed for my tent. I wasn't about to let bureaucracy get in the way of me finding Dave, war or no war. As I walked to my tent, I thought of the pilot I shot down.

The horrible truth that I killed a human being sank in. His children, if he had any, would never see their father again. How would I explain this to my dad? If I kept it to myself, would I supplant Grandpa Devers as the family nut job? I tried in vain to put the incident out of my mind, maybe when all of this was over, I could make peace with myself. My outburst with Billy about the stockyards only made matters worse. I returned my thoughts to Dave and to when if ever, I'd see him again.

While I stretched out on my cot, I tried to formulate what I'd do next. With Devers's whereabouts unknown, Dave missing, not to mention an evil angel racing me for the last page, I felt I needed more information. Turel could've killed me if he wanted to. So why didn't he? If he waited for me to find Devers first, he could kill us both then screw my lineage for all eternity. No matter how I thought it through, the result pegged me as a dead man.

My tent flap swung open and Marcus entered. In my eyes, he wasn't a colonel but rather a guy holding my nuts over a fire to get what he wanted. I looked at him but didn't bother to salute. However, I had a question.

"Tell me about that *Book of Ancients*. If it was guarded before, how did Lucifer get a hold of it?" I asked.

"That, I'm afraid, is a long story. Unfortunately, there isn't time to go over the circumstances."

"Then give me the highlights," I said and sat up on my cot. Several flies buzzed around in front of my face. I fanned them away only to draw their ire for me.

I motioned for Marcus to sit on Dave's cot. Marcus sat and removed his hat while he took a long breath.

"When the *Bible* was assembled in 364AD, the selection process was manipulated by Turel. He's a fallen Watcher sentenced to Hell along with many other Watchers for violations committed against humankind. When the Archangels in Hali saw this, they attempted to stop Turel by opening the *Book of Ancients* for a proper solution."

"That sounds reasonable."

"However, they didn't have permission from the Powers and thus exposed the book's location. Before Lucifer could strike, the book was scattered among the Archangels for safekeeping. Each angel was punished to live as a human and carried a single page. They're also devoid of the knowledge of other archangels in their vicinity so they couldn't divulge any information should they face torture or death."

"Being human is a punishment?" I asked.

"For the Archangels, it's severe, for they're without their full complement of powers. Turel learned of this and found a way to extract the pages from them. In time, he acquired all but the last page."

"Why didn't the good angels do anything about it? How come the powers that be let the book get scattered among defenseless humans?"

"That way they could conceal the book until it could be reassembled."

I swatted at the flies as they came within inches of my face.

"Since the last page remains at large," Marcus continued, "a provision in the *Book of Ancients* permits the use of humans to gain the last page on behalf of those in Hali. That's when you entered the conflagration."

While Marcus spoke, I found myself believing that angels were real, yet they hated being human. Interesting.

"Then Turel needs me alive," I said.

"He does. He's smart, and if he has Dave, he won't harm him so long as he believes Dave will lead him to the last page."

"How does Colonel Devers fit into this game?"

"I believe he has the last page since Turel's looking for him. There's confusion because we don't know where Devers is or even who he is. Tomorrow you'll begin your search for Dave. Perhaps along the way, you'll find Devers."

"Wait, you want me to look for the last page now?"

"Since Turel is now aware of you, remaining on your current natural course is no longer prudent. You must be more proactive from this point forward. Consider your efforts to locate Devers and the last page to be the same. If you find Devers, you'll find the last page as well."

"Did Devers have a choice in this stuff?"

Marcus tapped his lip with his finger. He seemed to choose his words carefully.

"He's involved, but his safety is assured."

"What about mine?"

Marcus shook his head. I cringed away as a stupid fly buzzed my eyes.

"This is bullshit," I said and stood up. I grabbed a shirt and swatted at the damned flies. I got a couple of them, but the others remained intent on annoying the crap out of me.

"I know this is a colossal task. But you must succeed," Marcus said then walked out of my tent.

A single buzzing sound caught my ear. The little bug, a small dark blip in my field of vision, taunted me. He got too close and I angrily clapped my hands on that little nuisance. Unfortunately, I couldn't solve my other problems that quickly.

After Marcus left, I stood outside my tent and watched the sun burn an orange sunset. While I breathed in the cool, damp air, I felt as though I lost my best friend forever.

As darkness intensified and speckles of stars grew brighter, I went inside my tent and lit an oil lamp. I shut out my rampaging thoughts of guilt when I heard steps sweep through the grass outside.

"John, we need to talk," Ray said as the dim light of my oil lantern cast a muted glow on his face. "I was with Marcus and the other flight leaders."

"Are we still going to look for Dave?" I asked.

"Yes. We'll escort you to Dave's crash site. After the ground troops begin advancing, it should be safe for you to search for Dave. Another man will join your search, a local from Chalons familiar with the region. Colonel Marcus considers you ineffective as a fighter pilot, so we think you should find your friend."

Renewed hope flowed through my beaten heart at the prospect of searching for Dave.

"Ray, do you think he's still alive?" I asked.

"I don't know, John. If he has his guns as you say, he has a chance. Besides, the German presence there is minimal at the moment."

"That's encouraging, except for the German soldiers I found by his wreck."

"They were likely a scout patrol. John, about what happened earlier with Billy."

"Oh, that. I was pissed at the time. All that crap about him calling me a meatpacker boiled my blood."

"Yes, well, I wanted to mention the stockyards didn't close at all this past summer."

Beads of sweat sprouted and trailed down my back. Then, my ears grew hot. The flashing lights of a police car in the rearview mirror had the same effect on me.

"Why do you say that?" I asked.

"Everyone knows, John. Closing the stockyards is big news."

"What are you going to do about it?"

"Considering the current climate, I see no need for further discussion. We'll pick up this conversation again at a proper time."

Wonderful. Ray decided to focus on business for now and then kick my ass at a more convenient time later.

"Okay, Ray," I said. Ray barely cracked a grin then left my tent.

Ray had me pegged. Apart from making my biggest screw-up since arriving in 1917, a new confidence to find Dave reignited inside me. The guilt that consumed my thoughts for the last couple of hours melted away.

I sat on my footlocker and stared at Dave's empty cot across from me. If I had survived a crash, what would I do? What could I do? Knowing Dave was good at self-defense was comforting, but I wasn't sure if he'd be able to think of what to do in a life or death situation. I had no choice but to make the most positive assumptions.

CHAPTER 13

I GAZED IN speechless awe as thousands of winged human-like creatures engaged in battles in the skies above me. They soared among the ivory clouds, fought and killed each other around a massive temple-like structure. I ran for cover and headed toward the temple entrance. High above the entranceway, I saw the word *Library* carved in bold limestone blocks. Too curious for my own good, I dashed inside.

While angels slammed against the hallowed walls, part of the dome collapsed in a crumbling avalanche of divine destruction. The stacks of bookshelves, thousands perhaps, ignited as lightning fire shot across the room. Angel corpses fell to the floor and onto the shelves in contorted, mangled, heaps. None of those in battle seemed to take the slightest interest in my presence.

Suddenly, one of the creatures landed in front of me and shook the ground like earthquake aftershocks. The beast stood tall and spread its bat-like wings. The flames of its fiery sword lapped through the air as it raised its weapon above its grotesque face.

The beast spoke in a mash of syllables then shrieked sounds of unknown meaning yet altogether terrifying. Its skull cap of molten lead clung fast to the crimson-stained flesh of its chiseled jaw. I tried to run away, but my feet held fast to the ground as if glued there. The creature stood more than twice my height, let out a hellacious war cry, and lowered its sword on me.

A crash of thunder and flash of lightning rocked the heavens, as I leaped out of my cot toward the tent opening. A soft rumbling and a gentle blowing mist soothed my panicked heart. It was only a thunderstorm. God, why are you screwing with me like this?

According to my watch, it was after four in the morning. The Chalons offensive would begin shortly.

I returned to my cot, coiled up, and closed my eyes. Faint images came into view of broad waterfalls and two maidens walking among brilliantly colored gardens with ornate, sweeping trellises that supported fragrant, colorful blooms. One of the maidens of indescribable beauty reached for my hand and smiled. I smiled back at her as we walked across a wide green grass field. We then approached a tranquil pond surrounded by closely cropped grass. I took in a deep breath and felt a peaceful warmth. The place was like nothing I ever saw before and I didn't want to leave. I had not worries, problems, or troubles of any kind. I turned to the maiden and wanted to ask her a question.

"John, wake up. Time to get ready," Ray said as he tapped the bottoms of my feet.

My eyes burned with fatigue as I arose like Dracula out of his coffin. The tent opening revealed daylight then my dream quickly vanished.

"Man, that was weird," I said.

"What was weird?" Ray expressed in a disinterested tone. He gathered my flight gear while I recapped my bad night's sleep.

"I got up earlier when I heard the thunder. Then, I closed my eyes for a second, then it's daylight."

"Time can go by quickly around here. Here's your coat."

Ray tossed my jacket to me then left the tent.

"Are you all right, Ray?" I asked loudly. He returned inside and acted jittery. I yawned so hard my jaw popped.

"Yes, splendid. I simply get a little nervous before a big mission like this."

I eyed Ray curiously while I pulled up my boots.

"Splendid, my ass. You're making as much sense as a dog with wings." I said.

"I said I was nervous, nothing more," Ray said.

"Okay. What are you nervous about?"

Ray paused then set my flight gear beside me. He wiped back his hair then wrung his hands.

"With the Germans following us back here yesterday, I'm distressed about this whole arrangement," Ray said.

"Look at it this way. If we face a lot of Germans up there, then let's blow them out of the sky all at once instead of one at a time."

Ray huffed slightly. "I wish I had your spirit, John. Colonel Eldridge's tank squads will move out soon. Time is precious," Ray said.

We walked to the mess tent and observed twenty tanks rumbling for the Gate. Two lines of what could be hundreds of men each trailed the tanks. The remaining tanks held positions on the western edge of the airfield. The bold wedge design with oversized tracks looked bigger in person than in the pictures I saw in history books.

"Looks like the offensive is getting started," I said as I buttoned my coat.

Ray checked his watch while I noted the infantrymen taking positions along the eastern edge of the airfield.

"Yes, I believe so," Ray muttered.

Being able to empathize with people's feelings was something I was good at, but Ray was a tough nut to crack.

"Ray, I have to ask. What's up with you? You clam up on me, and then you tell me you're nervous. It doesn't add up."

Ray stopped walking. He looked like a kid caught raiding a cookie jar. With his hands on his hips, he eyed the ground while he scratched the back of his neck.

"Not considering our discussion last night, I think this offensive is in dire straits," Ray said.

"Why?" I asked.

"When we first surveyed that location a couple of days ago, there was little German activity. Then yesterday we saw bombers and many fighters. To me, it seems the German efforts are concentrating somewhere else. All my calculations suggest the Germans will strike the Gate sector."

"The Gate is being reinforced right now," I said. "Eldridge will be there in plenty of time to back them up. We're covered."

"The Germans split our principal force in two. If the Germans strike the Gate, it won't take them long to overrun it if their arsenal is substantial enough."

"True, if the Germans knew we were shorthanded, which they don't."

Ray paused and looked me in the eye. I hadn't known him for long, but I understood Ray's concern by the drawn expression on his face.

"What if they did know?" Ray asked.

The commotion of the passing tanks and marching foot soldiers made too much noise for us to speak softly anymore.

"How could the Germans know?" I shouted. "We scoped it a couple of days ago and didn't find anything."

"The Chalons offensive has been in the works for months. Marcus, Edmund, Eldridge, Weatherby, and everyone in high command worked to orchestrate this effort. This move could potentially lead to the end of the war. I have an ill feeling that the Germans have gained information about the offensive. If I'm correct, then they have prepared for us."

Ray made sense, yet I started to feel a little worried. I watched as the tanks backed into the western edge of the forest then stopped inside the tree line.

"Do you think there's a spy someplace?" I asked.

"That's my fear."

Devers's letters suddenly jumped to mind. I remembered thinking the letters read like an apology or a confession. Was Devers part of this insane plot with Edmund and Turel? Asking Ray about Devers now seemed out of line, so I resisted the urge.

"Who do you think would sell us out?" I asked.

"I see two scenarios. First, the individual could be an Allied officer bribed by the Germans. Only an officer is able to gain confidential information worth anything to the enemy. Second, the individual may be a German spy who infiltrated Allied ranks. Either way, it spells dark times for us unless something good comes our way soon."

Ray's frown made me nervous. I didn't like the idea that my mentor for the last several weeks doubted the integrity of his superiors.

"You think it's an Allied officer, don't you?" I asked.

Ray nodded.

I trailed Ray to the mess tent like a lost puppy. The events that occurred since I arrived fit together like pieces from two different jigsaw puzzles. A small Frenchman in a brown beret dressed in infantry clothing stood outside the tent entrance as we approached.

"Ray, who is he?" I asked.

"He's your escort."

My escort. Turel and Marcus mentioned something about an escort, but this guy didn't look angelic to me. Then again, I wasn't sure I'd be able to spot an angel in human form if it stood in front of me.

"John, this is Rene Leveque. Rene, this is John."

Rene, with narrow brown eyes and a well-groomed, pencil-line mustache, appeared determined. His rough, calloused hand suggested he was a man of labor and his grip strength rivaled mine. Rene's disguise was perfect for the part.

"John, take the trainer because it has an extra seat," Ray said.

"Okay, but let me get my stuff out of my plane first."

Rene climbed into the back seat of the trainer then silently watched me stow my weapons in the front cockpit in the same manner I'd done with my plane. Pouty-lipped, he nodded his approval.

A ground crewman waited with his hands on the propeller as I climbed in. I strapped on my flight cap, pulled down my goggles, and gave the word.

The crewman flipped the propeller, and the engine coughed to life. Ray and nine other pilots accompanied me into the overcast sky. The drizzle stopped and a warm, summer wind drifted across the field.

We shaved the clouds at 1,500 feet as we headed to Dave's wreck. Dave had a fourteen-hour head start since his crash. Below, thousands of men double-time marched to the front.

Rene and I landed while our other fighters circled above to protect us. We met no resistance, which was in eerie contrast to the ground fire we encountered yesterday.

Shubert landed his plane and stopped beside mine. An extra pilot climbed out of Shubert's plane and hopped into my plane to return it to Chalons. As Shubert and the other pilot revved their engines, Rene and I waved. Shubert waved back then they took off to rejoin the others circling overhead. The Sopwith Camels then continued southeast along the front toward Eldridge's position.

Before embarking on a hike of unknown peril, I verified that my guns contained live rounds.

"All right, Rene, let's go," I said. We then trekked into the woods.

CHAPTER 14

WHILE RENE AND I trekked across the countryside, I brought him up to speed on what happened to Dave. I at least felt pacified that I was doing something to find him. I wasn't sure how eventful my search for Dave would go, but I knew I had to do it with a clear and alert mind. Rene explained how the Underground worked with the Allied forces. To pass the time on what was probably going to be a long hike, I asked Rene about his family.

"Since the war started, more so in the northern regions, the German assault on my countrymen has been horrible," Rene said. "The French government was slow to give needed help. Many men helped form groups for the Underground network. Others fought the Germans alone, but with no success."

"Your English isn't half bad," I said.

"I come from a wealthy family. I studied at Oxford University."

"That's cool. Do you think the Underground has Dave?"

"*Oui*, Lieutenant Harrod. Members of the Underground live in every French town. They could be old women, children, or crippled men. I believe the Underground has your friend and may be trying to return him. The Underground path leads this way. The countryside holds many places they can hide."

I switched my rifle to my opposite shoulder then rubbed a muscle knot in my neck. Weightlifting, no matter how much I grunted through over the years, didn't prepare me for long hikes in the woods with a ten-pound rifle that got heavier by the hour.

"Do you know all the hiding places?" I asked.

"I grew up here. Chalons Sur Marne is my home. If there's any place to hide, I know where it is."

"What do you do when you're not helping Allies find lost pilots?"

What did I know? As far as I knew, everyone was a peasant.

"I'm a vigneron," Rene said. "My family has made wine for over one hundred years. You must try our label."

"Maybe, but I never really liked wine."

"Ah, you're too sophisticated, then?" he asked with a sly smile.

"I suppose so. You got a family?"

"*Oui*, six children. My father and sister live with us. Do you have a family?"

We paused to take a few swigs of water from our canteens. A sharp breeze cut through the forest and struck my sweaty neck like frozen rain. A chill streaked down my spine, so I turned up my coat collar.

"There's just my dad and my two brothers. My mom died last spring. I'm glad the war hasn't split up your family."

Rene grew somber, broke a dead branch with his boot, then took a deep breath.

"We left Peronne during the Somme and went to my sister-in-law's farm north of Vitry le Francois. A sniper killed my mother soon after we left our home. We buried her near Montdidier, away from the bombs. After leaving the cemetery, German soldiers take my two oldest daughters. The soldiers murdered them."

"Holy Mother," I said flabbergasted. I thought I had it bad. Rene's real life experiences had my fears of the unknown beat by a mile.

I knew about Nazi atrocities but never heard stories like Rene's from a firsthand witness. He delivered his personal horror story to me like room service. My heart went out to him. I never experienced the pain of losing a child, and hopefully, I never would.

"Jeez, that's rough," I said. "What happened to your vineyard?"

"Part of it is gone. Much of it is in this region just over those hills."

He adjusted his gunnysack and resumed walking through the forest. I hooked my canteen to my belt and joined him.

"You are from Chicago?" he asked as he ducked under a low branch.

"Yep, been there my whole life," I said.

"Is it beautiful?"

"Chicago's a lot like Paris. There's always something going on. The lakefront is a great place to watch the girls," I said with an easy grin.

Rene smiled. "You're married, no?"

"No, not me. I'm not ready for marriage."

"I find that's where happiness is. When you do get married one day, have many children."

"Let's just get through the war first."

"Very well, Lieutenant."

We hiked across a grassy meadow and passed through clusters of old growth trees separated by wide fields that once served as vineyards and pasture before many of the residents moved out. We took advantage of tree cover at every opportunity. Soon, we discovered the shambles of what was once a stone house. Rene appraised the building then ventured inside.

"I don't think anyone lives here, Rene," I said as I scanned the condemnable dump. "Let's go."

"Of course nobody lives here, but that doesn't mean nobody comes here. This is an Underground stop. Come, I'll show you."

Rene took me to a far corner of the structure where he showed me a tunnel entrance.

"See? The grass covers the tunnel opening," Rene said as he moved aside a large leafy branch.

"Has anyone been here?" I asked.

I squatted for a closer look and the moist, earthy aroma of damp soil wafted into my nose. Moss covered the shadowed wall remains.

"*Oui*. The grass is matted. Someone was here not long ago."

I took Rene's summation to be a sign that Dave was nearby although we had no evidence he'd been at this particular hiding place. I was about to turn away when I saw a wristwatch pressed into the dirt. I eagerly picked it up and recognized it as Dave's.

"What is that?" Rene asked with curiosity.

I pressed the Indiglo light button. The soft greenish glow illuminated the watch's face.

"This is Dave's watch. Why would he leave it here? There's no way he could expect me to find it," I said then gently tapped the watch on the palm of my hand.

"How can there be light on it?" Rene asked.

I pocketed the watch.

"It's a special watch. Look, Dave's not far ahead of us. I have no idea how he thought I might find his watch, my guess it was out of desperation. Either way, we have to hustle."

"They will go to the next stop. I know the way."

A rash of goose bumps enveloped my body as I looked about the ghostly ruins. I wasn't sure, but it felt like the ghosts of the prior inhabitants either didn't want us here, or they wanted me to catch up with Dave.

"Come on, Rene, let's get out of here. This place gives me the creeps."

CHAPTER 15

RENE AND I continued our hike through the woods under an overcast sky. A fine mist blew and dampened my clothes enough to match my gloomy mood. A robin or other small woodland bird took off from a bush when Rene suddenly froze in his tracks.

"Do you hear?" Rene asked then turned toward the unmistakable sound of approaching aircraft, lots of them.

While we peered up through the lacework of branches, the images of man-made wings passed over us. Large black crosses on the underside of the wings were visible even through the dense cover overhead.

"Why are you so nervous? They can't see us," I said.

"I don't know where they come from, but we're seeing more of them. I think they may advance in this direction," Rene said.

"This region is supposed to be clear of Germans."

"I don't think the Germans will fortify this sector. They'll likely only set up a scouting post."

"We better get moving then, huh?"

"*Oui.* There's a broad field divided by a stream ahead of these woods. We need to cross that stream before night. Crossing open land in daylight is treacherous."

While we rushed through the woods, more airplanes raced overhead, some British, some French. Using the cover of the forest, we were relatively safe from aerial attack as long as we stayed in the thick parts of the forest. Before we knew it, we encountered the vast, wide-open field.

I caught my breath then crouched beside a rotted tree, which hosted the remnants of a large vacant wasp nest. Again, the sound of aircraft carried across the field. This time, the source was German, and the planes landed about a hundred yards northeast of us.

"You might be right about that German scouting post, Rene."

We crawled beside a large bush and watched a dozen German fighters land a short distance in front of us.

Rene removed a pair of small binoculars from his front pocket then scooted to a better viewing position. I shuffled across the grass to stay close to him.

"I count twelve planes, a couple of trucks. There are no tents, not many men," Rene said.

He handed me the binoculars. I took a long look at the pilots then at the planes. I watched with wonder as these vintage warriors of the sky went about their business.

"Who are those guys next to the pilots?" I asked.

"Where?" Rene asked and took the binoculars from me.

"Look on the far right of that last plane. Are those farmers? I thought Frenchmen hated Germans?"

Rene focused the glasses while he surveyed the men in question. I scraped the grass with my chin to stay out of sight. A large Garter snake quickly slithered past my chin and, thankfully, didn't give me a chance to freak out.

"They're not farmers," Rene said.

"Who are they?" I asked.

"They're Underground."

"Underground? Why are they hanging out with the Germans?"

"They might be trying to talk their way out of being captured."

"Hm."

Rene's head leaned forward slightly as he observed.

"What is it?" I asked

"There is another man, a pilot. I didn't notice him before."

"Let me see," I said and took the binoculars.

I viewed the men again and my jaw dropped.

"Holy crap, that's Dave," I said. I handed the binoculars to Rene and grabbed my rifle.

I removed the safety and aimed the rifle on a large Frenchman in a red beret. Rene gently pushed my gun barrel down.

"You can't shoot," Rene said calmly.

"What are you talking about? I can pop them from here, no problem."

"There are too many of them. You might get one or two before we are overwhelmed."

I looked back at the group with Dave then pursed my lips. Rene kept his eye on them.

"They are shaking hands, cursed traitors," Rene said.

"Damn. Okay, so what do we do?"

"We stay a safe distance back and follow them. We can't let them know we're here. They're plotting something, so the more we can observe the better."

"You have a point," I said.

I set down my rifle to look back at the group. I watched helplessly as they pushed Dave along at gunpoint. It was evident to me the Underground hadn't rescued Dave. They captured him.

"The party's breaking up," I said. "Dave and the Underground guys are leaving. The Germans are going back to their planes."

Rene hugged the ground while the German planes took flight and headed east. The two trucks turned around then went in the same direction.

"Something's going down, Rene," I said.

"What?"

"All those Germans and Dave in the hands of crooked Underground. Something tells me there's a plan in the works. Right now, Eldridge's division with four tank squads is a few miles south of here. We're bound to meet with our guys any time now."

"That's possible. Let us follow them," Rene said as he pulled out a dark blue handkerchief and then wiped the sweat from his brow.

"Where do you think they're going?" I asked.

"The next safe house is about twelve kilometers ahead. They won't get there by sundown, so we'll need to make camp close to them before nightfall. We'll check them at first light."

"Okay."

Rene and I made bounding strides like gazelles through the field's knee-high grass to keep up with Dave's group. The wreckage of two German Fokkers appeared as we approached a stream. One plane along with its pilot smoldered in the creek. The other rested in a crumpled heap with the pilot's covered body on the grass beside it.

With a running start, I leaped over the creek and landed with room to spare. Rene ran his best step but fell on his chest with a grunted thud. I pulled him up as he lost his grip and started sliding down the bank. We got a closer look at the plane wreck as well as the shot-up pilot on the ground. Whoever he was, he was out of his plane when he was killed.

Rene stepped around the body then squatted for a closer look. He delicately lifted the coat off the head of the deceased. After a quick peek, he jerked away and threw up.

"You all right, Rene? You know this guy?"

"I don't know that man," Rene said as he tried to compose himself. "This is upsetting."

He removed a handkerchief from his back pocket. He wiped his mouth while I stooped down to study the lifeless body.

"Who do you think covered him up?" I asked as I lifted his arm and let it plop down. "He hasn't been dead long. Rigor hasn't set in yet."

"I don't know. Perhaps your friend can tell us when we reach him."

I've gutted deer on hunting trips with my dad, so I was familiar with the sight of blood and innards. The pilot suffered a bullet wound through the left temple and it blasted out of the side of his head.

"From what I see, I'd say this guy got nailed by a machine gun. God, half of his brain was blown out." Tears streamed down Rene's face. "You sure you don't know this guy?" I asked again.

"*Oui*, I'm sure," he said and wiped his eyes. "This is too much."

He bent over, dry-heaved a couple more times, then took deep breaths.

I tried to ease Rene from his affliction, but I grew impatient. The search for Dave had to continue, hell or high water. At the same time, I couldn't stand here and watch Rene crunch his guts all day over a dead guy he didn't even know.

"Forget about him, Rene. We can't lose track of Dave. How much further do we have to go?" I asked.

Rene took several deep breaths. "About ten kilometers," he said.

We then heard distant rumbling sounds.

"Things will get ugly here real soon and turn this place into the next Somme."

"*Oui*," Rene said as he stole glances at the man on the ground.

"Quit looking at him." I grabbed Rene by the collar then dragged him away from the disturbing scene. "We don't have time for this."

We headed west for the woods then eventually caught sight of Dave and his group. The gloomy overcast sky did little to lift our spirits and even though sunset was still a couple hours away, it felt like night was an hour away.

We stopped trailing Dave for the evening as darkness rapidly consumed the forest. Dave's group couldn't progress any further than we could, so there wasn't much chance we'd fall far behind.

"The safe house is about eight kilometers northwest," Rene said. "They're heading in that direction, so we should catch up to them by first light."

"Sounds good, Rene."

The chilly forest air cut us to the bone, so Rene built a small fire. I buttoned up my flight jacket, flipped up the sheepskin collar, and leaned against a large tree. Rene rubbed his hands in front of the crackling fire. I set my rifle across my lap then crossed my arms.

I pulled up my legs then wrestled with the idea of attempting a midnight move to get Dave back. I felt my face drop as each conclusion of a rescue attempt ended with me getting dead. Man, it sucked being a human being. Why couldn't an angel help me at a time like this?

I lowered my head then made myself as comfortable as I could. Once I closed my eyes, a tidal wave of exhaustion washed over me. I took a few steady breaths and my mind raced into a dream.

The once magnificent tree I saw guarded by fierce winged creatures stood rotted. The tree's mottled leaves and charred branches stood lifeless under a massacred sky. The angel guards lay strewn around its trunk, ripped to shreds, and writhed in agony.

While consumed in cold terror, I watched as that winged bat-like monster with its flaming sword land before me once again. It slowly paced around me while I subconsciously matched it step for step to size it up. It spoke again as if it were trying to elicit a response from me. I didn't know how to answer. Like swinging a baseball bat, the beast swung its fiery sword at my head. The flames roared through the air as it approached my face.

I awoke with a shiver then saw a faint column of smoke rising from our campfire. The creature's horrid screeches still echoed in my mind. My rifle remained on my lap as I left it. My pistol was still in its holster, and my bayonet fixed to my belt. I recalled the horrifying dream and the cold, lifeless death of no tomorrows. I grew more defiant about my fear of these creatures yet sensed a yearning to engage them, to find out what they wanted from me, even if it meant death by fire sword.

Rene continued his slumber and snored loudly. I noted the time was 5:47. I set my rifle next to a tree then walked about the campsite to stretch. I reached for the highest branches then suddenly felt lightheaded. Sometime today, I'd have to find something to eat.

I thought of my last couple of dreams and, instead of blowing them off as nightmares, I thought about their meaning because I'd had similar dreams since my involvement with angels began. I reasoned that they were setting me up for a faceoff of sorts, or maybe training. No other explanation made sense, but I knew I didn't want any part of it. Ultimately, it seemed like it didn't matter what I wanted.

The forest sprung to life as brief sunlight poked through cloud breaks. I heard the knocking of a far away woodpecker and a host of scurrying noises rustling beneath the wet, rotting leaves. Then, I listened to what sounded like the voices of men in the east. I dropped behind a cluster of bushes and tried to spot the unseen visitors.

My heart pounded as I studied the woods for anything that moved through the staggering array of tree trunks. The towering thicket of maple and elm limited my vision to about fifty yards, but then the voices were gone. I chalked up the sounds to a tired mind coupled with rattled nerves.

"Do you see something?" Rene whispered.

My heart rate skyrocketed and my eyes nearly popped out of their sockets.

"Jeez, man! You scared the crap out of me," I said and fought to catch my breath.

"My apologies, my friend," Rene said then patted my shoulder.

"I thought I heard something out there."

We scanned the woods and listened.

"I don't hear anything," Rene said. "If you spend enough time in the forest, your mind can play tricks on you. You see faces in bushes. Branches look like arms. Animals and birds sound like people."

"I suppose. Are you ready to go?"

"*Oui*, the sooner we leave, the better. If your friend is ahead of us, maybe we catch up. We should get there in about an hour. Let us go."

CHAPTER 16

RENE AND I made good time as we traversed the forest and we expected to arrive at the safe house soon. Though the war was all around us, we managed to avoid any direct contact with planes, tanks, or infantrymen. With our ammo rather limited, an extended firefight was the last thing we needed.

"Boy, what I wouldn't give to see the sun again," I said. "I hate this gray, crappy, overcast sky. How much farther is it to the safe house? Shouldn't we be there by now?"

Rene looked at me and nodded with an agreeable smile.

As we passed one expansive vineyard after another, the outline of a small building took shape through the veil of trees and shrubs ahead. We gently stepped toward the house then spotted a German supply truck parked a dozen yards away. I unshouldered my rifle and loaded it. I noticed a group of people assembled in front of the house near a stone well, so we crouched down.

"Is that the safe house?" I asked.

"No, the safe house is a kilometer east. That's my home," Rene said.

"What? That vineyard of yours must be huge. "

"*Oui*, it was. Get down. Be quiet," he whispered then pulled me to the ground where we knelt beside a fallen tree. A group of people rushed out of the house. "That's my family. What are German soldiers doing there?"

Several German soldiers and Underground fighters corralled Rene's family near a stone water well. The German leader, an officer of some rank, pushed Dave aside. Two German soldiers, one small and rather lanky, the other, large and beefy, aimed their pistols at Dave who stared angrily at the officer as he rattled off questions. From my vantage point, I could hear everything they said.

"What'd he say, Turel?" Dave asked.

My heart soared at the sound of hearing Dave's voice. Now, I had to find a way to get him out of there. Turel looked angry. After what he did to me, I owed him big time.

"The captain wants to know who you are," Turel said in his deep, resonant voice.

I gripped my rifle tighter as a fire burned inside me.

"John, wait," Rene said and slowly rose to listen to the conversation.

"My friend wants to know if you know Edmund," Turel said.

"Edmund? What's Edmund got to do with anything?" Dave asked.

"If you give him what he wants, he'll kill you quickly. If you don't satisfy him, he'll kill this family one by one, until you do. Tell me, where is the last page?"

"I don't know anything about that. What's Edmund to you?" Dave asked again.

Turel grinned. Good move, Dave. Make that jerk spill the beans.

"I tire of Edmund, Marcus, Weatherby, and Eldridge. They don't work quickly enough to end the war in my favor. I need the last page."

"The last page of what?"

Turel moved closer to Dave's face. Dave always hated that. Why didn't he shove that thug away?

"I don't know anything about any pages," Dave said.

"Then explain these things. Edmund brought me these."

Turel removed my fanny pack and my portable tape player from a worn burlap sack. Our secret was out now.

"John, what's that thing Turel holds?" Rene asked.

"Not now," I said then looked back at Turel and Dave.

"Edmund told me about you Americans," Turel said with an arrogant swagger. "Edmund's such a coward. I shouldn't have taken him. Tell me what this is!" Turel smacked Dave on the head with the tape player.

I watched Rene's family, the women, children, and the old man. The terrified looks on their faces clawed at my heart and appealed to my sense to help them.

"Fine. I'll tell you everything," Dave said.

I reassessed our options but struggled to come up with a suitable plan. Two German soldiers firmly restrained Dave. From my position, they were sitting ducks. I aimed my rifle at the officer who then shouted an order. The soldier closest to Dave pointed at a family member then shouted his own order.

The short German soldier went to the elderly man, grabbed him by the collar, and shoved him to the captain's feet.

"Don't do it, man," Dave pleaded.

The old man pushed himself up and rested on his knees. His hands trembled with fear as he looked up at the German officer, who placed the barrel of his pistol an inch away from the man's head, then pulled the trigger. The family screamed as the old man fell back and blood poured from his wound.

Rene and I recoiled to the ground then planted our backs against the log. Rene was in shock.

"Who was that, Rene?" I asked hastily.

"My father," he said. Seconds later, his eyes flowed with tears.

Rene was in near hysterics. I shoved his head into my chest to muffle his cries and held him tightly. Death surrounded me ever since I got here, but all I could do was watch. With my rifle loaded, I set my revolver beside Rene.

I suddenly recalled being on a moose hunt with my dad several years ago and what he'd said. 'Moose are one of the largest animals in this part of the world. It will drop like a rock with a well-placed shot. If you're off by even an inch, the animal could survive for days before dying, most likely miles from here. You get one shot, John, so make it count.'

A commotion stirred as Dave freed himself from his captor and tackled Turel. Dave connected several furious punches on Turel's head.

"You sonofabitch!" Dave shouted. The larger German soldier and two other Frenchmen grabbed Dave by the neck and dragged him off Turel. Dave was like a rabid pit bull as his captors struggled fiercely to get him under control. Instead of rushing to his aid to beat those bastards into the ground, I reluctantly stayed put. I could help Dave another way.

Turel pressed a large hunting knife against Dave's neck. I thought for sure Dave's number was up and I feared I had waited too long to act. Turel shoved Dave to one of the German soldiers. He then grabbed a boy of about twelve years old, and ran the knife's blade across the child's throat. Blood spurt from the boy's neck then Turel, with a smile, let the boy fall to the ground. Within a minute, the boy stopped moving. Dave's horrific shouts will forever echo in my ears and the intensity of Turel's coldness froze me to the bone.

"Strike me again, and I'll kill everyone!" Turel shouted then wiped his bloody knife on the boy's shirt. Turel ignored the horrific cries of the women who threw themselves at the dead boy then shook him in vain to revive him.

"One last time, where is the last page?" Turel demanded.

Dave wiped his eyes then shook his head in frustration. He didn't know its whereabouts any more than I did. Turel turned to the officer in frustration.

The officer shouted an order to one of his subordinates, who then grabbed a girl of about four years old from a terrified young woman. He pushed back the screaming, hysterical woman then shouted at her.

"Abelina!" the woman cried.

The soldier removed his gun and pressed the barrel against the terrified girl's head. Tears streamed down the girl's cheeks while she struggled helplessly in her captor's grip. The officer then placed the end of his own gun barrel above Dave's right eye.

I couldn't take anymore bloodshed. Blood flowed too quickly around here. Dave stood in shock and his eyes wandered. I watched the little girl, Rene's daughter, cry for her mother. Dave breathed heavily, and I could tell he was in a desperate way.

"If they want to overwhelm me, let them," I said as I readied my rifle.

"What are you doing, John?" Rene asked.

"I'm going to make one shot count."

I set my sight on the German officer immediately threatening Dave. Dave wasn't going to die if I could help it.

The sun broke through the clouds, and golden streams of light fell upon the forest floor. Dave didn't speak as the German officer continued to demand answers. Dave's eyes wandered uncontrollably then locked on me. He focused harder and saw how I counted down from three with my fingers supporting my rifle.

Dave closed his eyes then dropped to the ground as I squeezed the trigger. A loud crack echoed throughout the woods, and a flock of quail took flight. The German officer's body collapsed on top of Dave. The family screamed in terror at my surprise attack. I fired several more shots, striking the house and the German truck. Everyone scrambled for cover. The larger German soldier let Abelina go. He ducked behind the water well and took cover with his fellow thugs.

I fired more times toward the water well to pin down the Germans and allow the kids a chance to get away. Bullets chipped the stone well. The Germans drew their weapons and returned fire.

"Get out of here! Go on! Go on!" Dave bellowed then waved the terrified family to go into the woods.

Turel and his men dashed inside the house. One German soldier fired a shot at the family as they rounded the corner of the house, but he missed. Meanwhile, my calmer nerves scored another German death.

The two remaining German soldiers behind the well returned blind fire into the forest. Dave struggled as he tried to get out from under the dead officer. When he got up to his haunches, he glanced at the officer's lifeless body. He scrambled to his feet and ran to the fleeing family. He caught up with them and they ran into the safety of the woods.

The shooting stopped and the forest abruptly fell into a tension-packed silence. I wasn't sure if I was still breathing.

In the stillness, I heard Dave shout. He sounded far away.

"John, I got the kids! If you're alive, whistle!"

In the quiet of the forest, I whistled like a cardinal. The Germans fired in my direction, and their bullets struck the tree that shielded me.

I strained to see through the brush but couldn't secure a clear shot at my assailants.

"Rene, can you see anything?" I asked.

"No. The Underground men went into the house. The other soldiers are by the well. I don't think I could hit them with this pistol. You best try with your rifle. If you move along this tree, you may get clear shots."

Rene handed the pistol to me with a shaky hand.

"Keep the gun, Rene. If I can get those Krauts out of the way, I'll need you to cover me in case those guys inside are still around. Don't hesitate to shoot. You saw what they did to your family. Dave is with the others, so they should be safe. Wait until I give you a thumbs-up. Fire a couple of times toward the well. That'll keep them busy."

I bellied along the fallen tree to its end roughly forty feet to the right of Rene. I gradually poked my head up. The German soldiers crouched behind the well busily searching for me. The soldier most exposed would get it first.

I gave Rene the thumbs-up. He stood and fired three shots at the Germans, who immediately returned fire. During the barrage, I fired once and struck my target square in the chest. He arched in slow motion then went limp. The others continued to shoot, ignorant to the fate of their comrade.

With another shot, I struck the second soldier in the neck. He clutched his throat while blood gushed wildly. The last German soldier stopped shooting to help his mates, then two shots from Rene's gun struck the lone surviving German soldier in the back.

I looked at Rene as he surveyed his house for any movement in the stone silence.

"Hey, Rene," I said in a firm whisper. "You okay?"

"Yes," he said then gave me a thumbs- up.

I shouted away from the house to disguise my location.

"Hey, Dave! Those guys out front are dead! You okay?"

"John!" Dave shouted back, "We're okay. I saw the others cut out the back! The house should be empty!"

In the distance, the sound of detonating bombs permeated the depths of the forest. Like an approaching thunderstorm, the rumbles got louder. The Chalons offensive had officially started, and the battles would reach here soon.

Rene and I approached the house with our guns ready.

"Okay, all's well. Dave, come on out!" I shouted.

Dave led the family to the front of the house. The bodies of the old man, the boy, as well as the German soldiers lay motionless in pools of blood, well absorbed by the spongy soil. Rene fought back the tears on seeing his father and son on the ground. The surviving children, with their arms outstretched, dashed to Rene.

When Dave saw me, he breathed a massive sigh of relief and we hugged like sumo wrestlers. This last incident was much too close to death for comfort.

"Man, I was afraid I'd lost you," I said. "If I hadn't found your watch, I would've pegged you a goner."

I handed Dave his watch.

"I almost was. Thank God you got here when you did." He hugged me again.

"Is everyone okay, considering?" I asked.

"They'll be all right. Say, John, one of those Underground guys was the one at the cabin with Edmund. It was Turel."

"That was him, all right."

"He ran out back with the others into one of those time windows. Turel's after the last page."

"I heard. The pieces are starting to fall into place," I said then viewed the bodies spread about the yard.

We shared some reassuring banter then pondered how we could get the colonels out of trouble before Turel got them. Without knowing how to use time windows, I couldn't think of a quicker way back to Chalons so we would have to run.

The little girl, Abelina, tugged on my pant leg. I bent down and looked the girl in the eye. I gave her a smile, and she said something in her innocent little voice.

"What did she say, Rene?" I asked.

"She said you're a big Doughboy," he said then smiled as he watched his daughter. To the girl, I must have looked like a giant.

"You're a brave little girl. You look out for your family, okay?" I said to her and turned to Rene. "Tell her for me, please?"

He translated and the girl smiled. She gave me a hug while I gently caressed her head.

"You and your friend must get going," Rene said. "Chalons is about forty kilometers straight west-northwest. You'll find a large open field. I believe that's where Colonel Weatherby is."

"That'd be the Gate. Thanks, Rene," I said.

"Let me get you more bullets. You may need them," Rene said then went inside the house. Within moments, he returned with a small burlap sack of bullets.

"Here, you take these," Rene said. "Maybe they'll last you until you get back to Chalons."

"Thanks for everything you've done, Rene," I said. "I owe you big for all your help. I'll tell Colonel Marcus everything that happened, but before we leave, we'll help you with your loved ones."

Dave and I stayed to help dig graves for Rene's father, son, and the German soldiers. Even though they were the enemy, we couldn't leave them exposed the way they were.

"I hope you all can find some peace soon. I think you've suffered more than enough," I said then leaned my shovel beside the front door. I wiped the sweat off my forehead with my shirtsleeve.

"Thank you. I don't know how we will fare, but we will survive," Rene said then set down a few sticks for a cross beside the mounds where we buried Rene's father and son.

I nodded.

"If you ever make it to Chicago, be sure to look for me," I said.

Rene gave me another hug.

"Good luck to you, my friend," Rene said and kissed my cheeks.

A grateful smile spread across Rene's face. He hugged me tightly. It was nice having a friend like Rene at a time like this.

"Are you ready, Dave?" I asked.

"I'm ready," Dave said as he rested his rifle on his shoulder.

We waved at the women and children as we made our way into the woods. Dave paused then glanced at a young woman, who gazed at him gratefully. She nodded and blew him a soft kiss. If Dave had a hat, he'd have tipped it in typical cowboy fashion.

"What was that all about?" I asked.

"Nothing, she's just a sweet lady. Look, I won't mince words, John. We're in deep here."

"You have no idea."

CHAPTER 17

DAVE AND I raced through the woods while constant mortar explosions thundered in the distance. He told me everything about his experience with Turel and the Underground and how he left his watch as a desperate bread crumb for me to find. I, in turn, disclosed what I'd pieced together about Edmund and what Marcus said to me regarding the last page. Turel being a fallen angel was icing on the cake. We stopped running to catch our breath but continued a brisk walk.

"I'm trying to figure out how Devers's letters figure in all this," I said. "I believed all along they were likely some kind of confession."

"Tell me something about them," Dave said while he ducked under a low branch.

"There was one letter with a November 1917 date on it. Those letters must've been written about something happening right now."

"Like what? Fallen angels?" Dave asked.

"There wasn't anything about angels, but we know Edmund has a confirmed link to the French Underground, who in turn has a connection to the Germans. We know the colonels are involved in a secret deal, probably for a lot of money. Remember how Edmund threatened me when we first met?"

"Yeah."

"We interrupted something that day. Maybe they were planning a deal then. He might think we're hot on his trail," I said.

"So, Edmund screwed up with Turel and now Turel's going to stick it to the colonels. Seems Edmund is the ringleader here. What should we do?" Dave asked.

My mind struggled to come up with a plan to save the colonels, but with no gift for strategy, I felt like I raced down a mountain road at night without headlights. Unless I had an idea where the road went, there wasn't much chance I'd survive.

"We have to tell someone, but not Ray," I said then drew in a deep breath.

"Why not?" Dave asked.

"I screwed up the other day."

"Crap. What now?"

"After we came back from looking for you, I got into a little argument with Billy. One thing led to another, and I blurted out something about the Chicago stockyards being closed."

"So? They've been shut down forever."

"In our time they have. In 1917, it was a booming place. Thanks to my big mouth, Ray and Billy got us in their sights."

"Perfect."

Dave's mouth hung open as we resumed our dash through the dense trees. We straddled over the remains of a tree trunk a few years away from full disintegration. I stepped on it, and my foot crunched through the rotted bark up to my knee.

"Do they think we're from the future?" Dave asked.

"I wouldn't go that far."

"Does Ray think we're more than just pilots?"

"Well, yesterday morning Ray told me he suspected a spy was among us. I wasn't sure if he was talking about us or someone else. Anyway, if Edmund has his way, the whole offensive is a bust. We have to get to Marcus fast."

Bomb explosions continued behind us and more planes zipped overhead. It seemed nobody wanted to miss the party at the Gate.

We approached the edge of the forest then encountered the vast field Rene described. British, French, and German planes flew in all directions in dogfights spread across the sky.

"I wonder how everything's going?" I asked as I observed the planes in their lethal acrobatic show. The greasy burning stench of mechanical destruction and gunpowder intensified.

"I don't know," Dave said as he wiped his forehead with his sleeve. He took a close sniff of his armpit then cringed. "I suppose it depends on how much time Edmund and Turel had with the Germans. I think the Gate is baked on this one."

"Look over there at the base of those trees. See it?" I said.

"It looks like a trench."

"That must be the Gate."

Dave studied the terrain carefully.

"You're right, John. Colonel Weatherby's supposed to be there."

A mortar shell whirred louder and exploded about 200 yards away from us. We then shielded our eyes from the shower of dirt and rocks that rained on us.

"Let's get out of here!" I shouted.

Dave and I dashed for our lives as several hundred German soldiers stormed over a nearby, grassy hill. Bombs exploded all around and annihilated the once quiet pasture.

"Are those our guys?" Dave shouted.

"No!"

We sprinted across the open ground toward the trench. I then saw German tanks clamber behind the advancing enemy soldiers. I stopped running to confirm we headed in the right direction. Thousands of men swarmed across the field like competing ant colonies on a candy bar.

The overcast sky of the past two days gave way to clear skies and bright sunshine. The beauty of this day would make a final serene memory for the many who would soon perish.

"Now ain't the time for sightseeing, John!" Dave shouted.

"I'm coming!" I said.

"They're right on our ass!"

The gods must've been with us as bullets zipped overhead, pelted the ground around us, and luckily never hit their targets. The faster we ran, the closer we got to the trench.

We were too busy running for our lives when we stumbled into the trench and landed on several Allied soldiers.

"You're the good guys, right?" I asked and gazed up at the men dusting themselves off.

"You're an American, ain't yah?" the scrawny soldier replied in what sounded like a Tennessee drawl and his rifle aimed at me.

"Hell, yeah," I said.

He set down his rifle, extended his bony hand, and struggled to help me to my feet.

"What are you all doing out yonder? Don't you know there's a war heading this way?"

"No kidding. Is this the Gate?" I asked.

The aerial battle continued unabated as the German tank battalions crawled closer toward us. The flurry of planes that chased each other looked painfully similar to the dream I had with the angels fighting in the heavens.

"Yep, this is the Gate," the soldier said. "Say, you're big. You got to be a might three hundred pounds."

"Close enough. How did the offensive start up? Did Eldridge's men get through?" I asked.

"Well, we know the southern shoot into Germany went okay. They ain't seen hardly any action. Weatherby knows more about that. They say we're expecting some Krauts this way. See our tanks back yonder?"

I turned around and looked into the forest.

"Yeah," I said.

"That's in case them Heinies get any ideas. We got buried mines about a hundred yards out yonder. We dug enough of them to send them all back to Berlin."

Neither Dave nor I were about to hang around to have tons of dirt and mangled bodies rain down on us.

"Plenty of Germans are heading this way, all right," Dave said. "Something tells me things didn't go right down south. Can you tell us how to get back to Chalons? It's important."

The smile on the soldier's face faded. "I suppose it's about ten or twelve miles west."

Machine gun fire erupted along the trench and showered the field with bullets. The sudden outburst rattled my ears, and I reflexively covered them. Dozens of enemy soldiers fell to their deaths. The German tanks continued advancing toward the Gate, unaffected by the barrage. Line officers blew whistles when the German tanks came within 500 yards of the line.

"I think you better cover your ears. They aim to do it," the Tennessean shouted.

"Do what?" Dave asked.

"Set off the mines!"

Allied and German cannon fire burst everywhere. On both sides of the Allied trench, shells exploded endlessly. Intense vibrations and impact tremors rattled my innards. Shrapnel sliced through the war-weary men indiscriminately. Zipping bullets splintered trees, and deflected off tanks. The screams of the casualties resounded between the brief moments of relative quiet between bomb impacts.

The bellowing cry of a steam whistle near the center of the line clued the men to cease fire. Everyone balled up on the trench floor in unison.

The deafening roar of the Gate mine detonation had no equal. Other than the blast at Hiroshima about thirty years from now, it was the largest man-made explosion in history. The force of the blast sent shock waves that vibrated my bones. No artillery barrage compared to the destructive force inflicted on the French countryside along the two-mile Gate line.

The spectacular explosion cast soil and rock high into the sky. Some parts of the blast even caused several low-flying planes to crash.

The first shock wave threw me onto my back, and I felt my brain slosh inside my skull. With my fingers shoved deep into my ears, I opened my eyes. I watched awestruck as the massive wall of soil soared for the heavens, then collapsed like an earthy tidal wave.

The indeterminate tonnage of dirt struck the ground with deep, powerful thuds. Fragments ranged in size from dust-sized particles to clods as big as steamer trunks.

When the downpour subsided, everyone in the trench rose to see what remained of the German army. The blast flipped over the first line of German tanks and killed thousands of German soldiers.

Only seven tanks of the second line were still functional. Machine gun fire from the trench resumed, their stark bursts tolerable compared to the thunder of the Gate detonation. The surviving Germans recoiled to the safety of their tree line.

"My God, my maker," Dave said as he observed the massive craters that remained.

"I still don't believe what I see," I said.

A mile-long string of craters, each about fifty feet deep and a hundred yards across, perforated the earth. All along the line, men dug out to assess the damage. As I climbed out of the trench, I saw several German soldiers strewn about the forest and in front of the trench. In front of me, I saw the partial remains of one of them draped over the trench ledge.

"Oh, God," I said as I pushed myself out of the trench.

"John, what's up?" Dave asked.

I took several deep breaths. The gruesome discovery caught me off guard. I got a strong whiff of the man's chest cavity, which reminded me of the musky stickiness of a gutted deer. That oily, humid smell can permeate and take root in the nasal cavity for days.

"There's only part of a guy here. All of his guts are gone," I said.

Dave spotted the inside of the man's hollowed chest. He turned away and quickly climbed out of the trench. Two medics arrived and removed the remains.

"Man, how much more of this do we have to take?" Dave asked.

I shouldered my rifle then turned to a soldier in the trench. "Hey, buddy, which way to Colonel Weatherby?"

"He should be down the line a spell, a good hundred yards," the soldier said.

"Thanks," I said.

We hiked behind the trench along the tree line. Soldiers continued digging out and took care of the wounded. Other soldiers piled up the German casualties.

"You know it'll only get worse," I said.

"You don't have to tell me," Dave said.

In moments, we came upon a large tent next to a boiler with a steam whistle attached to the side. The boiler hiss decreased as two men opened the boiler's pressure release valve and unleashed a blasting hiss. After covering my ears too late, I gave the men a dirty look.

"Give a guy some warning next time," I said.

Dave pushed aside the tent flap, then entered Weatherby's tent.

"Colonel Weatherby, sir?" I asked. His white curly mane and beard did little to hide the worry in his eyes. His dignified English manner seemed uncharacteristically edgy.

"Lieutenants Harrod and Sowell," Colonel Weatherby said.

"Yes, sir. You remember us?"

"Of course. Colonel Marcus said I should be on the lookout for you two. I'm glad you're both safe. Can I get you anything? Food, drink?"

Eating was the last thing on our minds after what we'd seen, but since it had been a couple of days since I last ate, the thought sent my stomach into a defiant growl. I patted my stomach then looked at Dave.

Weatherby asked his assistant, Captain Keary, to bring some food for us. It was when Keary left the tent that I noticed Weatherby had two missing fingers on his left hand.

"Sir, is there a way we can get a message to Colonel Marcus? It concerns Captain Edmund. We think he's connected to the Germans," I said.

Weatherby blushed bright red.

"Do you realize what you're implying?" Weatherby asked.

"Yes, sir. We can tell you what we know and how we know," I said. "You're not going to like it."

"Please tell me."

Weatherby listened to our testimonies. Dave related his experience with Turel and the German soldiers connected to Edmund, but we left out everything related to angels and the last page.

"Sir, I know this is incriminating stuff, but I swear it's all true," I said.

Weatherby stopped cold, and his eyes darted about the tent. I thought he was having a stroke.

"Sir?" I asked firmly.

Weatherby snapped out of his trance then explained why he set off the mines. I didn't know if he went into denial or wanted to deflect the conversation on purpose. Regardless, he looked like he was in a psycho-panic of sorts.

"Earlier reports from Eldridge suggested more German troops were on the way to the Gate," Weatherby said softly. "He should've been here by now to assist, but he claimed his instructions led him on an erroneous path and he's presently trying to recapture lost time."

If everything about Edmund, Marcus, and Turel were right, then Turel had double-crossed the Allies and had the German arsenal redirected toward the Gate. Weatherby, in a panic, set off the mines too soon. The detonation only delayed the inevitable and likely slaughter. Without a word, Weatherby escorted us outside to a communications tent where we found men scrambling to put things back in order.

"What's the problem here, Sergeant?" Weatherby bellowed.

"Sir, the line to Chalons is down. We sent three men to find the break," the radioman replied then returned the headset to his ears.

"Men, until the line is repaired, I'm afraid you'll have to stay here. Colonel Marcus's orders are to keep you until we prove communication with him. The line should be up soon."

"Okay, Colonel. Maybe we can catch up on some rest, provided those guys don't come back," I said as I tilted my head toward the German side.

"Sound reasoning, Lieutenant."

Captain Keary entered the tent with a bottle of wine, a bread loaf, and a dried sausage.

"Here, men," Keary said.

We devoured our unexpected meal. I missed the beer we'd usually drink on a busy day like this. However, we felt lucky to have what was available, considering everything we went through.

The euphoric effects of the wine hit us fast. Neither of us was a wine drinker, but given the circumstances, any booze would do. We spoke to Weatherby and Keary at length about our adventure over the last couple of days. I took a risk when I asked Colonel Weatherby if he knew Harrison Devers. He hadn't. The more we spoke, the more anxious Weatherby appeared. His behavior only solidified my belief that a conspiracy of sorts likely existed.

Outside the tent, we observed a hellish scene. Streaks of fading, golden sunlight sifted through the settling dust and created an eerie presence as the men continued digging out. With a reality like this, who needed nightmares? For the moment, I felt safe for the first time in two days. Two days, it seemed like weeks.

Darkness fell on the wasted, wiped out meadow. Dimly lit kerosene lamps cast a dull, amber glow inside the tent. The radioman created a dust cloud when he pushed the tent flap aside.

"Sir, I have Chalons on the line," the radioman said.

We ran out of the tent to the radioman's station. The radioman handed me a black, weighty handset.

"Colonel Marcus, sir? It's Lieutenant Harrod."

"Lieutenant Harrod, it's good to hear you're well," said the tinny, bold voice of Colonel Marcus through the primitive phone. "Is Lieutenant Sowell with you?"

"Yes, sir. He's okay too. I have information for you about the offensive. I learned from the Underground that Captain Edmund— Hello?" I looked at the handset and turned to Weatherby. "I think the line is dead again."

Weatherby put the handset to his ear then shook his head.

"I guess we're spending the night, Colonel," Dave said.

Dave and I left Weatherby's tent then went into the trench. We dug out little alcoves in the dirt walls that served as our sleeping quarters for the night. We marveled at the horrifying, hellish brilliance of the flares and the gunfire that raced across the prairie like streaks of white lightning. Then the bombardment began.

The German assault at the Gate continued for hours, and I didn't sleep a wink.

Weatherby's heavy artillery returned fire with vigor. Explosions on the German side flashed like strobe lights and the earsplitting crescendos of the tank firings echoed for miles.

As quickly as the firing started, it stopped. A haunting peace descended across the battered French prairie and I was never so scared in my life.

CHAPTER 18

AS THE MORNING sun rose over the Gate, the Allies assessed the damage sustained during the overnight attack. Thankfully, they suffered few casualties during the nighttime assault than during the previous day. Night vision didn't exist yet, therefore hitting a target in the black ink of night was a challenging task for both sides. However, that didn't stop the snipers who took shots at the slightest flicker of a lit match. More often than not, he'd hit some careless soldier who let his guard down or relaxed at the wrong moment.

Continuous explosions nearby made any effort to flee through the forest a fatal proposition. The southern portion of the Gate suffered the most. Hundreds of men died, while thousands more suffered life-altering injuries.

Colonel Weatherby and Captain Keary dove into the trenches as well. Unfortunately, Keary died when shrapnel ripped through his chest. He was dead before he landed in the trench. Weatherby injured his shoulder after falling on top of another soldier.

Impact craters from the artillery fire and the mine blasts left the once grassy prairie reminiscent of a pockmarked lunar landscape. The stillness of the dry morning air gradually gave way to muggy, swamp-like conditions.

A brown haze wafted across the plain as men continued brushing the dirt off equipment. After we took notice of the battered field, we knew there was no way we could stay here for long.

"When the line's ready, we'll call Colonel Marcus once more," I said. "After that, we get the hell out of here whether Weatherby says we can or not. We could swipe one of those trucks back there." I pointed to a row of ambulances and supply trucks lined up about fifty yards in the forest.

"You don't have to waste time convincing me," Dave said.

"Come on. Let's see what's going on with the damn phone."

We climbed out of the trench then headed to the communications tent. Several infantrymen stacked sandbags and rebuilt the walls surrounding the radio equipment.

Colonel Weatherby and the sergeant toiled endlessly to restore contact with Chalons. Weatherby watched us as we approached.

"Lieutenant Harrod, I believe what you said yesterday about Captain Edmund. The Germans have far more artillery than we originally anticipated. We'll request reinforcements once we set up communications with Chalons. That aside, how are you men holding out?"

"We're okay, sir," I answered. "Sorry about Captain Keary. He seemed like a nice guy."

"He was an excellent officer but stubborn at times. We should have the line to Chalons repaired within the hour. I wish to speak with Colonel Marcus to find out if we can gain more air support. If what you said earlier is correct, I anticipate an attack directly."

"Okay, sir," I said then wiped my forehead.

Weatherby retreated into his tent.

"It looks like we're waiting some more, Dave. Is it me, or is it getting hotter out here?" I asked and wiped my face with my sleeve again.

"I think the humidity is getting worse. It reminds me of our Florida job. Boy, what I wouldn't give to be there now cutting lawns instead of ducking for cover," Dave said.

I thought for a moment about that one summer during high school when we worked in Florida on a lawn maintenance crew trimming grass with gas-powered weed trimmers. That peaceful daydream gave way to a shout from one of the men down the trench.

"Colonel, we have a problem! Take a look!"

Weatherby's jaw dropped as he scanned the other side of the no man's land.

"My God, I never expected this," Weatherby said and took a long look at the thousands of German troops that had gathered during the night. "How is the repair on that confounded wire coming?" He shouted and headed for the communications tent.

Weatherby's reaction to the German assembly made us all uneasy. Tension mounted as the German forces continued to amass in the east.

"Maybe we should pull back. The Germans have a lot more guys than we do," Dave said.

"Retreat isn't an option, Lieutenant. We're the last line of defense before Chalons and Paris. We will hold this line!" Weatherby bellowed, determined to fight to the end. His nervousness suddenly faded.

"Then I think we should be on our way to Chalons while it's quiet," I said.

"You'll remain until Colonel Marcus approves your clearance. Is that clear, Lieutenant?"

"Yes, sir," I said disappointedly.

All eyes focused on the battlefield for an impending enemy advancement. I thought about how the huge craters from yesterday's blasts would make a crossing attempt a difficult or likely fatal proposition. Unless it rained, the craters would do little to slow the tanks.

Dave and I sat in painful helplessness while an hour of nerve-racking inactivity battled our patience. The radioman trotted over then announced that Chalons was again on the line. We went to the communications tent where Weatherby snatched the receiver from the radioman.

"Yes, Colonel Marcus," Weatherby said. "We had to detonate the mines yesterday. The Germans have assembled significant numbers of men. Along with Lieutenant Sowell's report of Captain Edmund, I believe the Germans will begin their advance within the next few hours."

We carefully listened to Weatherby's half of the conversation.

"I can't say at the moment, Marcus. The, uh, plan is for naught. Take whatever action is necessary to defend yourselves."

"Plan? I think we know enough about their plan," I whispered to Dave, who then nodded.

In the distance, the deep rumbling sound of aircraft grew louder.

"Yes, Marcus," Weatherby said. "I can hear their engines now. Is Captain Edmund about? I see. Don't count on him returning. From what Lieutenants Harrod and Sowell have disclosed, I'm certain Edmund has left indefinitely."

"It figures that jerk bolted," I said.

"Hey, John, these guys are crapping their pants. Let's get out of here," Dave said.

"I'm way ahead of you."

Weatherby continued speaking on the phone with Marcus.

"Marcus, I believe we've been, well, compromised. That's correct. After the planes leave here, I'll call with a report. Good luck to you as well."

Weatherby passed the receiver to the radioman.

"Colonel Marcus has ordered air support," Weatherby said.

The encroaching drone of Allied planes grew louder with each passing second and appeared a thousand feet overhead.

"They're already here," I said.

A German air strike now would severely cripple the Gate, which would then open a clear path to Chalons. Six de Havilland Airco bombers escorted by twelve Sopwith fighters rumbled ahead to the German fortification.

The Allied bombers, nearly identical to the Gothas we saw earlier, ambled across the sky. Thousands of Allied soldiers who occupied the trench at the Gate cheered as the planes passed overhead.

The whistle of the descending payloads resonated across the battlefield. First, plumes of dirt blossomed into the air. Seconds later the sound wave reached the Gate.

I grabbed Weatherby's binoculars to see the bombers' results. Above, twenty more Sopwith Camels joined a dozen French Spads. They dove and strafed the German fortification with constant machine gun fire. Along the way, the fighters dropped several of their own smaller bombs. Once the Allied bombers completed their delivery, they retreated to the safety of the west.

The Allied fighters crushed the German ground forces. The sudden appearance of German Albatroses and a dozen Fokkers quickly squelched the Allied cheers of triumph.

The fighters attacked each other with fury. One Allied bomber spewed smoke from its starboard engine after two Fokkers cut it up. The plane then spiraled into the northern forest. A billowing trail of black smoke marked its end. The remaining Allied bombers managed to escape but drew enemy fighters with them.

A Fokker barrel-rolled to shake off a determined Sopwith Camel, while another Fokker slotted behind the Camel. The Fokker fired. Moments later, the Camel caught fire and corkscrewed into the trench.

"Man, no way I could fly like that," Dave said.

"I imagine if we get back to Chalons, they won't be putting us back into the air," I said.

"What if Marcus orders us to? He can make things tough for us," Dave said.

"Marcus is the least of our problems."

We watched two Fokkers crash in the distance. One, shot down by a Spad, crashed in the middle of no man's land. The pilot of the second doomed Fokker guided his plane toward the Allied trench. We dropped to the trench floor as the aircraft then spun out of control and crashed thirty yards away from of us. Many Allied men died in an inferno when the fuel tank exploded.

The intense fighting continued for an hour. The battles ended when two Camels chased two surviving Fokkers south away from the Gate.

The Germans took a beating, and with only twelve planes, they caused unrecoverable damage to the Gate. Infantrymen could only watch the planes burn, but at least the immediate enemy threat was over.

"Sir, every minute we spend here is a minute we could be heading to Chalons. Can we take one of those trucks?" I asked. At this point, his answer didn't matter much to me.

Colonel Weatherby surveyed the rear where men unloaded supply trucks. Several ambulances stood by, waiting to transport the wounded to field hospitals.

"Very well," Weatherby said. "Inform the driver of that supply truck where you want to go. When you get to Chalons, give this letter to Colonel Marcus. Tell him we're faring well at the present time. However, we need reinforcements urgently. Take some ammunition and rations with you, whatever you can carry."

"Thank you, sir," Dave said with sincerity.

"We'll tell Colonel Marcus what happened. If you get through to him anytime soon, will you tell him we're on our way?" I asked.

"Yes, Lieutenant, I certainly will. Godspeed."

I pondered what was in the sealed envelope, then wondered if Weatherby was, in fact, Devers himself and gave me one of the letters. I couldn't open the sealed envelope, so I put it into my shirt pocket. Dave and I went to the ambulance where a short, robust man with his back to us barked complaints at an infantryman.

"Hey, buddy, Colonel Weatherby said you could give us a ride to Chalons."

The man turned around. To our surprise, the man was a woman.

"Call me buddy again, and you can walk! Hey, Chicago! Texas! I was worried about you guys. Hey, what's the news with you calling me buddy, huh?" Helen asked with crossed arms. The infantryman scurried away from Helen's verbal torture.

"Sorry, Helen. From behind you looked like everyone else," Dave said. "You're the driver?"

"You were expecting President Wilson?" she asked.

"Boy, you get around," I said.

"I'm always where the action is, Chicago."

I did a double take. The familiarity of her comment caused a memory flash. I felt a sudden, odd spiritual connection with her as she briefly looked into my eyes while she said it. This was too weird. Then again, it was probably *déjà vu*.

"Where are you boys heading?" Helen asked as she observed the frenetic action taking place around us.

"Chalons. Colonel Weatherby said we could use your truck. Can we get going?" I said with a hint of impatience.

"Well, why didn't you say so? Climb in, time's wasting!" she snapped back.

We climbed into the truck, a 1916 Ford Model T.

"Hey, Chicago. Can you give me a crank?"

"Say what?" I asked.

She pointed to the front of the truck.

"Oh right, sure," I said. I jumped to the front of the truck, gave the crank handle a hard turn, then the engine started. The sound of the motor was more like a tinkering collage of metal parts than any truck engine I'd ever heard. I'm sure all twenty horses under the hood were anxious to hightail it out of here as much as I was. I climbed back in, and we were on our way.

The steamy, late summer air continued to drain my spirits, while the sun blazed overhead. Military vehicles of all sorts ground the dirt road smooth between Chalons and the Gate.

"So, what brought you into all this mess?" I asked.

"Shortly after my brother left for Europe to fight, I answered a call for women drivers. I drove my father's Ford good and didn't see myself getting to Europe any other way. So, I signed up at the Red Cross. How'd you end up here?"

Boy, if she only knew.

"It's a long story," I said, with a heavy sigh. "Dave got shot down, then I came back to find him. We hiked back to the Gate, now we're going to Chalons."

"You boys must not be good flyers seeing this is the second time you got plucked," she said with a wink.

"Did you hear that, Dave? Everywhere I go, there's always a smart aleck," I said.

Helen elbowed me. I smiled then returned my attention to the countryside.

"Nobody can bother you when you're floating up there among the clouds. Sometimes I wish I could fly," Helen lamented.

The bumpy, gravelly road wound through hills and across shallow streams. We approached a small village bustling with Allied infantrymen and devoid of any wartime destruction. A dozen soldiers mingled around fuel trucks parked under a camouflaged canvas canopy. Helen pulled up beside a fuel truck where three idle soldiers stood by smoking cigarettes. Smart boys.

"Hey, boys, can we get some gas from you?" Helen asked with a smile.

"Sure, beautiful. You can have anything you want if you give me a kiss first," one of the soldiers answered followed by laughter from his friends.

"How about being a gentleman and just giving me some gas?" she asked nicely once again.

"How about you come around to the back of my truck and showing me your patriotism, sweetie?" he said with more laughter from his friends. He was quite the comedian, and I didn't feel like laughing.

I walked around the truck toward the soldier. I'd gone through too much crap to have to deal with this nonsense.

Helen slid out of the truck then stepped in front of me. Before I knew what happened, she kicked the soldier's groin then clutched his wavy black hair as he dropped to his knees. His face grimaced in pain as she lit into him.

"You giving me trouble, Pasquale? We're fighting this war together see? Don't go making the experience any worse than it is, or I'll polish your head with my truck. Get me?" Helen demanded. I liked this girl.

The soldier looked at her with terrified eyes. I was glad she was on my side.

"Yes, ma'am," he murmured.

"Good. Get busy with the gas," she said then let him go.

Helen calmly got back in the truck. I stood dumbfounded.

The soldier looked up at me. His jaw dropped as I crossed my arms and stared at him. I still wanted a piece of him, but Helen did a better job.

"You heard her," I said.

"Yes, sir."

The soldier untangled a hose then set to his task as I returned to my seat in the truck.

Helen smiled.

"You're okay, Chicago," Helen said.

"Thanks. I would've kicked his ass, but, you know," I casually said.

Dave nudged Helen then turned to me. "Old John's a regular powder keg, ain't he?" He said as he wiggled my cheek a couple times.

Helen giggled at my silly, blank expression.

"Thanks for the gas," I said then waved to the soldier.

"Yes, sir," the soldier replied with a smile. "Sorry for what I said, ma'am. Didn't mean any harm."

"Bygones, pal. Give us a crank so we can get along," Helen said.

With no more obstacles, we resumed our drive to Chalons.

The road was again quiet, except for the truck's puttering engine. The early afternoon humidity continued to stifle. Sweat trailed down my back and breathing became more difficult.

We'd driven about fifteen minutes when steam billowed from the radiator. Helen pulled up close to a stream next to a large grouping of trees. The remains of a blown apart farmhouse stood across the road from us.

She got out of the truck and opened the hood.

"Well, that's just dandy!" Helen proclaimed. "We'll need some water, or we're stuck here. There's nothing in the truck worth saving, so I'm not afraid to leave it if we have to."

Dave looked around nervously.

"What's the matter with you mugs?" Helen asked.

A shot rang out from he forest, and Helen fell back as if someone shoved her to the ground.

We dragged Helen with us as we scurried around the truck. Several more shots ricocheted off the truck body. One of the tires hissed, then went flat. More shots from the trees pinned us behind our truck. We looked at Helen's wound as she struggled for breath.

"Oh my Lord," she said.

Her face cringed as I gently removed her coat.

"You got hit in the shoulder," I said. "Breathe easy. Try not to panic. You'll be fine." I tore off her coat sleeve and used it to pad her wound. "Dave, those shots came from up high. They have to be in the trees. I guess two, maybe three of them. Go under the truck to see if you can spot them, okay?"

"You got it, buddy," Dave said.

"You'll be okay, Helen. Breathe slow and easy," I said softly. Pain contorted her face while tears welled in her eyes. Helplessness consumed me again, like it did before I started my search for Dave.

"Burns, like a poker," Helen said. "John, I don't want to die in this place."

"Easy does it, Helen. Let me get a look at this," I said. "I need to roll you over for a second."

I carefully turned Helen onto her side then saw a large gaping wound in her right shoulder. She was on borrowed time. The bullet passed through her shoulder blade. There was no doubt she likely suffered lung damage as well.

"See anything yet, Dave?"

Two more shots ricocheted off the truck as Dave made his way out from underneath.

"I saw two. One is almost straight ahead about thirty feet up, some twenty yards back. The other is to the left, same height maybe a little deeper in. It looks like they're in a treehouse. How are you, Helen?"

"It hurts bad," she answered. She dragged her sleeve across her face and wiped her eyes.

Dave looked at me while I gently shook my head. He gave Helen an empathetic gaze as he loosely held the rifle.

"You said you saw a treehouse? You mean a deer blind?" I asked.

"I guess it could be that," Dave said.

"Do you have a clear shot at them?"

Dave itched his head then set down the rifle.

"If they have a clear shot at us, then we should have a clear shot at them. You're the expert shot, John. I think you got a better chance at plugging them than I do."

Dave wiped the sweat off his defeated face. "I think with the angle, they couldn't see me too good," Dave said. "I don't believe they can see us on the ground with all that grass out front."

I grabbed an ammo magazine off the truck seat, crawled underneath the truck, and slid alongside the rear axle. I poked the rifle through the wooden spokes of the wheel and lined up my shot. Dave did what he could to make Helen comfortable.

I searched for my target in the woods then saw movement up in the trees. Through the gun sight, I saw my opponent aiming back at me. I took several steady breaths, held the last breath for a moment, and squeezed the trigger. A piece of wood from the blind fluttered to the ground. My target appeared and I fired again. My foe tumbled out of the blind, and struck the ground with a muffled thud.

I then set my sights on the other sniper. I fired then he too fell to the ground. Easy pickings.

"I got them, Dave. Did you see if there were any others?"

"No, I only saw the two."

I surveyed the trees but couldn't see anything else resembling deer blinds. I crawled out from under the truck and wrapped my coat around the end of the rifle barrel. While I moved the gun barrel beyond the back of the truck, a shot rang out and struck the tailgate.

I spied through the trees then spotted the remaining sniper. The branches obscured him since he was deeper in the forest, but I spotted him. I crouched next to the rear wheel then adjusted my rifle sights for a longer shot. I rested the rifle on the tire, which gave me a steady sight line. I made out the image of the blind through the branches then fired.

"I think I see him," I said.

The unseen sniper fired again and struck a wooden wheel spoke. I shot back. This time, I saw his arm dangle over the edge of his roost.

"Okay, I got him that time." I shuffled out from under the truck. "How are you holding up, Helen?"

"My head is spinning like a top," she said. "Could you get some water for me, over by the stream? There's a canteen in the truck."

"John, can you watch her while I get the water? I'll be right back."

"Yeah, go ahead," I said.

Helen's dizziness told me she bled internally. I looked into her eyes while I caressed her cheeks. For a moment, I swore I saw what looked like an aberration of some kind. I blinked, and the anomaly was gone. My heart ached as Helen fell deeper into hopelessness. The more I looked at her, the more my eyes welled with tears.

"What's wrong?" she asked.

"Nothing. Must be allergies," I said. I feigned away to see if Dave was on his way back with the water. Her expression of disbelief when the bullet struck her replayed in my mind.

The heat and humidity were at their peak when Dave returned with the canteen.

"Here you go. It's cold," Dave said. "Take a few sips then pour some on the wound. It'll help," Dave said.

"There you go, Helen," I said as he held the canteen to her lips. "Hey, Dave, can you soak these torn sleeves in the stream so we can make a cold compress?"

"You got it," Dave said.

Dave grabbed the bloodied sleeves then dashed to the stream. He hurried back and applied the wet sleeves to both sides of her shoulder. She jolted, then let out a heavy sigh of relief.

"Oh, that feels better. I'm afraid one of you will have to drive the rest of the way," Helen said as she took deep, agonizing breaths.

"We can't drive now. Let's go inside that house. We have to stop the bleeding first," I said.

I scooped up Helen then hustled her inside the blown apart cobblestone farmhouse. I set her beside a wall on the dusty plank floor. A whiff of lilac from her hair filled my nose. A memory of Mary flashed through my mind. I never realized how much I missed her.

I looked deeply into Helen's eyes as she winced in pain. I gently smoothed away the hair off her cringing face. My lips slowly cracked open as I watched her face reform into a familiar image. I couldn't believe my eyes. The metamorphosis completed and I sat in shock.

"Holy crap! Mary? My Mary?" I asked in surprise.

She smiled then grimaced at a pain tremor.

"It's me, John," Mary said and smiled.

Dave and I sat in bewilderment at the unexpected revelation. What the hell was going on here?

CHAPTER 19

DAVE SPOTTED A worn mattress covered in broken bricks, dust, and timber debris. He yanked at the mattress then flipped it over to the less filthy side. I picked up Mary and gently set her on the mattress. I took the leather strap from my rifle and fashioned a makeshift sling to support her shoulder.

Dave broke apart a couple of chairs and stacked the pieces in the fireplace. He lit a match, set it under a strip of the bone-dry wood, and started a small fire. Mary's presence stunned me, and I couldn't fathom how her disguise worked.

"You're a good man, John," Mary said. "Don't worry about me. Keep searching for Colonel Devers."

"What the hell's going on? How'd you change your face like that? How did you get here?"

Mary groaned in pain.

"An angel turned me into an Escort after your mother's funeral. That's why I cried so much that night at your parent's house when I told you a ghost spoke to me. The ghost was an angel. The angel disguised me and restrained my free will so I couldn't tell you who I was until now. I was able to keep an eye on you easier that way."

"Mary, talk to me. Will you please tell me what's going on?" I begged.

"Every March in the sixty-fourth year of every century, they've searched for a human worthy enough to pursue the last page of the *Book of Ancients*. You're by far the best they've found."

"I doubt that."

Mary grabbed my shirt with a firmness I never knew she possessed.

"You're the last Interceptor, a human wedged between opposing angels to keep the last page until the Redemption Moon."

I was glad I found out what an Interceptor was, but I didn't like it one bit.

"What the hell's the Redemption Moon? What last page?" I asked embittered.

"The teachings of the *Bible* are incomplete. With the absence of the excluded books, religious leaders manipulated man for the sake of evil, unaware they were doing so. The true, complete message has been veiled for centuries."

"What does evil want to do with that last page?" Dave asked.

"Recreate mankind in an evil image. Turel is leading that effort for Lucifer," she said.

She confirmed everything I'd heard about evil angels up to this point, and it didn't take me more than a microsecond to realize that I was a dead man.

"John, you've been granted divine endorsement, powers of high physical strength, along with an ability to traverse time," Mary said.

"You mean the time windows? I can make my own time windows?" I asked.

"Yes. You've already begun derailing Turel's plans. He's been successful for almost two thousand years. However, he's almost at the point of reclamation."

"What's reclamation?" Dave asked.

"That is the moment when the recreation of man begins at the full eclipse of the Redemption Moon. Before Turel can do that, he must possess the entire *Book of Ancients*. I believe Marcus told you about this."

A chill overcame me as Mary's eyes expressed urgent concern.

"What do I do?" I asked as my eyes flooded with tears.

"Follow your heart. In your heart, you'll find strength. Turel can't detect your intentions if you're acting solely on your heart's desire. All through your life, they've been helping you train for this task by giving you glimpses of the past then reinforcing your strong desire to exist during times other than your own. You're strong, thus far you've impressed many of the Protectors in Hali."

"Where's Hali?" I asked.

I caressed Mary's soft cheeks then wiped my eyes. I never knew how much I loved her until this moment. I had to get her to a doctor, but I refused to accept one wasn't anywhere near here.

"Hali is where angels are trained. They are Protectors, and they consist of three groups called Watchers, Archangels, and Powers."

"How many Protectors do I get to help me?"

"There's only you and Dave."

I wondered if somewhere along the way the angels would want me to perform open-heart surgery or rebuild a locomotive engine in less than an hour. Unreasonable expectations abounded here.

"Turel gets as many demons or whoever as he wants, but I get only one guy?"

"Quantity isn't relevant. It only takes one being to bring down Turel."

"How many guys like me tried stopping Turel before?"

"Sixteen."

"God is zero and sixteen against Turel, so he picked me to finish the job?"

"There isn't time to bicker. You must find Devers. He'll lead you to the last page. Your love for him is your strength. Your wish to save him is your desire."

It wasn't enough that I had to find a relative I never met, but accepting the reality that I had to face a fallen angel, find part of a mystical text, navigate the colonels movements, and somehow stay alive in an open-cockpit airplane, was a lot to ask.

"I never get a chance to look for him," I said. "What about the nightmares I've been having? We keep seeing a large tree with fighting angels. What about the angel I saw?"

"Those dreams were revealed to you to help you understand your purpose. The tree you saw was the Tree of Knowledge. The angel before it was Zateel. The war you saw occurred at the Battle of Heaven. You didn't imagine it, John. You saw the same parts of Heaven that Enoch saw. The battle was real. Eden is a real place, but if Turel succeeds, the nightmare you had will become the new reality."

My brain felt ready to explode. After I had endured shelling, snipers, and everything else, Mary told me that God had a job for me to save the world. Unbelievable.

"Then my whole life was a sham. This whole thing is nothing but a setup for some angel game I had no say in. What about our plans to get married? What about that?" I asked as a lump swelled in my throat.

"They asked us to help them with a much bigger purpose. Mankind's survival depends on you."

"I haven't won anything in my life, and they think I can save the world?"

"There's more. Getting the last page isn't enough. You'll ultimately have to face Turel. Then, you must kill him."

If there was ever a real straw that could break a camel's back, that was the one. There's no way a man could kill an angel. I was never a religious man, but this convinced me that God had a real mean streak.

"No way. You can't dump that on me. How can they expect me to beat an angel, huh? That's impossible," I said in shock.

"John, please. You must help them," Mary pleaded.

"How? I'm just a middle-of-the-road man. Mary, what am I supposed to do?"

"Win. Win for me, for us, for love's sake."

My jaw fell open as I watched her eyes close.

"Mary? Come on, girl you can't leave me like this," I begged while I stifled an urge to wail like a baby.

I held Mary tightly while abandonment filled my heart. My body trembled at the anguish of another lost person near and dear to me in my life. I didn't have any leads to get us out of our predicament, and I was awash with plenty of dead-ends.

We rested Mary flat on the mattress. I put my head to her chest but heard nothing. I put my face close to hers and felt no breath. I touched her skin, and it ran cool. My eyes flooded with tears again, so I shook my head violently in extreme denial.

I dashed out of the house and stood in the moonlight. I punted a brick fragment and looked up at the night sky. I stared at the full moon, the stars, and wanted blood. My heart felt betrayed. My spirit felt manipulated by unforeseen forces that took it upon themselves to take over my life and make me their personal pawn. My breaths grew short, an intense anger surged from deep in my heart then burst past my lips.

"You killed my mother. You killed my girl. You dragged me back in time to a war I have no business being in to find a relative I never met so I can fight an angel for some bullshit cause you're too scared to handle yourself. If you want me dead, then kill me yourself, you bastard!" I bellowed.

Nearly out of breath from my rant, I looked up at the dark sky then saw a spark of light in deep space grow brighter. It appeared as if it came right at me. My feet clung fast to the ground as if held by powerful magnets. I hoped it was a shooting star fixing to put me out of my misery.

Instead, an intense pillar of light, like a force from the creator of angels, crashed in front of me then knocked me flat on my ass. I looked up and beheld angels circling the light pillar high above. Three-dimensional symbols scrolled in front of me. Then, the light pillar suddenly zapped away in fading, rolling thunder.

The ground smoldered oddly, curiously even. I never knew dirt could burn. I crawled toward it for a closer look. There, branded into the ground, was a seven-pointed star. I looked at the unusual shape, then back up at the night sky.

My curses didn't sway the greater powers. No matter what I said or thought about them, I had to do their bidding whether I wanted to or not. Either way, I was going to feel more pain and heartache and this was just the beginning.

I went back into the farmhouse and sat beside Mary's body. I found a torn blanket, shook out the dust then covered Mary to her chin. I tucked myself against the stone wall while anguish consumed me. I never cried so hard.

Early the next morning, we dug a grave for Mary. After carefully spreading the last of the dirt over the soft mound, I placed my hands on it while my tears dripped on her grave.

"Okay, Mary," I whispered. "I'll do it for you."

We started our daybreak drive to Chalons. In our wake, we left the body of the girl I thought for sure I would one day marry. It was evident who controlled my life and it sure as hell wasn't me.

Sunbeams peeked through the trees before engulfing the day. I had a big job to do, and we had serious muscle on our side. However, when, if ever, would the wondrous angels help me? I didn't feel as though God helped me at any point in my life, yet so far, the only way He reached out to me was by killing my mother and Mary.

"I still don't get why they picked me," I said. "I don't go to church. I don't pray or even think that much of religion. I'm a free believer."

"John, have you considered that maybe that's exactly why you were chosen?" Dave asked.

"No."

"You're not bogged down by ritual or strict beliefs. You can think independently. You're unencumbered by any religious sect or rule."

"I don't know about that. I can't think straight anymore."

Mary's last words explained the nightmares as well as the news that God had a plan for me to head off a fallen angel. This was too surreal to accept as real. The big boss picked me, the most unreligious, average guy I knew, to save the world. Well, ain't I the lucky little bastard. Why couldn't they leave me in obscurity and let me figure out my own damn life?

CHAPTER 20

I STARED BLANKLY as I tried to comprehend the most tumultuous day of my life. Rampaging thoughts sped through my mind about my new role in searching for a piece of divine text hunted down by an evil angel as well as the unbelievable experience of an enormous power burning a calling card into the ground. What did a seven-pointed star mean? What was I supposed to do with it? Marcus, Turel, and Mary never mentioned it. Dave didn't know what to make of it. The more I thought about it, the less sense it made to me.

Dave and I entered the Chalons air base and parked the truck beside the Command Center. Marcus emerged from inside then stood beside our truck. Men continued to prepare the base for an attack that was likely imminent.

"Men, I'm most relieved in your successful return," Marcus said.

"We would've gotten here sooner, but we ran into some sniper trouble and, uh, lost our driver," I said then took a deep breath. My heart squeezed as I spoke of my fiancé who would never hug me, comfort me, or be my voice of reason ever again.

"I'm sorry about your driver. The most recent communiqué from Colonel Weatherby reported disastrous losses, and the Gate was in grave danger of collapse. When we last spoke, you mentioned something about Captain Edmund," Marcus said with concern.

"Yes, sir. Where is he?" I asked.

"I sent him to get a report from Major Thomason in the northern sector. The, uh, communication lines were down in that sector all day."

"Sir, we have reason to believe Captain Edmund sabotaged the offensive."

Marcus retreated inside the Command Center. Dave and I followed him then stood on the far side of the map table. One of Marcus's assistants, Lieutenant Duggin, a bug-eyed Brit with an acne problem, looked up as we entered.

"Are you saying Captain Edmund's a traitor?" Marcus asked softly. "That's a strong accusation, John."

"I have some strong proof," I said.

I collected my thoughts then described how the last several days evolved, but I didn't mention anything about angels with Duggin in the room.

"This is most unexpected," Marcus said as he paced around the map table and exchanged worrisome glances with Duggin. "Do you believe any of this?"

"Sir, I've always had reservations about Captain Edmund," Duggin said. "I don't doubt his skills. However, on many occasions, men have seen him leaving the base alone. I've personally witnessed him leaving on two occasions. Some of the pilots have heard rumors as to why he goes. Espionage has been a frequent topic in the latest discussions, but nobody came forward due to lack of proof."

Marcus supported himself with stiff arms as he stood over the map table. He grabbed a compass then tapped the map with it.

"Are any of those pilots you're referring to here at the moment, Lieutenant?" Marcus asked.

"I don't know, sir. They've been coming and going all day."

Marcus's face trembled, and then he erupted in anger.

"Then find whoever is here and bring them to me!"

Lieutenant Duggin dashed out of the Command Center to search for the pilots in question. Several pencils on the map leaped into the air after Marcus struck the table with both fists. He awkwardly composed himself, gathered the pencils, and grouped them neatly on the center of the map.

"Sir, our ambulance driver, Helen, told me more about why I'm here. Do you know anything about a seven-pointed star?" I asked as I proceeded to draw the star on a blank space on the map.

Marcus's lips parted as if he saw something astounding.

"She said I'm the last Interceptor," I said. Marcus stayed quiet but stole an occasional peek at me. "She was also my fiancé in disguise. It seems Dave and I weren't the only ones you bums brought to 1917. She told me an angel reached out to her. A sniper shot her, but before she died, she told me the whole story. Do you know anything about her?"

"I must confess that I was the one that brokered her to be your Escort. It was imperative that someone close to you serve that role. I apologize for your loss. However, do you understand the gravity of our situation?"

"Yes, sir. I believe it all. I don't like it, but I don't have a choice now, do I? So, do you know what that is?" I asked and tapped on the drawing of the star.

Marcus glanced at the star then walked around the table.

"It must be a symbol from the *Book of Ancients*," Marcus said. "The whole text is composed of symbols."

"Do you know where Devers might be?" I asked.

"I received word that he's missing in action."

I didn't need to hear that. Not only did Marcus know who Devers was but also lost track of his whereabouts.

Lieutenant Duggin rushed inside the Command Center. Collishaw, Bishop, Miller, and Shubert entered behind him.

I felt I hadn't seen them in weeks. Billy still wore the same sour expression since my stockyards misstep.

"Men, Lieutenants Harrod and Sowell have apprised me of information about Captain Edmund. I want to know your thoughts about him. You can start," Marcus said as he pointed at Ray. Marcus sat on a wood chair then crossed his arms.

Marcus listened intently to the accounts. The theory on Edmund was consistent with everyone. Edmund had exposed Chalons for weeks, yet everyone outside the colonels' inner circle failed to recognize it. The evidence that showed him connected to the Underground was overwhelming. The confirmation that a connection to the Germans existed was icing on the cake. Marcus excused himself from the Command Center. I followed him and stood beside him at the door opening.

Marcus lit a cigar then looked toward the planes as they took off down the airfield.

"Sir, uh, is there enough men at the Gate to stop the Germans?" I asked.

"We've procured four divisions from Reims," Marcus said. "Two are already in place here. The remaining two should be in our sector by morning, but I seriously doubt that either will reach the Gate in time."

"That's what Turel meant by building his armies, by getting our guys killed and taking their spirits for his own use. Sir, when did you last speak to Colonel Weatherby?"

"About two hours ago," he said.

"I think you should call him again to see how it's going," I pleaded. "Colonel Weatherby's in big trouble, sir."

"You have a point, Harrod. However, Captain Edmund hasn't returned yet. I believe we owe him the chance to account for himself," Marcus said.

"Colonel, how long should a round trip to the northern sector take?" I asked.

"About an hour."

"Seems to me Edmund skipped town," I said.

"We're going to have to do something about that boy," Dave said.

"How do you propose we do that?" Ray asked as he joined us. "If what everyone here has said is true, he likely will not return given the current status of the Gate."

"I don't know, but there has to be something we can do," I said.

The room filled with conversation to develop the best approach to salvage the offensive. Everyone gathered around the map table, and offered whatever information they had about the locations they'd flown over during the last several days.

Shubert and the other pilots determined there had to be a German aerodrome near the Gate, possibly more than one. Allied ground forces could hold a German advance at Chalons for only a short time before reinforcements arrived. The phone rattled and Marcus went to his side desk to answer it.

Marcus answered the phone. Shubert took a compass then performed some calculations while his mate, Miller, observed.

"What are you doing there, Shubes?" Miller asked.

"I believe I know where the German fighters are coming from," Shubert said then put down his pencil. "Remember this morning on our second run when we met all those fighters?"

"Yes," Miller replied.

"At first, I thought they came from the east, but I remembered the sun was on my right when they attacked. That means they had to come from behind, probably from the south or southeast. The only place close enough for them to amass that many planes would be right here."

Shubert pointed to a place on the map indicating flat ground surrounded by hills. He nibbled his lower lip then nodded.

"That was Major Thomason," Marcus said as he hung up the phone. "Captain Edmund never arrived. Therefore, I've determined him a deserter. Thomason said action in the north is minimal. The other two divisions from Reims should come by morning. I fear to think what the current Gate situation is now." Marcus looked at the map and nodded. "Shubert, your theory seems sound. We'll attack tonight."

"Tonight?" Ray asked with raised eyebrows.

"We have no other choice. There will be a full moon, so you won't be completely in the dark."

"Yes, sir."

"The mission will consist of two flight groups," Marcus continued with a determined, calculating intensity. "The first will be trackers led by Shubert. The second group will escort the bombers. We must find the location by first light or risk exposure by their dawn patrol. If you don't encounter the target by first light, then go to the Gate. Afterward, return for rearming."

If the Germans overran the Gate, then Chalons was the only obstacle preventing them from reaching Paris. Weatherby couldn't hold off a massive frontal assault since most of the forces went with Eldridge.

"Sir, what do we do if we get to the Gate and find it sacked?" Ray asked.

"Pray and return here immediately."

CHAPTER 21

DAVE AND I left the Command Center more nervous than ever. We tried to keep our minds from slipping into an all-out panic as we headed to our tent to change our clothes. I broke our nervous silence the moment the tent flap closed.

"So, Edmund left his bride at the altar," I said. "Why would he bail on a likely king's ransom?"

"Maybe he thought he had no way to retrieve it. Maybe Turel screwed him over."

Dave peeled off his grimy, sweat-stained shirt over his head then tossed it on the cot. It felt strange that given my new responsibility to save humanity, I felt a surging need to shower first. Sure, it seemed weird, but I hated my own body odor, it was too distracting. If I was to save the world, I wanted to be fresh as a mountain stream.

"We're going to have to do some laundry soon, or we'll be smelly for the duration of our stay," Dave said as he cringed at the stink coming from his dirty shirt.

He flung his coat over his shoulder.

"We don't know everything there is to know about these guys," I said excitedly. "Either way, I still don't like this Turel thing. If Turel's everything Marcus says, then he can pop in on us at any time."

"All right, John. Try to relax," Dave said. "I know you're jacked over about Mary dying, but we're still here and there ain't anything we can do about her. We have to move on."

I buried my hands in my pants pockets and felt as though I rode a bicycle into a brick wall. I went to the tent opening where the sweet pine-rich air filled my lungs.

"John? What is it?" Dave asked.

"You'll think I'm nuts if I tell you."

"Come on, spill it."

"If I follow my heart like Mary said, do you think it'll lead us in the right direction? All it got me so far is insane news and lots of death."

"I guess that depends on whether you believe her. Besides, nobody ever said the right path would be without peril."

Dave had me on that one. I assumed our journey would be more like a woodland hike, than a bullet-riddled obstacle course.

"I had a dream the other night, but now that I think about it, the creatures fighting did look like angels," Dave said. He furrowed his brow perhaps to help his brain find the right words.

"You had a dream about fighting angels like Mary said?" I asked.

Dave nodded.

"Same here," I said. "There was a huge tree surrounded by angels in the middle of a lush, garden valley."

"Yeah. Then, a nasty looking beast swung a fiery sword at me. It said something in a language I never heard before. Mary was telling the truth. She told us about our own damn dreams," Dave said as he grabbed a towel and a cake of soap.

"I was in denial all along about this angel stuff, but I'm afraid it's the real deal."

The last orange streaks of late evening sun shone through a filtered thicket of trees. The temperature diminished yet offered scant relief from the daytime humidity.

I went to my trashed footlocker and found some clean clothes. We took what we needed then headed toward the bathing shed. The thought of being a player in a holy crusade consumed my mind, and I fought hard to resist my natural urge to panic. However, I never heard of anybody who fought an evil angel and lived to talk about, which meant nothing since I never thought angels were real until now. Then again, how could any man succeed at killing an angel?

Dave and I didn't speak during our walk to the showers. Darkness was a welcome friend that hindered enemy advancement, which equalized threats from both sides to the point of shut down.

After we had arrived at the showers, I stepped under the water barrel then turned on the water. I stood motionless, letting the ice-cold flush cascade down my overheated body. The shock waves from the frigid water that usually raced through me flowed by unfazed. I savored the cool refuge and tilted my head all around.

Dave stood still under the showerhead. He leaned forward and let the water roll off his head like a waterfall.

My skin had numbed to the bone, but I scrubbed myself well then shut off the valve.

I sighed deeply as I reached for my towel. We dressed and shuffled our way back to our tent. Four more planes landed, followed by six De Havilland bombers. Like condors swooping to their roost, the bombers landed moments later.

"You know, we'll never see a sight like that again," I said in introspect. "Despite everything that's happened, it's been one hell of a trip," I said.

"It's been hell at least," Dave said. He wrapped his towel around his neck. "This wasn't what I had in mind about seeing Europe," he said then wiped his face.

"Me neither," I said.

The Chalons air base was replete with activity in preparation for the night attack. While we walked to our tent, I felt that the hyperactive pulse of the base would consume any chance for peace.

I sensed a large ominous presence looming in the east as we finished getting dressed. At that moment, Ray and Billy entered our tent.

"Hello, men. Cleaning up, I see," Ray said with impatience in his voice.

"We haven't showered in a few days, so we were due. You guys look like you got something on your minds," I said.

Ray and Billy sat on the footlockers. Billy couldn't sit still, so he stood back up.

"I have plenty on my mind," Ray said. "I feel a bit presumptuous to bring this up now, but because of everything we've been through over the past weeks, I suspect you have at least some respect for us."

Dave and I wore puzzled looks.

"All right, Ray, what's up?" I asked then pulled up my boots.

"Frankly, since we met you two, we've noticed certain oddities," Ray said.

"Like what?" Dave asked.

"You have a strange Yankee manner. You speak more uniquely than any American I've ever known."

Ray was on the trail of a scent but didn't know what he chased.

"Ray, Dave and I have been through some tough times. We're practically brothers. I guess you could say we've developed our own way of speaking to each other."

"Perhaps that explains a little," Ray said.

Ray turned to Billy, then to me. "How would you propose an explanation for that then?" Ray asked as he lazily pointed at my arm.

I raised my eyebrows. "Explain what?" I asked.

"That object on your wrist."

I remained calm and buttoned my cuffs. God, I can be stupid sometimes. I glanced at my wristwatch but felt too seasoned with war experiences to get upset over it.

"What's the big deal about a watch?" I asked casually.

Billy grew impatient and angry.

"Where on earth can you get a watch like that? It is a watch, is it not? I've never seen anything like that," Billy said.

"You guys are getting all worked up over nothing," I said.

"Just tell me one thing." Billy stepped in front of me and wore a bitter, angry scowl. "Do you or your ranch hand here have anything to do with Captain Edmund? Anything at all?"

Reluctantly, I looked into Billy's intense eyes.

"No, Billy, not one damn thing," I said. "Hell, we figured him out and told Marcus. If I were involved, I sure wouldn't be stupid enough to stick around here. The guilty man ran off."

A sergeant whipped open our tent flap.

"All flight leaders report to command. The Germans have taken the Gate!" the sergeant bellowed.

Billy didn't flinch. His steely gaze locked onto me like an angry bull ready to charge while a bucket full of adrenaline raced through my veins.

"If you're allied with Edmund in any way, I'll kill you myself," Billy said.

My neck hairs perked up as a nervous cramp hit my stomach. I wondered if anyone else could dump more pressure on me.

"Come, Billy, we're not getting anywhere with these lads," Ray said as he pulled Billy out of the tent.

"Hey, Ray, we never lied to you," I said.

"That's right," Dave said. "Heck, we'd be downright uncivil-like to betray the same men who'd saved our butts more than once. We had nothing to do with Edmund, I swear on my mother's grave."

Ray and Billy glanced at us then left.

"Come on, John," Dave said as he swatted my arm. "I want to get in on this meeting too."

We left our tent and ran to the Command Center. Dozens of men jogged their way between tents to join the growing group by the mess tent.

Marcus hopped onto an ammunition crate. He raised his hands, and the crowd quieted.

"Men, I bear grim news. The Germans have taken the Gate sector held by Colonel Weatherby."

Gasps of concern followed by mild chatter erupted from the crowd. I knew Weatherby was in a jam, but the Germans overtook him quickly. Marcus raised his hands again.

"Colonel Eldridge's division has encountered the Germans at the Gate and is presently engaged in battle. Two divisions from Reims have arrived to help him with an additional two divisions on the way."

"I'm glad to hear Eldridge got there in time," I said to Dave.

"Too bad for Weatherby, though. I liked him," Dave said.

Marcus continued. "The launch of our counterattack on the German air command will begin at zero three hundred hours. Lieutenant Shubert apprised me of a possible German air presence south of here. If we remove their air threat, we can severely cripple the German offensive then, hopefully, restore our aggressive plans into Germany. Squad leaders take over."

Marcus returned to the Command Center with three other high-ranking officers. Squad leaders called out for their groups to assemble for an immediate briefing.

"Looks like this could be our last round-up," Dave said flatly.

"We can't afford to die yet. You know, since Ray and Billy saw my watch, I'm more paranoid than ever," I said.

"I don't think anyone cares about your watch anymore," Dave said. "If you'd put that thing away at the beginning like you told me, they never would've seen it. Come on, let's go meet with Ray. I thought I heard him call out our squad. We're number twenty-two, right?"

"I think so."

We remained by the Command Center where Ray, Billy, Robert, and James gathered. Six other pilots also joined the group. Ray and Billy coldly eyed us as the men milled about waiting for Ray to begin.

"Okay, men, gather around," Ray said. "The planes are being prepared as we speak. Tomorrow at zero three hundred, we'll fly along the road to Nancy. From there, veer south-southeast toward Colmar then east of there should be our target. On arrival, we'll make several strafing passes. All bomber squads will follow the standard formation. Deliver your payloads then head back to base for reloading. Daylight will be wide by then, so you should experience no difficulty returning. Unless anyone has questions, I suggest you get some rest. Tomorrow will be active to say the least."

The group dispersed, and Dave and I started for our tent. I had no idea how Ray or Marcus expected us to sleep at a time like this.

"Harrod, may I have a word with you?" Ray asked. We stopped while Ray jogged over to us.

"I apologize if we were brash earlier," Ray said as Billy stood by. "Billy can be a bit coarse. We've been here a long time. However, we don't care much for surprises."

"Ray, nobody is more surprised by these circumstances than we are."

"You men are unlike anyone else here. Now, before we let you go up tomorrow, we must know. Who are you and where did you come from?"

I never liked a direct question I didn't want to answer, so I had to spin my words carefully.

"If you must know, we aren't soldiers," I said and swallowed hard. "We lied about flying. Neither of us ever flew airplanes until we arrived here."

"We knew you couldn't fly. That accounts for the training. However, that's not what I'm referring to," Ray said with apprehension.

"What are you getting at?"

Deflection and outright lying were my weakest traits, especially when facing people I considered my friends. I knew I sucked at it, but I felt like I was on thin ice and had to do something about it.

"You won't tell us?" Billy asked through gritted teeth.

"Billy, there isn't anything to tell. Now, are we done here?" Dave asked with impatience.

"Okay, men. Have it your way. Remember what I said about catching you both in a lie," Billy said then pointed at us.

They had us cold, but I stuck to my story so I could get through the awkwardness.

"Billy, we're not lying, okay? I won't repeat it. Besides, you guys need all the pilots you can get, good or bad. Now excuse us, we want to get some sleep," I said.

I felt the weight of their skepticism on my conscience as we went on our way to our tent. Dave held open the tent flap, and I entered.

"You think we're not lying, huh?" Dave asked.

"Our days are numbered, and the clock is ticking," I said. "Those guys are too hot on us to walk away without an explanation. All I did was buy us some time. If we're still here after tomorrow, they'll corner us then call our bluff. Five minutes after that, they'll put us against a wall."

"You knew them from history class as being great pilots. That hasn't changed. Throwing the outcome of the war in favor of the Axis would definitely be a change. As Mary said, they picked us. Well, they picked you, but I'm here as well."

"You're right," I said.

Dave gave me a friendly shot on the arm.

"Maybe tomorrow we'll find out where Devers is," I said as my internal optimism machine clung to its weakest working gear that refused to seize.

"Boy, wouldn't that be sweet?"

CHAPTER 22

"WAKE UP! TIME to go, you sleeping beauties!" a voice boomed and shattered our peaceful sleep. The soldier left our tent and proceeded to roust the next exhausted souls. Dave fumbled in the darkness to turn up the oil lamp for light. We dressed silently then gathered our gear. The importance of the mission weighed on my soul and I felt time was running out for me. Given recent revelations, it was paramount that I survived this nightmare.

"How are you doing, big guy?" Dave asked in mid-yawn.

Dave strained as he pushed his foot inside a boot.

"I'm okay, I guess," I said while I rubbed my burning eyes. "How are we supposed to fly in the dark?"

Dave pushed aside the tent flap then looked outside. He took a deep breath.

"There's a full moon out," Dave said. "I think we'll be okay. It'll be freezing up there, but we'll manage."

Dave snatched his jacket and goggles, and we went to our usual pissing trees.

We answered nature's call then approached the group of planes poised in front of Hangar B. The chilling nighttime dew collected on my boots. Each step helped the dampness permeate the leather through to my socks. No wonder my feet felt cold.

The camp swarmed with activity. Ground crews aligned the planes for takeoff, topped off fuel tanks, and loaded machine gun magazines. The engines of the loaded bombers purred while they idled for this critical mission.

Ray, Billy, and other pilots stood beside a bomber, reviewing the plan once more. The fighter planes lined up in two wide rows in front of the bombers. Two ground crewmen stood beside each aircraft, ready to start the fighters. We approached just as our group scattered to their planes.

"Okay, men, you know the plan," Ray said then gave me an unimpressed glance. "John, you follow me. Dave, you follow Billy. Fly tightly, men. Any questions?"

"Yeah," I said while I strapped on my flight cap. "Last night, Colonel Marcus spoke of the outer marker. Where is that again?"

"Colmar is the outer marker."

"How far is it from here?"

"About 150 miles. Any other questions?"

Ray glanced over the group.

"Very well. Good luck," Ray said.

Ray and the others left for their planes while Dave and I finished preparing ourselves for a cold, dark flight.

"Can't we get some coffee first?" I asked.

"No time. Just don't fall asleep," Dave replied. "You'll crash and die."

"Thanks, smart ass."

We climbed into our planes. My ears shuddered as one by one the engines roared louder and the planes took off down the airfield. Dave's engine revved, as he trailed the others in front of him. I stuffed my watch into my coat pocket and shoved the accelerator lever with vigor. Within minutes, we were all airborne and heading for Colmar.

Nighttime flying was a unique thrill. The moon softly brightened everything in shades of indigo and black. I recalled how the moonbeams reflected off Lake Michigan on a calm, star-speckled evening.

The shimmering moonlight on the planes in front of me cast a surrealistic vision of these aerial ghosts from a time when manned flight was new. I half-hoped our adventure was a dream. I'd wake up, find ourselves back in our own time riding our bikes, and the last page would be nothing more than a twisted nightmare. The bike trip, it seemed so long ago.

Our flight breezed along uneventfully except for my twitching muscles and chattering jaw. I slapped my face a couple times in an attempt to hinder the spasms of early hypothermia. The coarse leather of my gloves stung my frozen skin like bees.

The lead group veered east into the first glimmers of the sunrise that backlit the German territory. The flickering lights of Chaumont, the last point Eldridge had encountered before he turned north to Weatherby's aid, appeared below.

As we banked to port, I turned my head to view the bombers that gently clung to my tail as if tied to an invisible tether line. I'd never beheld such a fantastic sight as watching those primitive flying machines as they soared in the brilliant moonlight. Back-dropped by silver-edged clouds in the distance, they gracefully sailed over the ground below.

Near the Rhine River, Colmar's choice flatlands provided plenty of space for an airfield. The Germans could ship supplies down the Rhine on barges without notice or threat of destruction. Locomotives, on the other hand, belched massive amounts of smoke and steam which boldly marked their location.

Dawn approached as our squads reached Colmar. With my face numbed, my muscle spasms slowly waned while the rising sun warmed my cheeks and spirit. As I searched below, I hoped the base would appear soon, so we could do our job then get out of there. Adrenaline raced through my body with each passing second.

We crossed the top of a huge hill, and descended on a particular building that came into view. Towering trees surrounded the building, and then I spotted the air base and confirmed Shubert's suspicion.

We quickly surveyed the base for suitable targets while we sailed over the site. Dozens of fighter planes, bombers, observation blimps, and two massive zeppelins sat primed for us in front of one of nine hangars. The chill left my body and I was soon wiping sweat off my face.

Ray and Billy's group of fighters turned to starboard then attacked the German fighters. Several planes exploded into small fireballs. The Allied bombers deployed a steady succession of ordnance that systematically toppled the hangars.

A yellow-orange blossom of fire lit the early morning sky and briefly highlighted every Allied plane. Shots soon erupted from the ground, and struck the bomber that flew beside me. The plane shimmied, banked sharply to port, and crashed into a burning hangar.

Flames erupted inside the hangar followed by a second brilliant flash that blew the building to bits. Dave and I dropped our bombs then continued strafing the idle planes.

The relentless onslaught continued mercilessly on the unsuspecting base. German soldiers continued to return fire into the smoky sky.

Dave, Robert, James, and I zeroed in on the zeppelins. Each airship, filled with flammable hydrogen, made easy targets. As we approached the zeppelins, we each released a bomb that landed beneath each airship. The resulting explosions shot searing bits of steel through the airships, which then ignited the hydrogen. The ships collapsed under their own weight as the inferno quickly weakened the steel frames. The brightness of the flaming devastation illuminated the entire valley.

We rained machine gun fire on the remaining observation blimps. They easily caught fire then burned out quickly.

Like soaring hawks, we circled the base several times in search of more prey. In a pair of white strobe-like flashes followed by an earsplitting shock wave, two huge hydrogen tanks between the burning blimps exploded.

Dense smoke shrouded the aerodrome, which impeded further efforts to survey the damage. Our surprise raid destroyed every bomber, zeppelin, balloon, and hydrogen tank we saw. At most, a pair of German fighters might've survived. All the hangars suffered massive damage while the enormous flames lapped at the skies.

Before returning to Chalons, I stole a few last looks at the air base that burned in our wake. Oily plumes of smoke obscured the emerging streaks of a new dawn. My fuel gauge showed less than half-full. With a successful strike under our belt, we headed toward the Gate.

Upon arrival at the Gate, I saw thousands of Allied and German infantrymen scattered around the assaulted countryside. The smoking remains of war machines dotted the wasteland.

The Germans held the Gate defensively. Eldridge's division prepared to strike from a position a half-mile to the east of the Gate's trench. We dipped toward the trench then strafed the German-occupied Gate with hellfire. The German line took to arms as machine gun nests attacked with ferocity. With our air support, Colonel

Eldridge's division ground their way across the no man's land to the Gate then flanked the German stronghold.

Artillery fire from both sides blazed with fury. Mortar explosions flung soldiers into the air like rag dolls and flopped back to the ground. Many men died in mid-stride without firing a single shot while others took an enemy or two before succumbing.

Miller and Shubert flew side by side ahead of Dave and me as their guns blazed away. The accuracy of the Allied shelling upset the German occupation and forced them out of the Gate. Unfortunately, our success drove the Germans on a westerly course into the safety of the forest. Two Albatroses dropped down and drove a wedge between Miller and Shubert.

Shubert looped his plane then swung behind his pursuer. Dave and I closely tailed Shubert for support. Shubert clung to the Albatros like static then squeezed the trigger. As the Albatros spiraled down in a smoky trail, Shubert fired on his foe all the way to the ground.

Dave and I climbed to a higher perch and surveyed the fighting below. I wouldn't call it cowardly, but my assignment to kill an angel forced me to let the expert fliers fight so I could face my own brawl, in a hopefully still-healthy state, with Turel later.

While in pursuit of an Albatros, Ray zipped in from behind then fired. A red burst flashed from the Albatros cockpit and the plane nose-dived to the ground. Robert waved in gratitude then joined Dave and me as we returned to the trench. Without any plan to follow, I shot at anything that looked German.

A stream of smoke appeared in my peripheral vision as I fired bullets on anything in my crosshairs. German ground fire ripped through Miller's wings. I watched in horror as his plane curved hard to the ground then erupted into flames upon impact. James zapped three machine gun nests with one last lead shower.

Our fuel and ammunition was dangerously low, so we left the Gate for Chalons.

The last support divisions from Reims finally arrived at Chalons. Every soldier helped dig out a trench to establish a mile-long barrier. Ground crewmen scrambled to service the planes and positioned them for the next sortie. In a short time, Dave and I became seasoned fliers.

After we had landed, we climbed out of our planes then headed toward Ray.

"Are we going back to the Gate?" I asked.

"Yes, as soon as the planes are prepared. Come, we need to see Marcus," Ray said.

Ray, Billy, Dave, and I started for the Command Center. Shubert sat on the ground next to his plane while the crewmen serviced it.

"Shubes, are you coming?" Ray shouted. Shubert didn't respond. He sat alone and wept, no doubt heartbroken over the loss of his best friend, Miller.

Ray pushed open the Command Center door. Marcus looked up with great anticipation as we filed in.

Marcus looked up with eager eyes.

"Colonel Marcus, Shubert was correct," Ray said as he spoke for us. "There was a large aerodrome east of Colmar. We struck at sunrise with indisputable accuracy and left the target in flames."

"Specifics," Marcus said then swung his hands behind his back.

"I confirmed nine hangars, approximately a hundred fighter planes, thirty bombers, and two zeppelins. We destroyed all the hangars, several fuel depots, and hydrogen storage tanks. The smoke became too thick to identify any more targets. Therefore, I can't guarantee total destruction of the base or its arsenal. However, I can assure you there won't be any threats coming from that base for a long time. During the attack, we lost one bomber, and I regret to say, we also lost Lieutenant Miller."

Marcus nibbled his lip while he eyed me. He smoothed out his mustache then gently nodded.

"War isn't without hard losses," Marcus said. "Were you able to assess Colonels Eldridge and Weatherby?"

"Yes, sir," Collishaw said. "The Germans presently occupy Weatherby's post. Colonel Eldridge is gaining ground east of there. Unfortunately, Eldridge had overshot the Gate, but his tanks were pushing west when we had to return."

"I see. Show me on the map how the attack played out," Marcus said. "The rest of you come as well."

"Well, sir, we cruised past Colmar as planned. Heading east, here, we came upon a ridge. Inside the ridge sat the base."

"Did you encounter any resistance?"

"None, sir. I suspect we destroyed any threats while they were still on the ground."

The door of the Command Center swung open. The burly sergeant, the one that went around shouting announcements through our tents this morning, breathed heavily.

"Sirs, the Germans are advancing westward, and Colonel Eldridge is giving chase," he said in a bold British accent.

The room went silent. Marcus returned his eyes to the map.

"They're heading right for us," Dave said.

"Get to your planes! Stop the advance!" Marcus shouted.

We bolted out of the Command Center while whistles blared across the airfield. The crewmen completed replenishment efforts with the planes while Ray finished briefing the bomber pilots. In minutes, the airfield roared to life with the sound of aircraft.

Shubert rolled to his feet then stood. I watched him as he glumly climbed into his plane. With a blank stare, he strapped on his flight cap.

He looked toward the heavens then closed his eyes. He wiped away his tears, clawed the goggles over his eyes, and *Nobody's Baby* sped down the airfield.

Once we were airborne, we met the German troops pursued by Eldridge within minutes. They advanced closer to Chalons in quick order since they'd met little resistance. Gunfire on the ground blazed continuously.

Startled by a stunning volley of cannon fire on his right flank, Eldridge must have felt the pressure of a tenacious enemy on two sides of him. The Germans didn't surround him yet, but, if my impressions of him held true, he wouldn't let anyone get the best of him. He charged forward, while we dropped down to engage the newcomers on his tail.

We pinned down the German forces thus giving Eldridge relief and scant time to regroup.

The newly arrived Allied bombers destroyed much of the new German arsenal. We fired at the scrambling men who tripped into craters or over bodies and wreckage trying to evade our relentless attack.

Deplorable German ground fire resulted in not one lost Allied aircraft. The engine buzz and rhythmic machine gun fire drowned out the screams of the dying below.

Despite the seemingly successful air assault on the German reserves in the East, the enemy west of Colonel Eldridge pushed closer to Chalons. The excellent sighting of the Allied bombardiers destroyed many German tanks.

Twenty thousand Allied men occupied a thin line and guarded Chalons against the German threat now about five hours away. A mile-long trench east of the air base was the most heavily fortified.

Ground crewmen released the next sortie after I taxied my plane beside the others in front of Hangar A. I climbed out of my cockpit then ran to Dave's plane.

"This is unbelievable," I said.

"There isn't going to be much let up either," Dave said as he rubbed his forehead with his rough leather coat sleeve.

I spotted Ray beside his plane. I shuffled through the hoards of soldiers as though I ran through a crowded shopping mall at Christmas.

"Hey, Ray, hold on a minute," I said.

Ray finished wrapping his scarf around his neck then strapped on his cap.

"What is it, John?" Ray asked.

"Since Dave and I got here you've taught us how to look out for ourselves up there. I never thanked you for that. So, thank you, Ray, for everything. If there's anything I can do for you, let me know."

"I'm not certain of what you can do for me, John, but maybe there is something you can tell me."

"Sure."

"When all this hell is over, most likely today or tomorrow, will you explain that object on your wrist to me?"

I thought about Ray's proposition. I considered that I'd probably never see him again after today, so I didn't see a problem with his offer.

"Sure, Ray. I think that's the least I can do," I said.

I extended my hand. The glow on Ray's boyish face confirmed we were back in trust mode.

Ray turned away then climbed into his plane.

I ran back to my plane with a relieved conscience. I felt a smile crack on my face as I strapped on my flight cap and watched Dave approach.

"Did you two make nice?" Dave asked.

"I think so. I thanked him for everything he's done for us," I said.

"That's it? You talked longer than that."

"I also said that if I could do anything for him to let me know. With everything going on, what do we have to lose?"

"Not a whole heck of a lot, I guess. Let's finish this round-up, okay?"

"You got it," I said.

With the engines hot and hungry, we cruised down the airfield and soared for the war-torn skies.

CHAPTER 23

THE LATE MORNING temperature was cool for an early September day. Yesterday's humidity dried up and the brilliant blue sky I loved so much returned, much like it was on the first day we arrived in 1917. Several cumulous clouds in the distance slowly floated and warped into every possible shape. Even sunny, seventy-degree weather felt frigid at a hundred miles an hour in an open-cockpit plane.

Our squadron soon met Colonel Eldridge and noticed his struggle on the ground with the Germans. We offered all the support we could and spent all our ammo. Eldridge's division had gained great strides in little time and even came within a couple of hundred yards of hand-to-hand combat with the Germans. Consequently, he pushed the Germans even closer to Chalons. Eldridge's assault with the continued aerial bombardment only slowed the German advance.

As we headed back to the base for rearming, I realized the Germans, at their current rate of advancement, would arrive at Chalons in about an hour. Shubert dropped out of formation to assess matters elsewhere. Several Sopwith Camels from the Ninth Squadron engaged the German fighters, which allowed us to return for refueling.

Shubert taxied his plane beside Dave's. He killed the engine then climbed out. He anxiously scanned the area and observed two ground crewmen refueling two other planes.

"Crewman! Gas up this plane now!" he said then ran like the wind to the Command Center.

"What's up with him?" I asked.

"Don't know," Dave said. "He must've found something after he left us."

A minute later, Shubert burst out of the Command Center. Ray and Billy grabbed Shubert by his coat sleeve and demanded an explanation. The three of them agreed on something, and then Billy and James ran to their planes.

"Eldridge encountered a surge in German troops that came in from the north," Ray explained. "Remember to stay in tight formation. Don't break off unless you engage another fighter and keep a sharp lookout."

The front row of fighters, Shubert, Ray, and Billy, took off down the airfield. The bombers were next, followed by our row.

My plane cruised down the open field as the bombers cleared the trees in the south. Repetitious thunderous booms rocked the ground behind me. Intense impact tremors rattled my plane then an earthen barrier erupted in front of me and stopped me dead.

Once the dust settled, I saw that our planes rested in fresh bomb craters. To my right, I saw a Sopwith Camel in flames. A shell from above blasted it to bits. I climbed out of my plane then ran over to Dave.

"Dave, you okay, man?" I shouted as the Allied tanks in the West fired shells toward the German army still deep in the forest yet advancing toward us.

"I think so. My head's pounding. What the hell hit us?"

High above, I saw several massive zeppelins floating a thousand feet above.

"Look at that!" I shouted as I pointed upward.

The attack left strings of impact craters from the mess tent all the way to the end of the clearing. With the spoiled terrain rendered unusable for landing, Ray and the others would have to land somewhere else.

The agile zeppelins began an effortless turnaround for a second strike. The zeppelin's six Albatros escorts engaged our remaining squadron and flew all about the sky.

"Good God almighty," Dave said as he observed the zeppelins turning around and heading back toward the Chalons air base.

"They're coming back, Dave. Get to the trench, hurry!"

We sprinted toward the trench then jumped into it. We watched as bombs from the zeppelins destroyed the hangers and obliterated the Command Center.

A row of tanks on the western edge of the Chalons airfield meandered their way around the craters toward us. Machine guns on either side of us erupted in an ear-crushing crescendo as they fired on the zeppelins. As trees exploded, wood shards sliced through anything fleshy. My hearing would never be the same.

Four Gotha bombers swooped down on the Chalons Air Base then deployed their deadly cargo. More debris soared into the sky. I looked up for a closer view of the Command Center. The building was nothing more than shattered planks scattered everywhere. Marcus and two other officers ran up to the trench and sought refuge with us.

"Colonel Marcus, what the hell happened? Where did all those Germans come from? How did they know we were here?" I shouted.

Marcus shielded his face from a shower of dirt. Sudden explosions uprooted trees onto men. A shower of bombs reduced the tanks to heaps of scrap iron. Between shell bursts, I watched salvation arrive. In the southern sky, one of the zeppelins fell under attack by three Sopwith Camels. A slight fire burst near the airship's nose blossomed into a raging firestorm.

"Heads up! It's coming down!" Dave shouted.

In seconds, huge flames swallowed the airship as it made its final descent.

A lone Sopwith Camel burst through the black smoke and swooped alongside the doomed behemoth. The Camel fired on the parachuting airship pilots while a red German Fokker triplane closed in on the Camel.

"Damn, it's getting hotter the closer it gets," Dave said.

"It's *Nobody's Baby.* That's Shubert's plane," I said. The white lettering on the fuselage was plainly visible.

The Fokker nipped at the tail of Shubert's plane like a leopard about to take down a gazelle. As they zipped under the burning airship, the German ace stung. Shubert's plane puffed out smoke as he headed west over the trees with the German close behind. The airship crashed nose first into the forest in a thundering cacophony of screeching, contorting steel. A huge wake of black smoke enveloped the sky.

The divisions from Reims finally arrived. Immediately, they blitzed the German advance. We crouched in the trench while bullets whirred overhead. The chattering volley of Allied machine guns erupted again. My head pounded, but I assured myself that this fighting couldn't last forever.

By early evening the shooting subsided. Able-bodied soldiers lent aid to the many casualties that littered the air base.

"This looks worse than Gettysburg," I said. "Would they have died if we never came here?"

"I'm not sure, but I'd guess not," Dave said.

"Then this is my fault," I said as the realization hit me.

"No, that falls on Turel and the colonels. I think all we did was swat a hornet's nest."

The cries of the wounded wailed across the airfield, while medics set up makeshift aid stations. The pungent stench of gunpowder and the charred remains of man and machine choked the air. We climbed out of the trench and scouted the airfield.

"Colonel, where will Ray, Billy, and the others land? This place is shot to hell," Dave said.

"They'll go to Vauchamps," Marcus said. He shook his head, and then a look of sadness overcame him. "It is unfortunate that Captain Shubert succumbed in that fashion. He always knew when an enemy fighter was about."

Whistles blew deep in the forest. The war cries of thousands of soldiers grew louder. The Allies quickly abandoned the eastern trench for a last defensive effort on the western side of the airfield. The tanks retreated across the field to the forest and joined the remaining tanks still lined up along the west edge of the field.

"Fix bayonets!" men shouted from down the line.

"Are you ready for some hand to hand combat?" I asked.

"Screw that. Let's get the hell out of here!" Dave said.

We drew our pistols and fired at anything moving in the forest. Six shots didn't last long.

"John, I'm out, but I think I got a few guys," Dave shouted.

"I got three. Quick, follow that tank!" I shouted.

We climbed out of the trench then chased one of the tanks heading for the forest. We trotted alongside the twenty-eight-ton peacemaker for cover with Colonel Marcus close behind us.

"If we get to the woods, we should be safe for a while," I shouted.

"You better be right this time," Dave said.

Machine gun fire strafed the airfield as the German fighters bore down on our position. The tank was about fifty yards from the forest when one of the German Fokkers shot at us.

We balled up on the ground as bullets struck all around us. After the planes had passed over us, I got up and made my break into the safety of the forest. Dave and Marcus stuck close to me, as best they could.

I didn't know how long I ran or how far. It had to be at least a few miles, but I didn't care. As long as I heard gunshots or tank blasts, my feet drove me faster away from it. In a way, I was a little panic-stricken since death missed me by inches and my need for self-preservation kicked in again. We zigzagged through the forest then encountered an expansive field.

In the field rested the charred remains of a German bomber. Then, I saw the burning remains of a crashed Sopwith Camel inside the tree line. When I saw *Nobody's Baby* painted on the fuselage, I knew we found Shubert's wreck and miraculously, the same place where we first entered 1917.

I walked closer to the plane as I caught my breath. Marcus struggled to keep up with us. Despite narrowly escaping death at Chalons, I decided I'd had enough.

"We're out of here," I said then started into the forest.

Dave looked about the quiet field then stretched out his arms.

"Where are we going to go?" he asked.

I concentrated on going home, then, everything appeared in slow motion. The watery ripple of a time window appeared before me on the other side of a fallen tree toppled over by Shubert's crash.

"In there," I said.

"Holy crap, you did it!" Dave said excitedly.

I took one last look at the smoldering crumpled wreckage of Shubert's plane. His burned, lifeless body draped over the side of the fuselage. I never knew the man, but I knew life dealt him a bad hand. His whole family was gone, but I wondered how effective I'd be against a fallen angel since I couldn't spare anyone I knew from death. Fresh explosions reached our open field, and plumes of dirt rose into the air.

Marcus breathed heavily, gasping for air as he trotted toward us. Without hesitation, Dave and I dashed into the time window and away from the horrific sounds of war.

CHAPTER 24

DAVE AND I tumbled onto the forest floor like we did when we first arrived in 1917. We rolled onto all fours and looked for any danger behind us. We had our revolvers drawn, ready for anything. The distant bird warbles filled our ears in the stark serenity of the woods. The leaves of summer filled the trees, and I quickly broke out in a sweat under the late afternoon sun.

"Where are we? Are we back?" Dave asked as he swallowed between heavy breaths.

"I don't know," I struggled to say between my own excited breaths. My heart raced like a stock car engine at Daytona and my mouth felt as dry as cotton. "We could be. We're in a different time period, that's for sure."

"It's too quiet for my liking."

"There's no blimp fire or tanks or nothing," I said.

Crickets and birds chirped, uninterested in our presence. There hadn't been any fighting here, not in a long time, many years perhaps.

I holstered my revolver, yet Dave remained in a defensive posture. Our uniforms were dusty and tattered. The grass in the clearing waved peacefully in the warm afternoon breeze.

"If we're back, why are we still in this getup? When we left the first time, our clothes changed to military uniforms. This time they didn't change at all," Dave said.

"The way I see it, there's only one way to find out."

"Let's get going, John," Dave said as he swatted my arm and headed into the forest.

Darkness consumed the woods as we headed for some sign that we walked in our own time of 1986.

The forest thinned and revealed the treeless sites of a modern campground. I saw a shiny red Mercedes across the way parked beside an elaborate tent. An older couple sat on comfortable lawn chairs beside a crackling fire. They clutched wine glasses while they gazed at the dancing flames, her head lovingly resting against his shoulder. All I could think about was that I'd never get to do that with Mary.

"What was that?" I whispered, referring to what sounded like snapping twigs underfoot behind us.

"I heard it too. It's probably a raccoon or a possum. It's a forest, you know," Dave whispered.

I noticed a picnic shelter as well as several pop-up campers nestled in designated campsites off the dirt road.

"What do we do?" Dave asked.

"With these uniforms on, we'll draw unwanted attention. Let's go to the shelter."

"Lead the way."

We found a vacant campsite near the picnic shelter with a brick fire pit. We gathered some dead branches and stacked them into a pit. I patted my pockets and felt a small box I didn't know was there until now. I reached in and removed a box of stick matches.

"I didn't know I had these," I said.

"Maybe your angel friends helped with that."

I started a small fire in the pit. As the flames grew, we sat on a rough-hewned log bench and stared at the lapping flames. A full moon bathed our campsite in a soft, blue hue. More twigs snapped in the woods, and then a chill raced down my spine. I wasn't sure if a firefight was about to break out, or a raccoon would emerge from the darkness.

Dave smiled as he stared at the fire.

"What are you so spooked about?" Dave asked.

"I heard more of your forest critters. I guess I'm still a little edgy," I said.

"I believe it'll take some time to forget everything that happened to us over the last few weeks."

"We won't forget jack. I hope we never hear anything again about war or angels."

"Well, we're back in our own time now if that Mercedes is any indication," Dave said then tossed a twig on the fire.

"We never did find Devers. With Chalons gone, I can only guess Devers is dead too. Maybe Turel got him."

"John, we don't know that. Maybe your angel friends, whoever they are, will bring Devers to us. I think we paid the price for that show."

"I think so too," I said. "If they want us, they can come get us."

I wasn't superstitious, but sometimes instinct told me when I uttered the wrong words at the wrong time. Karma was a royal bitch when I screwed up, but I didn't care anymore.

"I'm okay with that. So, does a bike trip across Europe still sound like a great idea to you?" Dave asked.

"It used to," I said.

"We were there for what, a month or so?"

Dave stoked the fire with a dead branch.

A feeling of failure overcame me as I looked about the moonlit campground.

"I think longer. I'm just glad we made it back in one piece," I said.

"In the beginning, you were so sure that Devers was the reason we went back. Maybe this is some kind of time-out."

"All I know is that the time window was easy to open," I said.

I contemplated the specifics on how the window opened right when we needed a way out.

"What do you mean? Are you saying you opened that one on purpose?" Dave asked.

"I can't explain how I did it, but it was like I knew I could do it, so I did."

"Can you do it again?"

"I can try."

I looked over at the restroom building. With little effort, I felt a window image project from my mind.

"Holy sweet Jesus! Look at that!" Dave declared as he stared in awe.

I shook my head, and the window vanished.

"I think I can do it anytime I want to," I said.

"Where would we go if we went in there?" he asked.

"I think Miami Beach around 1940. I thought about the art deco hotels when I opened the window."

The ability came easily which seemed unusual, but I welcomed its simplicity. I guess that divine endorsement was real after all.

More twigs snapped in the woods. Dave seemed oblivious to them. That stupid raccoon or possum didn't know how to avoid the dead branches.

"If we are back in 1986, we still have the rest of the month to finish the bike trip. Are you still up for it, I mean, if we get our bikes back?" Dave asked.

"Man, our bikes have to be long gone by now," I said, as my jaw popped in mid-yawn.

Despite being back in the safety of our own time, I remained in nervous exhaustion. Dave, however, had no trouble falling asleep. My previous nightmares were just as vivid in my memory as if they'd happened in real life.

Mary's words about my new job to face an evil angel still echoed in my mind, and I had no clue about what I'd do if I came face-to-face with Turel again. I didn't have Mary to go back to anymore. Two people in my life were dead all in the name of the last page. If I quit now and went home, I'd feel like I quit on them. Given everything that's happened, I figured the angels would probably follow me home and drag my ass back into the broiler whenever they wanted. Therefore, trying to escape seemed pointless.

I leaned against the wood bench, about to close my eyes when the blurry image of a soldier stepped closer to the campfire. At first, in my deeply exhausted state, I thought I imagined him. I blinked hard, sat up, and focused.

"Colonel Marcus?" I asked quizzically.

"Harrod, you startled me. I thought you were out. Please forgive my intrusion."

"Never mind that. How the hell did you find us?"

Marcus approached then sat in front of me. Dave snored rhythmically, so I didn't see the point in waking him. Now that I was a relative veteran of time travel, I knew the importance of keeping a cool head. Besides, a panicked mind can't think.

"There are those who make it possible for me to use time windows when necessary, like now or when I saw you at your sporting event. I merely followed you here."

Marcus once said he wasn't an angel but him being here only implied an angel somewhere pulled his strings.

"Do you know how dangerous it is for you to be here?" I asked.

"I'm confident I'm quite safe, for the moment at least. My case is without regard to where I am, only that we're in a desperate way."

"Desperate, huh? Why?"

Colonel Marcus opened his shirt breast pocket, removed a folded letter, and handed it to me.

I unfolded the letter. I instantly recognized the letterhead of the travel agency that booked our flight from Chicago to Paris.

"What do you want?" I asked.

"Since you're the last Interceptor, we still need you to get the last page."

"What do you mean *we*?"

"Colonel Eldridge and I."

"What did you guys do?"

Marcus turned back to the campfire. His lips quivered.

"That's not important," he said. "What is important is that you help us. I assure you our intentions are good."

I hated making decisions without knowing all the facts. Since we were in my time, I tried to make a deal.

"I need to know something first," I said. "You said Harrison Devers is missing. How do you know that when you denied knowing him the first time I mentioned him?"

Marcus looked at the fire for several minutes. He picked up a stick then stoked the burning logs. A grumpy sour expression fell over his face as the small glow of the fire radiated off him.

"I've been through too much to be screwed with," I said. "Are you sure you don't know where he is?"

"Yes, I'm sure. Harrod, I feel you need time to decide. However, there's little to waste."

"Who are you to push me? If you think I'm going back to that bloodbath, you're nuts," I said as I pointed into the woods.

Marcus readjusted his cap.

"Lieutenant, you clearly have your concerns. However, if you can find it in your heart to help us, your efforts won't be overlooked."

Marcus reached into his pocket and removed a folded piece of paper.

"This will explain further," he said then handed the paper to me.

Mary told me to listen to my heart. There, I'd find strength and needed answers. I could only look on as Marcus faded into the dark of night among the trees and bushes. I opened his letter, but my tired eyes failed to make out the calligraphic penmanship in the flickering firelight.

I put the letter in my coat pocket. I don't know how long I sat staring at the glowing embers, but at some point along the way, I fell asleep.

Morning arrived with the sun's life-giving heat. I wiped the sweat from my forehead then rolled onto my back. Unable to fall back asleep, I opened my eyes. I saw with great joy the blue sky of morning.

"Hey Dave, do you think we're back for good?" I asked.

"Oh, sweet mother of mercy it was a dream," Dave said with a sigh of relief.

"Wrong, buckaroo. We still have our guns and our uniforms. I had some nasty dreams again, but at least that tree with the angels wasn't in them."

"I had a whopper of a dream too," Dave said.

"Maybe we have shell shock," I said with scrunched eyebrows. I cleared my throat, hocked a loogie, and arced it into a nearby bush.

Dave rolled off the bench then stretched for the heavens.

"Marcus was here last night," I said.

"Marcus? Why didn't you wake me up? Wait a minute, how did he get here? Weren't we the only ones who could use that window thing?"

"He said he followed us. I don't know how it all works."

"What'd he want?"

I removed the letter from my shirt pocket and read it again. The fancy scrollwork-like penmanship was just as difficult to read in daylight as it was by campfire light.

"He gave me this," I said as I handed it to him.

"What's it say?"

"It's kind of hard to read. You try."

Dave looked over the letter then read aloud.

"Here goes. *Lieutenant Harrod, for the past several months we have been engaged in affairs of which we are most ashamed and deeply regret. Our treachery and willingness to consort with evil elements hostile toward the Allies are unforgivable. However, our actions to correct our mistakes caused our own undoing. The unexpected disappearance or rather abandonment by Captain Edmund has left us vulnerable and targeted by former accomplices, and I fear we'll not survive for long. I yearn to see my wife and daughters. Knowing they'd spend the rest of their lives bearing my shame is too monumental. If you could find it in your heart to help us, please do so expediently. Regards, Colonel James Marcus, Colonel Francis Eldridge.*"

Dave shook his head. "He wants us to go back to help him? What the hell did he ever do for us?" Dave asked as he handed the letter back to me.

"I know. Remember the orders I gave him on our first day?" I asked.

"Yeah."

"Those weren't orders, it was our travel itinerary. He knew all along I was an Interceptor, or else he would've busted us."

I reread the letter. Certain phrases in the letter seemed familiar.

"Hey, I get it," I said. "This letter isn't a confession. It was a call for help."

"Come again?"

I took an excited breath then explained.

"Edmund and Turel want to kill the colonels because Marcus and Eldridge had a change of heart. They wanted to save face and Chalons. Remember how determined Marcus was about saving the Gate by eliminating the German air base?"

"I was in the same room as you, John. I remember. So how does Marcus get this letter back so he can give it to Devers?"

Dave stroked his mustache and his eyes narrowed.

"A letter like this wouldn't be given to just anybody," I said. "My dad told me that Devers was mainly reclusive. I'll bet Devers has something to do with this. Maybe they left his name off to protect him."

"Either way, they're all in a heap."

"That's right. They'll charge the colonels with conspiracy and treason for starters. Then they'll likely face execution," I said.

"What do we do?"

"Before Marcus left last night, he threw a guilt trip on me to help him."

"You want to, don't you? You want to see whether Eldridge or Marcus can lead us to your great-grandpa."

Horrific memories flashed through my mind as I considered the prospect of returning to 1917, yet a strange sense of security blanketed me.

"Yeah," I said. "I do."

"How do we go about it?" Dave asked.

"The experience of going through the time window was the same for us both times. We went through the first time because Edmund and Turel forced us to. We returned with the knowledge of an espionage ring along with information that pointed to the possible location of my great-grandfather. I guess I was right. Time machines are nothing but fantasy. The only way to time travel is with permission, a divine endorsement."

"Makes sense seeing that we don't have to question the powers that enabled us," I said.

At that moment, a feeling of dread overcame me. There was no way around it.

"What?" Dave asked.

"This letter means we go back," I said as I waved the letter.

Dave rubbed his trousers anxiously.

"How do you figure?" he asked.

"I first read this letter at my dad's house last spring. Devers gave it to my mom. How could Devers or Marcus give a letter neither of them presently has?"

"If you gave that letter back to them and saved them, he'd have no reason to give that letter to your mom at all. That means we would've changed history," Dave said.

If we intervened further from this point on, we'd alter Eldridge and Marcus's future. Would their lives be any different if saved from seventy years of guilt? Would they be happier? Would they still marry, or have children? If I followed my heart as Mary instructed, changing my family history must be okay. Maybe if I changed things a lot and got the last page, the angels would put things back for me like they were before Mom died. After all, angels and time travel was a powerful pair.

There was no telling what would become of us if we helped Eldridge and Marcus. We might even help ourselves right out of existence. I read the letter twice more then decided.

"Dave, we're going back. It's like there's a voice in my head telling me in a language I can understand but can't speak."

"You mean like God is doing this to us?"

"No. I think angels are doing it."

Dave thought for a moment then shook his head.

"No, that ain't it," Dave said. "If God were to move us around in time, we would've heard a voice or seen something profound. All we get are nightmares and run-ins with psychos. Besides, why plunk us down in a war? Why would a loving God do that? You see what I mean?"

"I do. Maybe this is how God gets humans to do his dirty work. We've heard a voice, Mary's. She was real. I think time windows are strong convincers that a being greater than us lowly-ass humans exists in some form. What do you think? Go back or stay here?" I asked.

"I don't know, damn it!" Dave said while he paced around the fire.

"Mary said for us to follow our hearts. My heart says we go back."

"Sonofabitch," Dave said then kicked a small rock.

"I know this sucks, Dave, but we have God on our side."

"Well, I can't argue with that now, can I?"

We retrieved our war gear then went into the forest. In a short time, we arrived at Shubert's overgrown wreck. I viewed the wreckage then peered into the clearing. As we stood in the stillness of the forest and gathered our thoughts, I gazed at the clearing that served as our hellish foster home. The sounds of the forest and the breeze that blew across the clearing drew me in.

While we faced the fallen tree that was the entry point to a world of utter chaos, I looked at Dave then smiled.

"Are you ready?" I asked. "You look a little apprehensive."

"Of course, I'm apprehensive! What the hell do you expect?" Dave snapped.

"We'll be okay. I promise."

"Right. You promise. All I wanted was a little action and a little adventure," Dave said. "Got any clue on where we'll find Marcus or Eldridge?"

"Nope."

Dave took another deep breath then shook his head.

"All right. Let's go. There's nothing more exciting than driving blindfolded in a snowstorm."

I looked at the fallen tree and concentrated. The window appeared instantly. I felt the warmth of divine endorsement and an emerging power grow within me as if I had the strength of the angels at my disposal. It was a great feeling, but I knew damn well that I wasn't an angel. We stepped over the fallen tree and into the clear rippling waves of the time window.

We emerged from the window then stood still for a minute while our eyes adjusted to the brightness of the clearing. The time window closed behind us instantly.

Twenty feet in front of us sat three planes. The solid black cross on the fuselage indicated whose side they belonged to. Suddenly, grumbling noises emanated from behind one of the planes. Three German pilots were busy tying up Colonel Marcus. Colonel Eldridge sat next to him, bound and gagged.

"Holy crap," I said.

The pilots jerked their heads toward us then scrambled for their guns.

Three rapid shots rang out. I watched as the pilots dropped to the ground. I turned to Dave as he holstered his revolver.

"What?" Dave asked nonchalantly.

"Did you do that?" I asked.

"My timing's off a little, but I got them."

"We've only been here two seconds. Just like that, you take down three guys?"

"Sorry," Dave said with a shrug.

I never thought I'd see the day when Dave would gun down someone quick draw style, let alone three people. Damn, he was good. We went around the planes then untied the colonels.

"Lieutenants, I'm most grateful you decided to come to our aid," Marcus declared.

"Are you two okay?" I asked.

"None the worse," Eldridge said as he rubbed his wrists. "How did you bloody do that? You come out of thin air and kill three men."

"Simmer down. We just saved your ass," Dave said.

"Consider yourself lucky we even got here," I snapped back.

"You disrespectful ingrate," Eldridge said then lunged at me.

Eldridge would've been easy to knock out, but instead, I wrestled him to the ground. To keep him from hurting himself, I put him in a wrestling submission hold called a guillotine. I knotted him up tightly, and held him while he unleashed a string of impressive obscenities.

"Harrod, let him go," Marcus demanded.

"Come on, John, he ain't worth the hassle," Dave said.

"I'll let him go, but only if he promises to be cool. Dave and I can easily go back and let you two clowns take your chances. What do you say, Eldridge?"

Eldridge took his time answering, so I put on the squeeze, and he yelped.

"Very well, now let me go," he bellowed.

I loosened my hold and let him struggle to his feet.

"Here's the deal, colonels," I said as I brushed off my hands. "Dave and I will help you as best we can. After we're done, we're gone. We expect your full cooperation in any military encounter where our presence is questioned."

"Harrod, I've already explained everything to Eldridge. However, he's not used to anyone speaking to him in your fashion. Please understand."

"Hey, if we agree to work together and forget our petty differences, we'll help."

"Very well, Harrod," Eldridge said and we shook hands.

"Lead the way, colonels. I hear Edmund or Turel's after you, not to mention the favor I owe both of them. So, where do we go?" I asked.

"Vauchamps," Marcus said.

We left the pilots to the buzzards but left the planes alone. I wasn't about to set the planes ablaze and send smoke signals to mark our presence. Despite our first fight, I found it a weird sensation locking Eldridge in a wrestling move I hadn't used since junior high school. In time, I hoped our relationship would become more universally favorable, at least until we finally got out of this godforsaken place.

CHAPTER 25

THE COLONELS, DAVE, and I ventured across a small grassy field the war hadn't found yet. We hiked for about an hour through the waist-high grass after which we came upon a well-travelled dirt road. We followed the quiet road with the distant echoes of mortar blasts miles away. After a few minutes into our walk, a medical transport truck wavered about the dusty road then jostled to a stop in front of us. Two sergeants wrapped in wool overcoats didn't look a day over eighteen.

"Sirs," a sergeant covered in sweaty dust said followed by a salute. We saluted back. "By any chance, would one of you be Colonel Marcus?"

We stood quietly, then Marcus stepped forward.

"Sergeant, I'm Colonel Marcus. This is Colonel Eldridge, and Lieutenants Harrod and Sowell."

"Sir, you were reported AWOL after the fall of Chalons. You have to come with us to Chaumont to clear this up. We have orders to detain you. This must be my lucky day finding you here," the sergeant said with a cocky grin.

"Not lucky enough," Eldridge said as he drew his revolver then shot each sergeant in the head with cold determination.

Eldridge calmly holstered his revolver and put his hands in his pockets while he glanced at the dead sergeants.

"Francis, have you gone mad?" Marcus asked.

"Those lads relished our discovery more than they should have," Eldridge said then took a couple steps toward the truck.

"Your short temper will be your undoing. How will you explain this at our debriefing?"

"Given the circumstances, perhaps Edmund sent these scouts. I suggest you put the bodies in the grass away from the road. No person knows we're here. Thus we'll have no need to explain anything to anyone."

We carried the bodies to the tall grass beside the road while Eldridge and Marcus hustled into the truck.

"Harrod, you and Sowell begin down the road for Vauchamps. You can meet up with Collishaw and Bishop there. It's better if we arrive separately. Best of luck to you."

"What?" I asked. "You're ditching us?"

"Harrod, please. You have my word," Marcus said.

With that, they went on their way and left us in their dusty wake.

"Great idea helping those two no-goods," Dave said. "How do we know they won't pin the murders on us?"

"Good point. If anyone catches us near here, they'll blame us for sure. Come on, we better get out of here before someone else shows up asking questions."

This was perfect. Marcus and Eldridge took the only ride to the next base and left us to the wolves. Nothing but the chilly autumn wind blew through the barren, ghostly trees as we hoofed it along the desolate road. In the distance, the rumble of mortar fire assured us the fighting was far from over.

Our long, lonely walk ended when we found a barren patch of land. Perhaps it was the Colummeir airfield. We headed toward a collection of small wood frame buildings then found what looked to be the Command Center. The grounds appeared deserted. I knocked on the door a couple of times then went inside.

A captain seated at a desk tapped methodically at a manual typewriter. After he had completed his paperwork, he looked up at us. He was a lanky man, rail thin, large Adam's apple, skin whiter than newly fallen snow. His blazing red butch-cut hair left no doubt about his ethnicity.

"I'm Captain Sullivan. Can I help you, sirs?" he asked in a soft Irish lilt.

"Yes sir, I'm Lieutenant Harrod, he's Lieutenant Sowell. We got lost after the battle at the Gate. Is this Vauchamps?" I asked.

"No, Chaintrix. Vauchamps is thirty kilometers west. You said your names were Harrod and Sowell?"

"Yes."

Sullivan turned to a wall of slotted cabinets where he removed several sheets of paper. He carefully inspected them, and then glanced back at us.

"Please, sirs, have a seat," Sullivan said. He sauntered to a Morse Code machine and tapped away.

"Is there a problem?" I asked.

"Please, sir, don't distract me while I'm doing this. I'll be with you directly."

"Sorry."

I turned to Dave.

"What do you think?" I asked.

"If you hear a rattle in the tall grass, don't stick your face down for a closer look," Dave whispered.

"What's that supposed to mean?"

"He's rattling a lot at that telegraph machine."

I wasn't in the mood for one of Dave's Texas analogies right now.

"What are you trying to say?" I asked.

"We should get out of here," Dave said as he eyed the captain concentrating at the machine.

"You mean desert? They'll shoot us."

"That's the part that keeps me here."

Sullivan returned to his desk where he shuffled more papers into neat stacks.

"Sorry to keep you, sirs," the captain said. "You'll need to stay until you've been debriefed."

"What's going on?" I asked.

"You've been reported missing in action. An intelligence officer is en route to record your account."

"Are we in trouble?"

"That isn't my decision." A field phone rattled on Sullivan's desk, and he picked it up.

"Yes, this is Sullivan. Both of them are here," he said as he stole a glance at us. "Yes, sir." He hung up the phone then returned to his paperwork.

"Excuse me, what was that about?" I asked.

"Command is sending a security detail and will arrive in due course. You must wait here. If you leave, you'll be arrested and jailed as deserters."

"Of course," I said. Dave nodded.

I suppose I could've opened a time window and got us out of this jam, but running away wasn't an attractive choice. We could bolt if we had to, but I wanted to see where my so-called natural course with Marcus would take me.

An hour into our wait, the door swung open. A colonel of stately proportions resembling Grover Cleveland emerged with an aide of lesser stature. The aide carried a worn leather satchel slung over his shoulder. We snapped to attention and saluted.

"Colonel Lars Hutchins, Secret Service Bureau, MI6. Come with me," he boomed.

Colonel Hutchins hustled us to another building nearby. His aide sat at a table, removed a notepad, and began writing. Hutchins began writing as well. I didn't like Hutchins's brashness. I felt I couldn't answer convincingly without some answers of my own.

"Excuse me, sir," I said.

"What is it?" he asked while his calloused eyes remained fixed on the paper as he wrote.

"How long have we been reported missing?" I asked.

"Almost two months. Your last reported sighting was 9 September 1917 at Chalons aerodrome. Where have you been since then?"

"Best I can recall, after the battle of Chalons, we were knocked unconscious by a bomb. When I woke up, I found myself in some farmhouse."

The colonel wrote furiously as he captured every detail that came out of my mouth, not that it mattered to me.

"When you awoke, how much time passed until you tried to return to your squad?"

"I'm not sure. I had headaches and dizzy spells. I could hardly stand. Dave here was much the same."

"You've been missing for almost two months, yet you can only account for one of those months. What of the other?"

"When we gained enough strength, we ventured out, but we must've gotten turned around. Somehow, we ended up near the Swiss border. Luckily, we hopped a transport west, and then walked it back this way. We were trying to get to Vauchamps when we found this place."

"Why Vauchamps?"

"Colonel Marcus told us to go there so we could meet up with Ray Collishaw and Billy Bishop."

Hutchins stopped writing. His eyes shifted about the desk as he twiddled his pencil.

"Marcus? Have you seen Colonel Marcus lately?" Hutchins asked.

"I saw him about four hours ago," I said.

"Where is he now? Do you know his bearing?"

"No, I don't. He and Colonel Eldridge took off in an abandoned truck. I don't have any idea where they went."

Until I knew the truth why Marcus and Eldridge ditched us, I decided to protect them even though it went against my better judgment.

"Do you know Major Collishaw?" Hutchins asked.

"Yes, sir. Can we reach him?"

Colonel Hutchins ignored me. He took to the phone and called Vauchamps airfield. "Major Collishaw?" Hutchins asked. After several minutes of speaking with Ray, Hutchins seemed satisfied with Ray's explanation, whatever it was.

"You men are free to go to Vauchamps in the morning but you must remand yourselves to Major Collishaw's charge upon arrival."

Colonel Hutchins and his aide marched out of the building as quickly as they entered.

"That wasn't too bad," Dave said.

"No," I said. "Did you notice how Hutchins paused when I mentioned Marcus?"

"I caught that too. Do you think Hutchins is on to something?"

"That'd be my guess."

"Now that the heat is off for the moment, let's get something to eat."

We entered the crude mess tent, which made the Chalons mess hall look like a four-star restaurant. Stale, salty bread rolls and cold oatmeal was the only food available, but I wasn't about to complain. The cook explained that chow ended a couple hours ago. Maybe we'll have better luck tomorrow.

The cold night air was absent of war noise except for the distant volley of cannons many miles away. I hated the shelling even though we experienced only a few days of it. That was all it took to make a veteran out of me. I couldn't imagine being in the trenches for weeks at a time with bombs exploding all around every minute of the day.

After we had eaten, we found an empty barrack to use for the night. We created makeshift beds by piling several itchy wool blankets on the dusty plank floor. Hopefully, we'd get a quiet night's sleep.

I walked along a grassy path and took in the sweet scents of wild flowers, lilac, and lavender. A flock of geese honked across the wide, clear sky. As they descended toward me, a winged man twice my height with an indescribable face sidled beside me then sounded a golden reflective trumpet. The blare violently shot me out of my slumber, and I sat up to catch my breath. Dave stared back at me as if I was a mutant.

"Dave, those crazy dreams are back," I said then rubbed my eyes.

"I can see that," he said as he watched me.

I pulled up a blanket to help stop my cold sweat shivers.

"Ready to hit the road?" I asked.

"Yeah. I say we head out," Dave said.

We left the blankets on the floor and stepped outside. My steamy breath wafted across my face as I noticed several Model T trucks near the mess tent. Dave hopped in behind the steering wheel while I gave the engine a crank. Like an old lawn mower I once used as a kid, it took several tries before the machine came to life. We backed out then started down the road in the emergent daylight.

Air attacks and ground assaults bombed, shot up, or violated just about every building along our way. Most of the houses stood vacant. Some families loaded casualties onto wagons, which took them to a nearby cemetery or field hospital.

The thirty-kilometer ride to Vauchamps passed in a couple of hours. I hoped we'd get there soon as I wasn't sure my back could take much more bouncing around. The air base was small like Chaintrix. There was a cluster of smaller buildings surrounded by barbed wire and several armed guards. I assumed that was the brig.

"My ass is killing me. These old trucks leave nothing for comfort," Dave said. He grimaced as he hopped out of the truck.

"At least it got us here. It's about eight o'clock. Let's try that building over there," I said and arched my back.

The familiar buzz of aircraft echoed across the airfield as four Sopwith Camels landed. We stood by as the pilots climbed out of their planes and walked toward us. One of them removed his flight cap, revealing the youthful face of Ray Collishaw. He smiled at me, but his partner, Billy, did not.

"Hey, Ray. How's it going?" I asked.

Before Ray answered, his partner, Billy Bishop walked straight up to Dave and cold-cocked him across the jaw. Dave stumbled to the ground in complete shock.

"What the hell, Billy?" I demanded as I rushed to Dave's aid.

"I told you two bastards what would happen if you lied to me," Billy said.

"What the hell are you ragging about?" Dave bellowed.

"I'll show you."

My jaw slacked open as I helped Dave to his feet. We followed Billy to his barrack, a glorified shack at best. Ray closed the door. Billy grabbed a small, red sack from the drawer of a plain wood desk.

"Explain this," Billy said as he threw the sack at Dave.

Dave, still reeling from the punch, recognized the sack as my fanny pack. He looked at me as if seeking permission to speak.

"Don't look to Harrod to save your hide. I inspected everything. Start talking."

Billy's lisp took the edge off his demand. I exchanged glances with Ray, but I realized I couldn't talk my way out of this one. In fact, I didn't even want to try.

"Okay, guys, here it is. Like I said before, we aren't soldiers or pilots. We don't belong to any military branch. We're from the future, 1986 to be exact. We believe someone sent us here to save a relative of mine whose location is still unknown. Along the way, I was given the ability to do this."

I opened a time window in the back of the barrack. The purity of the rippling water-like rings remained long enough for them to get a good look before I closed it.

"At this point, I might ask if you have any questions, but I'm not going to," I said. "You two need to help us. There's no time for personal squabbles. We need to work together as time is short."

"Harrod, at first I didn't believe you, but after this display, your actions make more sense to me. I think I can speak for Billy as well," Ray said.

Billy sunk to his cot and, with a slack jaw, surrendered to my ability.

"Harrod, I know you said no questions, but I have a few I must ask," Ray asked.

"Okay, but I reserve the right not to answer. Go ahead," I said.

Ray opened his satchel, which contained my Walkman tape player. "First, what is this contraption?"

I looked at my damaged tape player, a hundred bucks shot to hell.

"Where did you get that?" I asked.

"It was confiscated from Edmund," Ray said.

I couldn't get into the science involved, but it made no sense to blow their minds with a bunch of technical stuff that even I didn't understand.

"You know what a phonograph is, right?" I asked.

"Yes," Ray said.

"It's like a phonograph but in a different format. A tape goes inside there, and music comes out of little speakers."

"This is small and weighs little. What else is there in the future? Who wins the war?"

"From our time, we won, but that may change. That's why we're here."

"But, John, one more thing," Ray said excitedly.

"No, that's it, new subject. Tell me what happened to you guys after Chalons got blown up."

Billy sat quietly as he tried to grasp my remarks. Dave waved his hand in front of Billy's face. Billy gently shook his head then looked up at Dave.

"You want to take part in our little discussion, or do I get to return the favor?" Dave balled up his rugged fist in front of Billy's relaxed face.

"No. No, carry on. I'm listening," Billy said.

His lisp grew more pronounced. I hoped I hadn't short-circuited his brain.

"After Chalons, we retreated to Vauchamp. Now we're performing recon for a new offensive at Cambrai," Ray said.

"Boy, Dave, they move right along, don't they?" I asked as I glanced at Dave.

"Recon continued for a month when we heard they captured Edmund. He's in the brig several yards over."

"Wait, Edmund's here?" Dave asked.

"Yes," Ray said. "They found him north of Chalons in an underground shelter. I heard there were some documents found on him. I'm not sure of the content, but they had high command in a tither."

In the back of my mind, I thought about Colonel Hutchins. Perhaps he's involved with Edmund and the Germans as well.

"A tither? What tither?" Dave asked.

"Details are scarce," Ray said. "I heard rumblings of sabotage at Chalons. I suspected some dealings with the Germans as well. They even named Colonels Eldridge, Weatherby, and Marcus. We haven't been able to make much sense of it. A matter for the courts, I assume."

"I guess so," I said.

"What became of you two?" Ray asked.

"After Chalons, we returned to our own time. We were there for a day. Marcus needed our help, so we came back. We saved them from German capture, and then watched Eldridge whack two sergeants."

"Whack?" Ray asked.

I didn't feel too badly about using that word, I could easily write that one off as a local term.

"I mean killed," I said. "Then they took the sergeant's truck. We haven't seen either of them since. We ended up at Chaintrix where we met a sea lion of a guy named Hutchins."

"Colonel Lars Hutchins?" Billy asked as he straightened up.

"Yeah. Have you heard of him?" I asked.

"He's not someone you cross. He reports directly to General Haig. He has a keen sense of rooting out spies on both sides."

"Then Hutchins would also know how to hide a spy too. When we mentioned Marcus and Eldridge, he let us go."

"I'm afraid my suspicion that a traitor was about was correct," Ray said as he paced around the barrack and brushed back his sandy mane.

"Men, this is serious. Hutchins wouldn't be here unless he had it on good authority that a legitimate spy was about," Ray said.

"If we're going to get a jump on this, we should start with Edmund," Dave said. "Think about it. Hutchins hightailed it to talk to us since we were connected to Marcus at Chalons."

"I know for certain that Colonel Hutchins was one of the first to interview Edmund after he was captured."

"Time's wasting," I said. "Can we see Edmund?"

"Sure."

"How long is he going to be here?"

"Until his hearing and likely execution are carried out."

"Execution?" I asked.

"Yes, for treason," Ray said.

"We have to get as much as we can out of him while we have the chance."

Ray led us to the stockade that contained its sole inmate, Captain Edmund. My spirit ached to wring his scrawny neck like a wet washrag. However, there was a remote chance he could actually help us.

CHAPTER 26

RAY AND BILLY identified themselves to the stockade guard who then led us down a narrow, musty hall to Edmund's cell. The guard closed the door then returned to his desk.

We found Edmund asleep face down on a dingy cot. The stagnant air instantly made my nose tingle.

"Get up," Ray said as he kicked the bottom of Edmund's foot. Edmund scrambled off the cot.

"What the devil?" Edmund said in confusion.

"Do you believe in miracles, Edmund?" I asked.

Edmund's jaw dropped. His eyes bulged, and then a look of fear fell over his face.

"What are you doing here? What do you want?" Edmund asked as he scurried up on his cot like a frightened child.

"We need answers, and you're going to give them to us," I said.

"Why should I help you?"

"Do you know a guy named Colonel Hutchins from MI6? I heard he spoke to you a while ago."

"Of course," Edmund said then sniffled.

"What interest does he have in you or Colonel Marcus?" I asked.

"Colonel Marcus died at Chalons."

"I have a news flash for you, Edmund. Marcus is alive."

Edmund faced formal charges as a deserter, but somebody still wanted that weasel alive.

"Marcus is alive?" Edmund asked. "They said they'd get them both when Chalons collapsed."

"Who would get them? What's your relationship with Marcus, Eldridge, and Weatherby?"

Edmund faced the corner of his cell. He smoothed back his tangled oily hair then spun around.

"I can't say," Edmund muttered.

"Captain," Ray said. "You've been charged with desertion, treason, and should've been shot weeks ago. Once Hutchins finds what he's looking for, he'll carry out your sentence immediately. Don't you want to see your family again? Don't you miss them? Believe me, when I say John can help you."

I shot Ray a quick glance. I couldn't deny his statement, but Ray knew how to get Edmund to soften up better than I could, so I let it go. Edmund's eyes glossed over.

"It was Turel," Edmund said. "He organized the compromise of Chalons."

"We figured that out. Does Hutchins know?" I asked.

"When Hutchins questioned me, I didn't mention Turel. I told Hutchins that Marcus and the other colonels conspired with the Germans for massive sums. That was more believable."

"Sums of what, money?"

"You catch on fast, Yank," Edmund said with a sliver of sarcasm.

I grabbed Edmund by the neck. With one arm, I pinned him against the wall while his weakened body flailed a few inches off the floor.

"Look, pal. I don't have time for games. Either you start talking, or I start squeezing."

I clamped down on Edmund's neck until his face turned dark red. I then let him fall to the floor to catch his breath. I grabbed him by the lapels and set him onto his cot. He gingerly rubbed his neck while his facial redness faded to its natural pasty whiteness.

"Chalons was to be the last reward," Edmund said. "After that, we'd vanish. Marcus and Eldridge went back on their word. I suppose they suffered from a case of self-preservation since they made it out of Chalons in one piece."

"Let me understand this," I started. "Marcus, Eldridge, Weatherby, and you were in bed with the Germans to throw the Chalons offensive for cash?"

"Yes."

"How much money were you clowns going to get if you pulled it off?" I asked.

"Two million pounds," Edmund muttered.

"My Lord," Billy said.

"What's the big deal?" I asked. "In dollars, that's about, what, a million? Thousands of lives are worth a hell of a lot more than that."

"John, in our time that probably bucks around fifty million or so," Dave said.

"Whoa," I said.

"Fifty million? In your time?" Edmund asked with a tinge of surprise in his voice.

"Never mind," I said. "What else did you tell Hutchins?"

"That was all."

Edmund dropped his head and looked at his feet. He then rubbed his thighs anxiously.

"What else do you have up your sleeve?" I asked.

"Nothing, I swear," Edmund said.

"Bullshit," Dave said. "Your days are numbered, buddy, and confession is good for the soul. Besides, the next time you see a preacher he'll be escorting you to the gallows or the nearest brick wall."

Edmund's eyes darted about the room, and a deep suspicion about Edmund boiled inside me.

"Very well. Before Chalons fell, Turel struck an agreement to thwart an effort at Cambrai. They captured me shortly after, so I don't know anything more. Perhaps Marcus or Eldridge can be of greater assistance since they attended more of the meetings."

"If we see them, I'll ask," I said. "Did Colonel Hutchins ask you anything specific about Colonel Marcus or Eldridge?"

Edmund sat still with a look of defeat. My eyes watered slightly then my nose tingled again. There must be a slather of mold plastered underneath the wood plank floor.

"He asked mostly routine questions," Edmund said. "Like when I saw them last, where they went, who he saw, matters of that nature."

"Do you know where Colonel Marcus could be now?" I asked.

"He may be at one of two underground hiding places. Nobody in high command knows about them. One of them is an underground dugout. The other is a small cabin in the forest."

"I can't picture Marcus or Eldridge crawling in the dirt. Where is this cabin?" I asked then went into a sneezing fit. The musty, moldy smell finally broke through my defenses.

Edmund rubbed his neck once more while I sniffled and dried my eyes.

"It's close. There's a road to Epernay. Along the way, you'll find Saint Martin d'Ablois. When you reach the church, take the road west to a bridge. Stop before the bridge then head north into the woods. Venture a hundred meters or so, and you'll find it."

"The secret hideout is in an old house outside of town?" Dave asked.

"The hideout used to be in the town's church basement, but we had to move it. Nevertheless, the money is there," Edmund said.

I could've railed on Edmund all night, but I backed off. Under my anger, I found a degree of compassion. Time was short so my playing the hard ass wouldn't help my cause. So, I chose the compassion route in the hopes that he'd voluntarily tell me more.

"If you have a soul, your last thoughts should be of your family, if you got any. Think about what their lives would be like without you. You might want to write to them. You don't have much time."

"John, I think that'll do," Ray said.

"I mean it, Ray. His family will want to know what became of him," I said.

"As it stands, none of them even exist yet," Edmund lamented. I looked at him curiously. I couldn't believe nobody else caught Edmund's meaning.

"We'll return if we have more questions. Guard!" Ray bellowed.

"Ray, Billy, will you excuse us for a few minutes? I'd like to talk with Edmund alone."

Ray and Billy eyed each other then shook their heads. Billy leaned against the wall then crossed his arms.

"I'm serious, guys. Give me a few minutes. I'm not going to hurt him."

Ray and Billy reluctantly left the cell yet spied us suspiciously.

"We'll be right outside," Billy said as he pointed toward the door.

"Okay," I said then closed the door. Edmund wasn't the weasel I first thought him to be. He was different. He must've known we were different too. His comment about his family not existing yet struck me as unusual. My heart beat faster while I thought it over, then I decided to take a big chance.

"You're not from here, are you?" I asked.

"No. Herfordshire," Edmund said.

"I mean, you're not from this time period, right?"

Edmund's eyes widened as if he found something nobody else could understand in 1917.

"No," he whispered.

"How did you get here? To 1917?"

I needed to know. If that time window had divine origins, then it made sense that other pawns like me might've gone through them as well.

"I was storing black powder barrels at the Alamo when Turel appeared and brought me to a log cabin in the woods."

"When was that?"

"It was in the spring of 1836. He showed me his evilness by threatening to kill my family if I didn't cooperate with him."

"What have you and Turel been doing all this time?"

"Since we met, there's been nothing but bloodshed."

"Do you know anything about a fallen angel?" Dave asked.

Edmund's jaw dropped.

"You know about Turel?" he asked.

"I do." I rubbed my jaw as I thought. I recalled the punch Turel threw at me in my tent. "What do you know about him?" I asked.

"He says lots of things, especially when he drinks. I didn't believe a word until I saw his angry red eyes. At first, I thought he was like any other human. He mentioned his leader, Samyaza, a few times. It was all too much to believe."

Edmund arose from his bed. He shuffled around the room, seemingly gathering his thoughts.

"Others are acting for a leader to perpetuate a mirage on the unsuspecting," Edmund said.

"What are you talking about?" I asked.

"The *Bible* is only part of the truth," Edmund said. "Over the centuries, the world's religious leaders have been praising the *Bible* to gain financial power, ultimately for world dominance. The power they believe they're wielding is all false but will be reacquired by the principal."

"Who's the principal?" Dave asked.

"Turel or Samyaza, I think," Edmund said. "Then they'll rule over mankind."

"Have you seen Samyaza?"

"No."

"Does Turel have any weaknesses?" I asked.

"I gather human vices," Edmund said. "He likes drinking. Turel has powers no human can stop. He wouldn't send me home when I demanded. Death is my only salvation."

"So, what is Turel's goal?"

"To recreate mankind on August 2, 1934," Edmund continued.

"You mean that's going down in about fifteen years?" Dave asked.

Edmund nodded then took a deep breath.

"How do you know all this?" Dave asked.

"As I said, Turel drinks. When he drinks, he talks. The only countermeasure to prevent a travesty at the Redemption Moon was to mask the third month of every sixty-fourth year of every century. During that time, the angels enlist a mortal at birth, to track Turel. That chosen mortal is called the Interceptor."

I looked at Dave for some reassurance.

"Dave, he confirmed everything we've been told."

"You must finish your search while you're here," Edmund said with a cracking voice and wiped his nose on his sleeve. "Time manipulation is always at risk as is the life of your great-grandfather. Save him as you intend then leave this place," Edmund said.

"How did you know I was trying to find my great-grandfather? Do you know where he is?"

"Turel's also looking for him since Devers's name was created here. Turel's been following you, hoping you'll expose the person with the last page of the *Book of Ancients* then take it for himself."

Edmund sat on his cot and covered his head with his hands. Dave and I took a few moments to gather our thoughts then left Edmund to his destiny.

An endless line of troops paraded past the base as Dave and I entered Ray and Billy's barracks.

I believed Edmund, but I knew now that I'd have to finish what the angels started. We entered the barracks then dissected all the information we had.

"One or both of them is a spy," Ray said.

"Who?" I asked.

"Marcus and Eldridge. Hutchins is after the colonels. If he catches them, he'll kill them on sight."

"Without a trial?" Dave asked.

"No, not for them," Ray said. "If this fiasco were made public, the Allies would face a compromised position here, not to mention the political embarrassment. Colonel Hutchins has a notorious history. Once he gets his man, he'll make a quick order, and carry out the sentence. I would suspect that he'd likely file a report that the colonels died in action somewhere to cover the impropriety."

"Hutchins doesn't screw around," Dave said. "He's as crooked as any politician."

"What do we gain by saving Marcus or Eldridge?" I asked. "It seems to me they'll get what they deserve. We'd only be delaying the unavoidable."

"I don't know. Maybe if we heard Marcus's side of the story first, we could help them without anyone dying. We have to find him before Hutchins does."

Dave wet his lips then groomed his Longhorn away from his mouth.

"What about Turel?" Dave asked. "What are we going to do about him?"

"Nothing yet. As Edmund said, Turel's role is observational for now. We'll start with the house in the woods Edmund mentioned," I said.

"Edmund only told us about the places Marcus knew about. He might know other places where Turel could hide."

We didn't have time for guessing games. Unless Turel's an idiot and shot his mouth off a lot, he'd be tough to find.

"I'm sure Edmund told us everything he knew," I said. "Let's check out that house and, if nothing comes of it, we'll grill him again."

"Okay. Edmund isn't going anywhere. Let's take one of them trucks parked out front," Dave said.

"No. We'll wait until dark. There's no sense advertising ourselves. Ray, you and Billy wait here. If this place is as close as Edmund said, we shouldn't be gone long."

"Very well," Ray said.

We had waited for the cover of darkness before we headed to the house in the woods. Edmund's description didn't put it far into the forest. With any luck, it would be less than a hundred yards from the road.

As our truck puttered its way down the rough, dirt road, we found the church then made the required turn. Nobody was outside. Only the sound of our tinkering engine echoed off the brick walls of the war-torn village businesses with punctured walls, blown out windows, and scars from countless fires. Once we encountered the bridge, Dave pulled the truck off the road. All said and done, the ride took about an hour.

"Good Lord, the nights don't get this dark at home," Dave said.

"Come on, let's try to find this place," I said.

We stumbled our way through the blackness of the forest. We bumped against tree trunks and snapped an occasional dead branch.

"Cold out here, huh?" I asked.

"It's nippy, all right. Hey, look ahead," Dave said.

"It's a light. Maybe that's the cabin."

We approached the cottage and upon closer inspection, I thought it nothing more than a makeshift shed. We crept up to the window and stayed below the light shining through it. From the lower corner of the window, I stole a quick glance and saw several men inside. Some were French, some German, the others British.

"What are they yammering about?" Dave whispered.

"I don't know. I heard Cambrai mentioned twice already."

"Do you see Marcus or Eldridge?"

"Yep, they're in there."

"Where's their truck?" Dave said then looked nervously around our position. The lanterns inside the house cast a soft light on us.

"Maybe it's on the other side. Now, keep quiet," I whispered harshly.

The meeting erupted in hearty laughter, so I looked back through the window. Marcus handed several sheets of paper to a German officer. The officer read then nodded. Another German soldier tossed a large duffel bag onto the table. Marcus removed several bundles of cash from the duffel and didn't smile. He carried himself as if he'd done this many times before. He returned the money to the duffel then set it down at his feet. The Frenchmen drank from many bottles of wine then broke out in a song.

"What are they doing now?" Dave asked.

"Marcus took a huge bag of money. A deal just went down."

Behind us, footsteps snapped dead branches. The room's light that reflected off our faces finally gave us away.

"Stay where you are," the English voice said then came closer.

I sensed Dave's willingness to make like Billy the Kid, so I slowly turned around with my hands up. I then found myself looking down the barrel of a rifle. Before he could alert the others, I shoved the rifle out of my face with my left and threw a right uppercut at the man. He toppled backward into a heap of leaves. Nobody inside was any the wiser.

"Hey! You there, halt!" a huskier, English voice boomed.

Dave spun around then plugged two shots into the unknown arrival. "Run!" Dave shouted. The party inside went stone silent. We bolted into the darkness.

Voices shouted behind us as we made our panicked run to our truck. How we didn't fall onto our faces during our sprint was miraculous. We reached our truck with panicked breaths. Dave leaped into the driver's seat. In the blackness, I heard voices grow louder. I gave the engine crank handle a hateful rip.

Shots echoed through the evening stillness and struck the truck with regularity. With his foot to the floor, Dave hauled our butts toward the relative safety of Vauchamps.

"Damn it!" I said.

"What?"

"I just pulled a splinter the size of a pencil out of my cheek," I said as I threw the splinter out of the truck.

"Glad you're not hurt too bad," Dave said with a cringed face.

"What are you talking about?"

"I got one in the arm," Dave said sadly.

"Oh crap. Are you okay?"

"No! I got shot, for God's sake!"

"Maybe I should drive."

"I'll be okay. Just help me stay on the damn road."

The hour-long drive back felt like it passed in minutes. We skidded to a stop, leaped out of the truck, then dashed into Ray's barrack.

"What happened? Are you men hurt?" Ray asked.

"Dave got hit in the arm. I think a ricochet got me on the cheek."

"I'll get a field kit," Billy said.

"We found the house all right," I said. "The colonels were there with some German officers along with some French guys."

Ray quickly unraveled a roll of gauze.

"Marcus was in on the scam, all right," I said. "He took a huge sack of money from the Germans in exchange for some sheets of paper. I heard them talk about Cambrai."

"That's not splendid news," Ray said.

"You're telling me," I said.

Dave winced as he removed his shirt. Blood oozed down his arm.

"Looks like the bullet passed through. Hold on, this will burn," Billy said.

"What will burn?" Dave asked curiously.

Billy opened a bottle of Mercurochrome then poured it onto Dave's wound.

"Damn, give a guy some warning! Sonofabitch!" Dave said angrily.

"Buck up, tough guy," I said.

"Until you've been shot, keep your damn mouth shut," Dave fired back. "There ain't any surgeons around here good enough to repair any damage. I might not be able to lift anymore."

"Hey, I'm sorry, Dave," I said. Sometimes, my lack of compassion was ill-timed.

"You should be sorry. How does it look, Billy?" Dave asked.

"There doesn't appear to be any bone damage. Billy said as he gently turned Dave's arm. You can move your arm, so I think you'll be okay. Keep it clean and change the dressing often. See a doctor as soon as you can too."

Dave grimaced while Billy dressed the wound.

"We need to see Edmund again. I have to ask him more about Turel and what they got in the works with Cambrai," I said.

Ray sat on a creaky pine chair behind his desk. He let out a defeated breath then looked at me with a sullen expression.

"What is it, Ray?" I asked.

"Edmund was found dead about ten minutes ago."

CHAPTER 27

"WHAT DO YOU mean, Edmund's dead?" I asked in disbelief. "He was in a guarded cell, for God's sake."

"I was curious about what you said to him privately, so I went to see him and found him dead in his cell," Ray said.

We weren't gone long, but with the base crawling with soldiers, I found it impossible to believe nobody saw nor heard anything. Then it occurred to me that if Turel killed Edmund only minutes ago, then he simply time windowed from the cabin to the cell and did the deed.

"This ain't going well," Dave said with a grimace while Billy tightened the bandage on Dave's arm.

"The guards didn't hear anything or see anyone," Ray said.

Ray stepped from behind his desk and handed Billy a folded sheet of paper.

While I gently stroked the bandage on my cheek, I paced about the room to gather my thoughts. I knew telling Ray and Billy that Turel was an angel would only cause more problems for me, so I kept that off the table.

Turel seemed fearless, yet his elusiveness made me nervous since he could probably use time windows more efficiently than I could. Intimidation wouldn't work on him. Wits and greater strength were the best one-two punch to beat backstabbing people like him, but not an evil angel of greater ability.

"Did they take Edmund's body away?" I asked.

"Military Police is investigating the matter," Billy said. "However, before they arrived, Ray and I discovered this paper under Edmund's pillow."

As I read the letter, everything Edmund wrote read as though a man from 1836 had written it. If Turel brought Edmund here as he said, then Edmund was powerless. That fact diverted my hatred from Edmund to Turel. However, I related more intimately to Edmund's situation. The angels brought me here in the same way, and that made me wonder when Turel would come for me.

"Turel and some of his men held Edmund's family hostage," I said. "Edmund spoke the truth."

"I agree," Ray said with a nod.

"They were all in it together. Isn't fighting a war bad enough that those no good cattle rapists had to throw their battles too?" Dave asked as he removed his coat and tossed it onto Ray's desk.

Ray shook his head as he eyed Dave with parental disapproval.

"Cattle rapists?" Ray asked in dismay. "Your choice of words lacks civility at times. However, we share your disgust."

"What is it with people who know they're about to die?" I asked.

"What do you mean, John?" Billy asked.

"They tell everything," I said.

"Well, as he said, John, Edmund wasn't able to say anything because Turel had him dead to rights," Dave said. "Maybe that's why Marcus and Eldridge left us to the vultures. They had to get to that meeting."

"Maybe, but why would Eldridge kill the MPs? That seems extreme," I said.

"Killing is nothing to guys like Marcus and Eldridge. With all the men they've slaughtered over the months, what's two more? Now they're going to do it again at Cambrai."

Dave studied his bandage then cringed when he moved his arm slightly.

"Tally another win for Turel, which in turn will make my life that much harder come Redemption Moon time," I said.

"Redemption Moon?" Ray asked. "Is that a holiday?"

"I wish," I said.

The distinct rattle of a Model T truck outside grew louder then it squealed to a stop outside our barrack. We listened intently for any sounds coming our way. Billy turned down the oil lamp.

I cautiously pushed aside the dusty burlap curtain. The new arrival parked behind the truck Dave and I used. The driver carefully glided his hands over the truck fenders. His hand appraised a puncture, or rather bullet hole, on the rear fender. Both of the men finished inspecting the truck then scouted the grounds as if to see if anyone was watching them.

"How many are there?" Ray asked.

"I count two," I answered then felt my chest sink. "Damn. It's them."

"You men best scatter," Billy said.

"John, we better get our act together and fast," Dave said as he threw on his coat.

"Right," I said. "As far as we're all concerned, we don't know what Marcus and Eldridge are up to. Got it?"

"The crap's going to fly loose and sloppy once we spring everything on them," Dave said.

Ray shook his head as he huffed annoyingly.

"Men, language, okay?" Ray pleaded.

"Sorry, Ray. He's a colorful one," I said while I thumbed at Dave.

Dave shrugged.

"Your clarity is sometimes sacrificed, but I seem to be grasping your manner with words," Ray said.

"Where can we bunk for the night?" I asked.

"There's a storage depot beside the hangar office," Ray said. "Return here in the morning. With any luck, the colonels will still be here, and we can learn the truth."

I stepped to the window and watched two dark silhouettes as they checked the other buildings. Once the figures headed toward us, I led Dave to the back door.

"Guys, pretend you're sleeping. When they come in, play dumb," I said, as we headed for the back door.

We stood close by the door and listened. My guts went into knots when I heard the familiar voice of Colonel Marcus as he burst into Ray and Billy's barracks.

"Where the bloody hell are they?" Marcus boomed.

CHAPTER 28

UNLIKE WE DID at Chalons, Dave and I managed to get some decent sleep in Vauchamps. I rolled off my cot then stretched my arms. I rubbed my shirt cuff across the grimy supply hut window. A plume of stale-smelling dust floated through the golden sunbeams. Not a soul stirred outside. The truck we used remained in front of our barrack and there was no sign of the colonels.

I didn't understand why Marcus was so pissed. Using Ray and Billy as buffers gave us time to regroup as well as give Marcus and Eldridge time to cool off.

"Dave, let's get over to Ray's barrack and see what happened with Marcus last night," I said.

"Looks pretty quiet out there," Dave said.

"Quiet is something they got a lot of around here. Ready?"

"No. I'm not about to get into a pissing match with Marcus and Eldridge on an empty stomach."

"Okay, then let's get something to eat at the mess tent first. Hopefully, we won't run into them there."

We opened the creaky supply depot door then jogged across the frost-covered grass to the mess tent. This base was nothing more than a filling station, a stopover for pilots en route to other air bases.

The mess tent was open, but nobody was around. We grabbed some tin cups from a table and a tray. There was some tea left, as well as some eggs in a cold pan. The smell of eggs cooked in lard didn't appeal to me, but in a war, beggars can't be choosers. We ate what we could then went over our plan.

"There aren't any planes around. Maybe Ray and Billy went on dawn patrol. I'll bet Marcus and Eldridge are in one of the other barracks," I said.

"Do you think Ray and Billy got reamed by Marcus last night?" Dave asked.

"No. I think Marcus knows we figured him out, though. I hope he'll be calmer now that he's had time to mellow out."

The tea was colder than I expected, but I couldn't eat or drink much since I was so concerned about our looming confrontation with the colonels. I stood from the table and stomped my cold feet.

"Do you think he suspects it was us who shot those men at the cabin last night?" Dave asked.

"No doubt. How's your arm?" I asked.

"Throbbing. How's your cheek?"

"The same. I hope we don't get infections. Whenever you're ready, I guess we can head over," I said. "I don't have much of a strategy in mind." My exhausted face showed Dave everything about my excitement at the prospect of facing the colonels and God knows what else.

"This is going to suck," Dave said.

We left the mess tent then went to Ray and Billy's barrack. I knocked on the barrack door, but nobody answered. Dave pushed the door aside. There on the cots, sat Marcus and Eldridge who watched us enter.

"A word, Harrod," Marcus said coldly.

Dave closed the door. Marcus fired a steely gaze at me while Eldridge struck a match and lit Billy's oil lamp.

"My thoughts exactly," I said.

"Been about in the evening, I see," Marcus said. "You've even gained an injury during the course."

I gently graced the bandage on my cheek then glanced at Dave's bandaged arm.

"We know you two were at the cabin last night," Marcus continued.

Before he could start his questioning, I spoke first. That way I could find a little room to maneuver, if possible.

"First things first, Colonel," I said. "Why did you kill those MPs?"

"That was necessary," Marcus said. "Certain people can't afford to have their efforts uncovered by the wrong sorts."

"You're not making a damn bit of sense," Dave said.

"Allow me to explain it another way."

"I don't care what your orders are or who you work for," I said. "We came here to help you two monkeys at your request. So lay off the demands, Marcus. We don't owe you squat."

"I'm a man of reasonable fiber. You've heard of what happened to Captain Edmund?"

The door flung open, and the abundant girth of Colonel Hutchins filled the doorway.

"Appears everyone is here," Hutchins said. "Colonel Marcus, come with me. You others remain here until we return."

Eldridge appeared dumbfounded, but I stared in shock at the intrusion. I didn't even have time to interrupt Colonel Blubberhead.

"Do you understand me, Colonel Eldridge?" Hutchins asked impatiently.

"Yes, sir," Eldridge said through gritted teeth.

Hutchins and Marcus left the barrack then closed the door.

"Colonel Eldridge, why is Hutchins so interested in you and Marcus? We saw you in the house last night with a ton of money among people you shouldn't be with. What the hell's going on?"

"Colonel Hutchins is a witch hunter. We've been trying to find a way out of our predicament for months. The Cambrai order was to be our last arrangement."

"A way out? Were you planning on sticking it to us while you two skipped town?"

"In so many words, yes."

"You piece of crap," I said then lunged at Eldridge.

Eldridge put up little resistance as I belted his midsection. He dropped to the floorboards and heaved for air. I was about to work on his face when I saw a large envelope protruding from his inside coat pocket. I yanked it out then smacked his face with it. I stared at him in disgust while I fought every instinct to kick his head in.

"Give those to me," Eldridge said.

He groaned as I stepped down on his forearm then tossed the envelope on Ray's cot.

"Look, to answer your question about killing those men, it was necessary," Eldridge said.

"Why?" I asked.

"We were gone for almost two months after Chalons fell. Those men would've taken us in and ruined everything for everyone."

"Keep going," I said as I sat on the desk.

"Once we learned what the current date was, we realized the meeting was only two days off and, if we missed it, there would've been dire consequences."

I shook my head in disbelief. Nothing annoyed me more than people who pawned off explanations in generalities.

"Dire consequences? Dave, do you believe this bag of nonsense?" I said with an embittered smile.

"It does account for some things," Dave said. "It's the escape that rubs me wrong. If you were so hell bent on leaving, why did you come here now?"

Eldridge scooted himself against the wall and massaged his gut.

"We told you when we parted to get here to Vauchamps. Marcus ordered Collishaw and Bishop to fly here because Marcus knew Chalons wouldn't be safe for Allied planes after the attack. I'm in awe at how you found us last night."

"We talked to Edmund before he was killed. He told us everything," I said.

"Everything?" Eldridge asked in a guilt-ridden, rising voice.

Eldridge didn't seem too keen on my having him on the ropes and preparing to knock him out.

"Everything," I said sternly. "He told us how you and Marcus sold out the Chalons offensive for a sack of money big enough to sail to America on your own yacht. Edmund said he stashed his money in some church. Where's your cut?"

"Cut?" Eldridge asked.

"Yes. Your cut, your share, your piece of the action. Jeez, follow the program, man," I said. I grabbed the envelope off Ray's desk, rolled it up, and swatted him. He covered up while I smacked him as if he were a disobedient dog. "So where's the money?"

"The money's in the same church," Eldridge conceded and I stopped swatting him. "I never told Edmund nor anyone else. The money was safe there because Edmund would never search for my share in his own hiding place."

"Where did Marcus hide his share?"

"In the same blooming church."

"Does anyone else know about it?"

"I've told no one. It's a sum of money you don't boast of."

My heart yearned for some encouragement or a thread of hope. These guys sat on a gold mine and were ready to start new lives. Out of curiosity, I broke the envelope's wax seal, and leafed through the contents.

"What are these, Colonel, travel papers?" I asked.

Eldridge breathed heavily then curiously closed his eyes as I read.

"We received them last night with the money," Eldridge said. "Marcus and I were to leave for the United States after the exchange, but you and Sowell interfered."

A slew of documents stuffed the envelope including a birth certificate, passport, citizenship papers, referral letters, and military discharge papers, all falsified with the same name, Harrison Devers. I'd finally found my great-grandfather in Colonel Eldridge and brutalized the hell out of him. As I looked at him sitting on the floor against the wall clutching his belly, I wanted to throw up.

"John, what is it?" Dave asked.

I passed the papers to Dave. "Check out the name," I said.

Dave's eyebrows arched up as he read.

"Holy mother," Dave said.

"What's the matter?" Eldridge asked.

"Change in plans," I said. "Look, we have to get you out of this mess somehow."

"Nothing would please me more," Eldridge said.

Eldridge struggled to use Billy's desk as a prop to stand up, so I rushed over and helped him to a chair at Ray's desk.

"Are you okay, sir?" I asked.

"I must admit I never experienced such a blow of extreme ferocity. You've completely winded me."

"Sucker punches have that effect," Dave said which made me feel worse than I already did.

The door swung open, and Colonels Hutchins and Marcus entered.

"I've spoken with Colonel Marcus and debriefed him. Colonel Eldridge, we have a few questions about your activities with Chalons," Hutchins said.

"We? What do you mean?" Eldridge asked in surprise.

"Where were you when the base was lost?" Hutchins asked.

"I was in pursuit of the Germans. Our drive headed west toward Chalons."

"How is it you found yourself in pursuit? Did you fail to advance to the Gate sector per Colonel Marcus's direct order?"

"I did, but we overshot the Gate location."

"You have a history of taking matters into your own hands, disobeying orders, and recklessly endangering your troops. Explain how you blatantly missed the German flank?"

Hutchins was a total jerk. Guys that cut off explanations like that aren't interested in truths. They'd cruise through the formalities so they could carry out punishment to save their own butts.

"I cannot. I was unable to reach Weatherby soon enough."

"Perhaps you waited long enough to begin your assault, so the enemy could take a stronger offensive position?"

"That's incorrect, sir. True, I went to help Weatherby, but that was because we faced less resistance than expected and advanced too far north."

"You admit going against orders. Colonel Marcus told me that he ordered you to stay where you were. He stated you were to only report activity as encountered, not as engaged."

"Excuse me for interrupting, sir, but what the hell is going on here?" I asked in protest.

"Silence, Lieutenant. I'll get to you directly," Hutchins said.

The muffled sound of aircraft engines grew louder then the engines of two planes roared over our barrack.

"Sir, I followed orders," Eldridge continued in his defense, but Hutchins condescendingly looked at Eldridge.

"Do you know a Frenchman named Turel?" Hutchins continued in an arrogant tone.

"I've met him. Colonel Marcus has too."

"Colonel Marcus has admitted no knowledge of this man."

"Like hell," I said.

Without flinching, Hutchins continued his interrogation uninterrupted.

"MI6 has known for months of Turel's existence," Hutchins said. "He's eluded capture. However, you've had regular meetings with him. How do you explain that?"

Ray and Billy entered the barrack then unbuttoned their coats.

"What goes, sirs? Having a flight meeting without us?" Ray asked as he removed his flight cap and jacket. He hung his coat on a nail then looked at me. Instantly, he seemed to gauge the seriousness of the meeting, so he didn't offer any small talk.

"Look, Colonel Hutchins, Colonel Marcus knows Turel," I said. "I mean, both of these guys met with his flunkies just last night. Even Captain Edmund admitted that he, Marcus, and Eldridge knew Turel. They've also made repeated deals for cash."

"I told you to keep quiet," Hutchins ordered.

"Colonel Marcus, what'd you do with Colonel Hutchins before you two came back in here with both barrels blazing, huh? Did you two cut your own deal?"

"Silence, I said!" Hutchins bellowed.

Marcus stood close-lipped then crossed his arms in defiance.

"Edmund wrote his dying words on paper confessing to everything. He named both Marcus and Eldridge as players," I pleaded.

In mid-huff, Hutchins paused right when his plump, red face was about to burst.

"I have no record of such a paper," Hutchins said. "Where is this document you speak of?"

I looked at Billy, and he went toward the desk. He opened a drawer and retrieved Edmund's letter.

"Here, sir," Billy said.

Hutchins read the letter then shook his head.

"Everyone here has read that letter, Colonel Hutchins," I said then put my hands on my hips. That way, we had more eyewitnesses in case Hutchins tried to tie us up in some bureaucratic bullshit inquest down the road.

"Colonel Marcus, how do you propose an explanation for this? You were told not to contact Turel or any of his associates."

I shot an evil stare at Marcus and wanted blood.

"What? So you knew him all along. You back-stabbing sonofabitch."

"Lieutenant, one more outburst and I'll throw you in the stockade."

"Jam it, big boy!" I bellowed.

Hutchins started for me, but Ray jumped in and held Hutchins back. Dave bear-hugged me so I wouldn't make fast work of that blow hard. An endless stream of obscenities flowed from my mouth as Dave held me a couple inches off the ground. Hutchins shouted back, but I couldn't hear him over my own verbal jabs. The tussle reminded me of several locker room fights I endured over the years.

Billy and Marcus yelled for everyone to settle down. When that didn't work, Billy fired a bullet through the roof.

"Everyone quiet down," Billy said as his eyes reviewed each of us. We exchanged calculating glances, so I decided to speak first.

"Here's how I see what happened," I said, as Dave let me go. "Marcus, Eldridge, Edmund, and Weatherby all hooked up with Turel. They made secret deals for whatever reason, so now you're trying to pin all the blame on Eldridge. Right so far, Colonel Hutchins?"

"Your lack of discipline is appalling, Lieutenant," Hutchins said.

"Am I right?" I demanded.

"In a manner."

"Look, I thrive on honesty. My friend here can confirm that. So, let's start with a couple questions to help us all out. First, what did you mean about Marcus not contacting Turel? Now, be honest. I guarantee you don't want to screw with me."

Hutchins looked about the room. He watched as Ray, Eldridge, and Billy shook their heads. However, Hutchins still didn't look convinced.

"I am not an individual to be trifled with by anyone, especially by a spunk American such as you," Hutchins said like an arrogant snob.

"I thought so. Look past my shoulder."

With a little effort, I produced a time window. The window's shimmer rippled hypnotically. Hutchins looked back at me with wide eyes. Ray and Billy stood awestruck at the unprecedented spectacle, at least for them.

"In case you're wondering, that's a means for me to alter future and past events. Meaning, I can go back in time to do whatever I want to your family, so I strongly suggest you cooperate," I said and closed the window.

"Colonel Marcus is with me," Hutchins admitted in defeat.

"What?" Eldridge asked.

Marcus brought me here to brand my great-grandfather a spy. What purpose would that serve? Was this the ultimate starting point that sent Eldridge down a long road of anguish that lasted his whole life?

"He's MI6," Hutchins said humbly. "Marcus was ordered to uncover any allied espionage factions and recommend any necessary eradications."

Eldridge's face grew ashen as he fell back onto a chair.

"Did Marcus find any spies?" I asked.

"He did," Hutchins continued. "Turel's one. Colonels Weatherby, Eldridge, and Captain Edmund were the others."

"When did Marcus first tell you about them?"

"Nearly six months ago."

I stepped in small circles as I thought.

"Did Marcus offer any recommendations on how to destroy the network?" I asked.

"Marcus was to deliver his proposal days before the Chalons collapse," Hutchins said.

"So, all that time he could've done whatever he wanted."

"That's one interpretation."

"Perhaps, but why didn't you do anything for all those months? Didn't Marcus get you any updates, or were you sitting on your hands the whole time?"

"You bloody insolent bastard," Hutchins shouted.

"I'm sure you can do better than that, Colonel," I said. "For now, just answer the question."

Hutchins squirmed, while beads of sweat streamed down his temples. He removed a white monogrammed handkerchief and dabbed his shiny head.

"Marcus sent updates every week. Operations like these take enormous amounts of time."

"You're defending Marcus a lot," Dave said.

"He's one of my operatives. It's in everyone's best interest that he not be exposed for the sake of national security," Hutchins said.

"Spoken like a true politician," I said. "What's to become of Marcus after we're done here?"

"He may or may not face a court-martial, but he'll certainly be dishonorably discharged."

I considered the facts while I paced in front of Hutchins. Hutchins seemed so sure that he sat in the driver's seat, but I had to make it clear to him that nobody drives my car. I had to get Eldridge in safe harbor one way or another. My brain churned methodically as a chain of thought emerged.

"I say Marcus won't be court-martialed and that he'll be honorably discharged," I said.

"That isn't my decision," Hutchins said.

"Maybe. Since you have General Haig's ear, he'll follow your recommendation to the letter. What about Eldridge?"

"Since he was so deeply involved, he'll face trial then possibly spend his life in prison or face execution."

Neither result worked for me.

"Maybe he deserves it," I said. "With Weatherby and Edmund already dead, you only have one more crook to hang. That would be a fitting end to this disaster, wouldn't it?"

"It would. Now may I ask you a question, Lieutenant?" Hutchins asked.

"Go ahead," I said.

"If Marcus, Eldridge, Turel, and Weatherby obtained so much payment, where is all this money now? I assume large payments would be had for the information they gave to the Germans."

Eldridge looked up at me sharply. His eyes begged for mercy, or perhaps he couldn't believe I was about to give away his war chest.

"The money is in a church. There's enough for the King to build a new castle," I said.

"It exists?" Hutchins asked.

"Yep."

"Then bring it to me."

"I got a problem with that, Colonel. You should too."

"How so?"

"Everybody in this room knows about the money and how it was acquired. If I bring the money to you, with Marcus being a willing participant from your organization, then technically that makes you an accessory. Marcus met with a known traitor. He got money in exchange for military secrets, and then kept the cash for himself. Did Marcus not tell you about that part?"

Hutchins jerked his head toward Marcus. I knew Hutchins wanted me to bring in the money. If I did, he'd no doubt keep it for himself. At the same time, he could get Marcus and Eldridge out of the way for good. He was slick, but not slick enough.

"That's absurd," Hutchins said.

"Sorry, Colonel. You knew Marcus might try to keep the money, but he couldn't spend a dime without laundering it first. When you felt he might have scored enough money, you descended on him like a hawk on a rabbit."

Hutchins looked around the room nervously. His chubby face quivered with each movement.

"Lies, nothing but lies," Hutchins said. I had him on the ropes then prepared my knockout punch.

"I warned you about being honest, sir."

Hutchins took a deep breath. He played his last hand, and he held nothing.

"Very well, what does your supreme intelligence dictate we do? Haig knows I'm here with Marcus and Eldridge at this moment. He'll demand to know the current state."

Since I wasn't a leader or ever sat with people like that, coming up with a lie to fool a general wouldn't be possible. However, if history taught anybody anything, it was that people loved their heroes.

"Colonel Marcus, last night at the house, what information did you give the Germans about Cambrai?"

"I told them we'd attack from the northwest on the morning of the 24th of November."

Now that I had the rats by their tails, the next question was what to do with them.

"November 24th? Edmund's letter said the Germans would start their attack on Cambrai November 20th. That's how Turel and the Germans were going to screw you once more by jumping on you four days sooner," I said. "Edmund was privy to that and Turel killed him to keep that secret hidden."

"Clearly, I wasn't aware of that development," Marcus said.

"Colonel Hutchins, instead of telling Haig that you found a spy, you say you found a double agent of sorts in Eldridge."

"He'll never believe me."

"Yes, he will. You contact Haig today and tell him you have first-hand information from a double agent that the Germans are planning an attack on November 20th from the northwest. Tell him to shift the attack then strike with everything from the southwest on the 18th."

Hutchins wiped his head while he considered my suggestion. "That might work," he said.

"Tell Haig that everyone in this room was involved in the discovery which saved the Allies from a potentially crushing defeat."

"What of the money?"

"Right now, you're in deep trouble if you admit that one of your own agents was in on a secrets-for-money scandal. If the press got wind of it, the public would demand your heads. If I were you, I'd forget about the money and forget about any court-martial. Instead, call Haig with the good news that you saved the Cambrai offensive from a catastrophic loss. If they ask any of us, we'll say you knew about it all along and what a freaking genius you are. What do you say?"

Hutchins mulled over the proposition then took a breath.

"How do you propose I settle this investigation?"

"If you carry out the attack like I described, then I think I have a solution that will work for everyone and put this matter under the rug forever," I said.

I turned to Dave and grinned.

"Whatever you do, make it low-profile. We don't need to draw more unnecessary attention our way," Dave said.

"No problem," I said.

CHAPTER 29

COLONEL HUTCHINS STOOD tall and dignified as he read off each of our names during a ceremony that recognized our heroic efforts that saved the Allies from a devastating defeat at Cambrai. Despite the lives lost because of Marcus and Eldridge's prior dealings, Colonels Hutchins, Marcus, and Eldridge were in the clear. Even though justice didn't kick their butts like it should've, my mission to get the last page was a much bigger priority.

General Haig presided over the ceremony with Colonel Hutchins, General Pershing, and a slew of VIPs. A company of infantrymen heading for the front also paused to take part in the proceedings. Nobody outside my circle of participants knew the truth about what happened, and it was going to stay that way.

After the requisite pictures taken by the press, Ray, Billy, the colonels, Dave, and I, gathered in Ray's barrack. Colonel Hutchins never wanted anything to do with me again, so he immediately parted with Haig the moment the ceremony was over.

"What more do you wish to say, Lieutenant Harrod?" Colonel Marcus asked.

"We saved your butts. Without Ray and Billy backing us up, you might have gotten away with your plans," I said.

"Yes, well, the beam of enlightenment has shined on me. Therefore, I view matters differently."

"Glad to hear it. Now, we still have a couple things to discuss."

"Regarding?"

"The money and Turel."

"Hmm."

"Colonel Hutchins took the whole revelation well. I doubt he'll go back on his word to forget about the money, so here's what I think we should do."

"Keep in mind we risked our lives to get that money," Eldridge said. "I trust you won't take all of it."

"You mean you sacrificed many lives to get that money."

Eldridge backed down and nodded with a sigh.

The money was worthless to me anyway. How would I explain a couple million pounds in 1917 English currency to our 1986 banks? The IRS would be all over us, not to mention the FBI.

"We're not taking any of it," Dave said. "There would be too much explaining to do on our end."

"He's right, guys," I said. "As ill-gotten as that money is, some good can still come out of it, so here's the plan. Give some to Ray and Billy. Fifty thousand pounds each ought to be enough since they stuck their necks out for you."

"Can you make it a hundred thousand?" Ray asked.

I looked at Dave then shrugged.

"I don't have a problem with that," I said. "How about it, Marcus?"

"Very well," Marcus said.

"Marcus and Eldridge can each keep five thousand. As for the rest of it, divide it evenly among English and French charities, anonymously."

"Why anonymously?" Eldridge asked.

"Neither of you deserve the recognition, considering how you acquired the money."

Marcus nodded.

"That sounds amicable," Eldridge said with a defeated breath.

"You guys also have to stay out of trouble. If you screw up, I'll come back and deal with you harshly."

"How will you find us?" Marcus asked.

"I can't explain it to you because there isn't any way you'd understand. Fifty years from now, they'll invent the microchip, and computers will be commonplace. Finding you will only take me a matter of minutes. That's all I'm saying."

"Damn it, John," Dave said. "Remember our little rule?"

"Right, sorry," I said.

Eldridge furrowed his brow curiously.

"What do we do about Turel?" Ray asked. "Colonel Hutchins has never been able to capture him."

"It doesn't make sense to chase him," I said. "We have to get him to come to us, but how?"

I went to the window then pushed aside the ratty curtain. I felt we might be close to going home, but those last few steps were the hardest.

"Come on, John, this one should be easy. What was it that got the colonels into this mess?" Dave asked.

"Money?" I responded in return.

"Bingo. What do you think old Turel would do if he found out that we railroaded him out of all that lettuce, not to mention how we jacked his plan with Cambrai?"

A smile of hope cracked my face as the pieces came together.

"No, money is only part of it. I have a plan. Dave, you and Eldridge get the money and meet us at Shubert's wreck. Marcus and I will meet Turel at the cabin," I said.

"What are you going to do to him?" Eldridge asked.

I paused then smiled.

"I'm going to piss him off."

CHAPTER 30

MARCUS DROVE THE supply truck while we ventured to the cabin for a showdown of sorts with Turel. The idea didn't sit well with me, but I had to do something. Certain apprehensions crept into my heart as we bounced along the road. Neither of us spoke. I was too angry to want to hear any more from him. He was one wrong word from my putting a bullet in his head. Instead, I focused on agitating Turel enough to get him to think I knew about the last page. I wasn't sure how Turel would follow me, but there was something important about the site of Shubert's wreck since I time-windowed from there twice.

The dusty road wound through the barren trees. We finally arrived at the house a while later. Fortunately, we wouldn't have to hike through the woods like last time. We stopped the truck in a plume of rolling dust.

"Marcus, we found out Eldridge is Devers," I said.

Marcus paused then stared ahead.

"You said Devers has the last page," I continued. Marcus still stared ahead.

"I can't afford to get into the details of his circumstance," Marcus said as he broke his silence.

"What's the story with you and Eldridge? How'd you end up together?"

"We have a unique friendship. However, some things about us had to remain silent. Please, there isn't time."

Marcus got out of the truck then headed for the cabin door.

"Wait a second. Are both of you angels?" I asked as I rushed beside him.

We approached the cabin door, but before I could say another word, we heard a bottle fall and roll across the wood plank floor inside. Marcus loaded his revolver, and then returned it to his coat pocket with the hammer cocked.

"Turel can be unpredictable. We need to assure him that he's been swindled," Marcus said.

"From the sounds of things I'd say he's been drinking. It shouldn't be too hard to convince him that we screwed him over," I said.

"Harrod, I need to say something before we go inside."

Boy, I hoped it was good. No teacher ever taught me how to call out an evil angel, let alone a drunk one.

"What is it?" I asked.

"Everything you witnessed to this point since we first met was all for your benefit and safety."

"You mean you played me?"

"Not in the manner you think. We had to give you a path to follow so that you wouldn't actively search for the last page. That's why Turel never moved on you. He has, however, been studying you, learning your mannerisms and behaviors."

"So you led me down a path that allowed and evil angel to study me? Other than him being a drunk, I don't know squat about him. I wasted all that time."

"No time has been wasted. It might not look like it, but we've been protecting you and training you for the harshness that will likely follow you after this evening is over."

I found it hard to believe that angels protected me, but I was still alive. Maybe there was some protection afforded to me over the course of this journey, even though I still never saw a real live angel in its true form.

"How do I know you, or Turel, won't kill me in there?" I asked.

"I give you my word, John. You'll know exactly what to do. Stick to your plan. Follow your instincts and remember your talents. If all goes as we wish, it'll be up to you."

"What will?"

Marcus opened the door then entered. I stayed close to his heels then closed the door behind me.

"Where's Eldridge?" Turel asked bitterly. He lowered his head as he scowled at me. "Why's he here? Marcus, you know to come here alone."

"There's a problem," Marcus said.

"What problem?"

Turel set down his bottle then angrily gazed at Marcus.

"Edmund's dead," Marcus said.

"I know. I killed him. He doesn't need his money. More for us."

"They found a note under his pillow that he scribed implicating everyone, including you."

"We don't need humans in our way. We have money. You and Eldridge have travel papers with free passage to America. New life for you."

"Eldridge confessed to his involvement with you. He took the money, but was captured," Marcus said.

"He took the money?" Turel asked.

Turel looked up angrily.

"All of it. They told command of your involvement with Cambrai. They're responsible for your loss."

"You have something to say?" Turel demanded then breathed heavier as he gawked at me through his bloodshot eyes.

"I wanted to get a good close look at your ugly ass face before I crushed it," I said.

"You threaten me? You are nothing. Where is my money?" Turel asked in total disregard of me.

"They're taking the money to a place several kilometers west of Chalons. There's no way your drunk ass will ever find them," I said smugly.

Anger washed over Turel's face. His breaths shortened.

"West of Chalons? That's the entry point," Turel said as his eyes shifted.

An entry point, no doubt Turel used that as an angelic term. I knew there was something special about the location of Shubert's wreck. It was a landmark for me, a reference point.

"You should know better than to trust a human," Marcus said then removed his pistol. He aimed it at Turel's head. Turel smiled.

"You're done, pal," I said.

Turel reached for the bottle in front of him then gulped it dry. In a blink, the bottle crashed across Marcus's head. He fell back onto the floor while he clutched his bleeding scalp. Marcus wiped the flowing blood off his face. Turel picked up the pistol. Turel's speed would've impressed Bruce Lee. I stepped toward Marcus to help him, but Turel shoved me against the wall. He snapped his face back to Marcus.

"You try to keep the money for yourself? You try to steal from me? We plant you with that stuffed pig Hutchins. Then you let Eldridge take all we worked for? Hali will be ours without you. I'll do you a favor."

Marcus looked at me with wide eyes, and then Turel pulled the trigger. The shot to Marcus's head startled me and for a few moments, there was no sound. Turel then faced me. He didn't look like he had anything fun in mind for me. He smiled then dropped the gun.

"Come on, tough guy. We both know you don't want any money," I said.

Turel laughed himself into a fit and gurgled up some wine. He looked into my eyes as he wiped his mouth with his sleeve. His eyes glowed red, then his breaths grew rapidly.

"Then what do I want?" he asked with a sly grin.

"The last page. I know where it is and you ain't getting it. Later, you sonofabitch!"

I opened a time window and got the hell out of there. The last thing I had heard before the time window closed was Turel when he shouted, "Interceptor!"

CHAPTER 31

I EMERGED FROM the time window then frantically looked around for Dave and Eldridge. Shubert's wreck still rested in a tangled mess among the trees. I saw a truck several yards away, then two men climbed out of it.

"John? You got here fast," Dave said.

"I time windowed here. Turel just killed Marcus. I expect Turel here any minute. Did you get the bags set up?"

"They're in the truck. John, they had a lot of money."

"Okay, leave it there. Turel's not after that anymore."

"What does he want?" Dave asked.

"The last page."

"You don't have it," Dave said.

"No, but he thinks I'm on my way to get it. I have to get him before he goes after Eldridge."

We trudged our way to the entry point next to the fallen tree steps away from Shubert's wreck.

"John, do you hear anything?" Dave asked.

I cupped my hands behind my ears. Other than a cold wind that blew through the barren trees, I didn't hear anything. I turned to Eldridge who stood eagerly waiting for direction.

"Maybe we're safe for now. Sir, you should wait in the back of the truck."

"Are you sure? I might be able to help," Eldridge said.

"Turel's fuming. You better stay out of sight. He might kill you for the fun of it."

As I unleashed an intense want to return to 1986, the watery, rippling rings of the time window appeared.

"Is this going to take us home?" Dave asked.

"It should," I said.

Dave and I ran into the time window. As I reached the time window's edge, I stumbled forward as if someone shoved me from behind.

I tumbled onto the muddy forest floor. Thunder and rain pounded the woods as I struggled to gain my footing in the wet leaves. In the shafts of early evening sunlight, I came face-to-face with my nemesis and the intense anger in his eyes. He was inhuman, yet I wasn't afraid.

"Remember me?" Turel said with a predatory grin.

"I never forget an ugly sack like you, Turel."

"I know you're the last Interceptor and why they sent you. You best deny your task. You can't win against me. I assure you, you will fail like all those before you. Give me the last page and save yourself."

One win. I have always wanted one win that mattered. I wanted Turel to die painfully for what he did to those around me and he deserved it. I wiped my hands on my pants and tried to work out my first strike attack plan. Before I knew what happened, Turel struck first. His speed was insane.

Turel threw a quick, vicious right cross which caught me square in the jaw. I spun to the ground as heavy raindrops pelted my blinking eyes. I lay stunned, and then heard several grunts behind me. Dave tackled Turel who dropped the gun onto the soggy, leafy forest floor.

I recalled what Edmund said about Turel and his weakness for human vices. Perhaps I could beat Turel badly enough so he couldn't hurt me.

I scrambled off the ground to rush to Dave's aid when Turel tripped me. He then snapped to his feet and struggled to stand straight. I slugged Turel hard and knocked him flat on his back.

I dove onto his chest then threw the hardest punches I could muster. Blood sprayed from his mouth as I knocked out several of his teeth. Despite my barrage, he seemed weakened but showed no sign of pain. I grabbed his hair then lifted him to his feet. I thrust him over my head military press style then threw him onto the ground.

He rolled to his side writhing in pain. I grabbed him by his coat and belt and curled him up to my chest. In an animalistic rage, I shouted and dropped him across my knee. He plopped to the ground and didn't move. He groaned endlessly as he struggled to orient himself. I fought the reality that I kicked the crap out of an evil angel. His pain didn't seem real enough and I didn't fully trust my effectiveness.

"Get up," I said with my back muscles flared wide. I felt my neck hairs spring high, then I took deep breaths expecting some unexpected angel move I wouldn't know how to counter.

Turel rolled over onto his back then looked up at me with an evil grin. I felt an ungodly strength course through my body and sensed I'd need every ounce of power left in me to finish him off.

He pushed himself up onto all fours. I kicked him in the head which sent him onto his back once more. I rolled him onto his belly, squatted over his back, and pulled his head back by the chin.

In the rain, I struggled to get a firm grip on his oily, stubbly face and end his miserable life. There was no way I was losing this fight. I craved success, like a lion thirsting for blood. Lightning flashed, and thunder crashed around as I finally got the grip I needed. Every muscle in my body flexed as I anchored myself for one last final move on Turel's neck.

"Harrod, stop!" a voice shouted in the distance.

"Who's there?" I yelled. I struggled to see through the downpour, my grip still firm on Turel's head. Dave stood beside me with his gun drawn and pointed at the figure in the shadows of the maelstrom.

"Colonel Eldridge. Get him, men," Eldridge commanded.

A squad of four British infantrymen intervened and grabbed Turel. They propped him up against the trunk of a nearby tree and pointed their rifles at him. Turel breathed hard as he clutched his abdomen. He shot me a final sinister grin.

"You think we're done, Interceptor? Guess again," Turel said then winked at Eldridge.

"He's mine, sir," I said.

"I'm aware of your desire, John. Men, you have your orders," Eldridge said.

Four shots rang out as lightning struck a nearby tree. In an instant, I saw a wisp of light dart from Turel's body, a soul or spirit perhaps. It floated in front of me with its reddish eyes fixed on mine. Then, it dashed into a swirling black void that suddenly opened on the forest floor and after he went into it, the void disappeared.

Turel's body fell forward onto the muddy, wet leaves of the forest floor. The last of his body's blood drained into the mud. The soldiers confirmed Turel was dead with two final bullets to his head.

"What did I just see? A ghost?" I asked.

"No, that was Turel," Eldridge said. "The body was just a shell. He won't be back for a long time."

"But he will be back, right?"

Thunder rumbled overhead and the rain tapered off.

"Yes, I'm afraid he will. John, I hoped I would catch you in time."

"How did you get here?" I asked.

"Turel arrived and followed you into the time window. I, in turn, followed him."

"How are you going to get back?"

"I hoped you could assist with that," Eldridge said.

I concentrated and opened a time window a couple of yards away beside a thick pine tree.

"Sir, did you write the letter that Marcus gave me before we returned to help you?"

"I did. We both inscribed, but the thoughts were ours together."

"After all the crap we've been through, I managed to find you but never found the last page."

"I have the last page. However, the handoff must happen under prime circumstances. There is too much time until the Redemption Moon for you to take possession now. You're also much too inexperienced to protect the last page effectively. The last page handoff must come when there's little to no attention focused between the parties."

"Sounds tricky."

"It is."

"If you had the last page, then that would make you—"

"Take care of yourself, my boy," Eldridge interrupted. "You too, Mr. Sowell."

"Remember our deal?" I said as I pointed at him.

"I won't disappoint you," Eldridge said then nodded.

"Good."

I stepped back, and we saluted each other. With one last look at me, Eldridge smiled then winked. The soldiers hauled Turel's limp carcass into the time window, with Eldridge right behind them. He was going to be a happy man. I knew it.

Dave and I hiked through the forest, soaked to the bone, while the rain tapered to a drizzle. I recalled that it started to rain when we first left to 1917, so I was confident we were back in 1986 and on the right day. We found the campsite shelter as well as the same rough-hewn benches we slept on before. I stretched out on one of the benches and Dave on the other. Perhaps this campsite was the one we were supposed to be at. I closed my eyes and didn't care what befell me during the night. My fears finally washed away and I could finally sleep in peace.

The sun arose, but a crisp breeze gave me a chill. Too tired to cover ourselves, we managed not to freeze to death during the night. I sat up and looked at Dave. His uniform was gone. Our uniforms had changed back to the clothes we wore before we first entered the time window to 1917.

"Dave, are you up?" I asked. I wished I had an extra sock to toss on his face. I owed him that.

I got up and rubbed my arms briskly. I walked over onto a grassy patch immersed in sunlight.

"Yeah, I'm up," Dave said as he tugged on his shirt. "Hey, our clothes."

"I think they changed while we slept, but I'd say we're back home."

The cool morning air sent tingles through my body. I rubbed my arms to warm up while Dave looked about the campgrounds.

"Hey, that family with the red Mercedes is gone," he said.

"I think this might be the campground we were supposed to stay at anyway."

I looked around the empty campsites. Over by a restroom building, I noticed an exposed bike tire. We walked over for a closer look and discovered it was our bikes and trailers.

"I don't know about you, John, but there's definitely a higher power at work here," Dave said.

"You don't have to tell me."

We retrieved our bikes then walked them back to the wood bench. I looked beside the bench and saw our revolvers nestled in their holsters.

"Our guns," I said.

"Why are they still here? What do you think it means?" Dave asked.

"It means they officially own my ass. Let's get a move on. I don't want to wait around for another time window to come along. It might send us to the Crusades or something."

We walked our bikes down the winding road toward the park exit. We approached the Ranger Station and saw a park ranger working at a desk inside.

"What are you doing?" Dave asked.

"I was thinking about how we changed Devers's life. I'm curious how it changed my life as a result."

"Do you want to call home?"

"I'd be lying if I said the curiosity wasn't killing me."

I asked the park ranger if I could make a call. He reluctantly pointed me to a phone on a desk behind him. I picked up the receiver then paused for a moment. How would I handle it if my family changed? What if I answered the phone? I didn't have an alternative plan for any surprises, so I dialed and hoped for the best.

"Hello?" a woman's voice asked.

"Mom?" I bellowed.

I couldn't believe my ears. A tidal wave of elation hit me that Mom was alive. I never imagined that I might've changed history enough to derail Turel from killing my mother.

"No, it's Nicole. John, is that you?" the girl's voice asked.

"What? Nicole who?" I asked in surprise. I didn't know anyone named Nicole.

"Your sister, you big ape. Who else do you know named Nicole?"

"No, I, uh, didn't recognize your voice, I guess. Is Dad around?"

"No. They're at the lawyer's office."

"They?"

"Mom and Dad."

Holy crap. There is a God.

"How's your trip going, big brother?" Nicole asked.

I have a sister and Mom's alive! This was too unreal to believe. I suffered so much in the war that I welcomed any good surprises.

"It was kind of, uh, exciting," I muttered. "We met some interesting people and saw some amazing things."

"Was exciting? Are you coming back home already? You've only been gone a few days."

A few days. I never considered that the time window skewed time. We only missed a few days of our own time period, while we went through hell for weeks on end in 1917.

"Uh, no," I said.

The park ranger tilted his head at me. I turned away awkwardly.

"Hey, I got accepted to UC," she continued.

"UC?"

"The University of Colorado. Pretty cool, huh?"

"Yeah. So, what are, uh, Mom and Dad doing at a lawyer's office?"

"They're going over Great-grandpa Eldridge's estate."

"Great-grandpa Eldridge? Don't you mean Devers?"

"No, Eldridge. Who is Devers?"

When we saved Eldridge, it wasn't necessary for him to change his name to Devers anymore, which made perfect sense.

"I didn't know he had an estate," I said.

"You're the one who did all that family history stuff at his ranch in Woodland Park. Did you forget about that?"

"I guess I did. Was he rich?"

"Big time. He was one of the richest men in the country."

"What? How?"

"Are you for real?"

"Humor me, Nicole. I've been through a lot."

The park ranger looked at me then tapped his wristwatch. I nodded but didn't want to hang up.

"He built a ranch in Oklahoma and found oil on his land. Then he got involved with electronics in the sixties. Then he got into philanthropy."

"How much did he leave you?"

"Almost a million dollars," she said under her breath.

"Oh, my God," I exclaimed.

After everything I did to get him to follow an honorable path, it looked like I'd have to go back and straighten him out after all.

"I know. Your letter came this morning," she said.

"Read it."

"It's certified. I can't open it."

"Just read it to me, I'm on a borrowed phone," I said.

"Okay, hold your horses. 'Dear John, Words can't describe my elation. Your help in the past has influenced me beyond rational thought. Giving to those without has been most rewarding.

"As you directed, I have given to countless charitable organizations during my life, all anonymously. You're a kind man whose heart is proper and spirit steady. Take this correspondence to the lawyer listed at the bottom of this letter. He will make the necessary preparations for you to receive what I have bequeathed.

"Establish a trust and contribute to any worthy organization or individual you see fit. Your giving isn't to bring praise and recognition to yourself, much like your terms to me.

"Second, tell no one of this inheritance, for if you do, they will look at you differently, sometimes not favorably. Finally, come visit me when you have the time. We have much to discuss. Your loving grandfather, Francis Eldridge.'"

"Jeez Louise," I said. I never expected Eldridge to strike it rich. I told him to give it all away. "Nicole, you can't tell anyone about the letter."

"I won't, John. Grandpa said in my letter that you two had a special arrangement and not to pester you about it, so I won't, even though it's been driving me nuts. Mom and Dad were gone before your letter arrived, so they don't even know about it yet. I'll give it to you when you come back."

"Thanks. I'll bet Grandpa Ray was thrilled when he got his share?"

"Grandpa Ray?"

"He's been working that janitor job forever. Now, he can retire."

"John, Grandpa Ray died when I was a baby."

"What?" I asked in shock.

The park ranger tried to take the phone from me. Dave intervened and got into a quick argument with him. He did his best to calm the ranger down while I tried to grasp the unexpected shock. Dave reached into his pocket and gave the ranger a few dollars. The ranger accepted them happily then went back to his business.

"When did he die?" I asked.

"In 1976."

"Get out of here. How?"

"Somebody shot him."

Losing my Grandpa Ray was almost as painful as losing my mother. Grandpa Ray was the best.

"John? You there?" Nicole asked.

"I'm here. Why would anybody kill a janitor?"

"Janitor? Grandpa Ray was the President of Chicago Mutual, the big insurance company that Great-grandpa Eldridge started."

Insurance? How does a guy go from being a janitor to president of an insurance company?

"Did they ever catch who killed him?" I asked.

"No. If you ask me, I think it was a hit," she said.

"A mob hit?"

"You didn't hear it from me. To Mom and Grandma, it's a touchy subject. I remember hearing tidbits from dad about the mob taking control of the company. There was something about Las Vegas too. He didn't know for sure how Grandpa Ray figured in. Of course, it's all hush-hush."

I didn't know who killed my Grandpa Ray, but considering how I meddled with the past, I probably had a significant role in it.

"I can understand that. Look, I have to get off the phone. The park ranger is giving my dirty looks," I said.

"I know I'm not supposed to ask, but one thing about this letter bugs me," Nicole said.

"What is it?"

"The part that mentions you visiting him when you have the time. He underlined the word *time*. What did he mean by that?"

"I can't get into that now."

"Okay, but you owe me when you get back."

"Sure thing."

The park ranger crossed his arms then stared at me angrily. He began a stream of French words in a typical French condescension I saw in countless movies. He got bitchy anyway despite Dave's gesture to pay for the call. Maybe the call cost a lot more than a few dollars.

"Look, uh, Nicole, I have to go. Could you tell Mom and Dad I said hello?"

"Sure. Tell the stud I said hello."

"Stud?"

"Yeah, Dave. I'm not a little girl anymore, you know. You don't have to keep protecting me."

"Bye, Nicole," I said in a long monotone.

I didn't know I had a sister let alone protect her all the time.

"Okay, bye," Nicole said with a giggle then hung up.

No matter how much I apologized to the ranger, his verbal barrage at my running up his phone bill continued as I backed out of his office. I gave him a couple more dollars, and we started pedaling down the road to get away from him. He kept scolding us until we went around a curve and thankfully, out of his sight.

"How's everything back home?" Dave asked.

"Well, my mom is alive, and Nicole says hello," I answered.

"Who's Nicole?"

"My little sister."

"You don't have a sister."

"Of course, I don't!"

"Holy moly."

"Anyway, my parents are okay. Eldridge lived a long, happy life."

"Mission accomplished, then," Dave said.

"Not exactly. Remember all that money we left with Eldridge to give to the poor?"

"Yep."

"The way Nicole was talking, I'd say he was worth well into the many millions when he died. He left money to each of his relatives. Nicole didn't know how much I got. I have to see a lawyer after we get back home."

"Holy Mother of Pearl," Dave said excitedly. "What else?"

"My Grandpa Ray is dead."

"What?"

"About ten years ago. They think a gangster shot him."

"Did we cause that?"

I nodded.

"I think so," I said.

It seems Divine endorsement didn't have any control over changing future events after manipulating history.

"Well, I'm not going back to 1917 to fix it. What else did Eldridge say in the letter?" Dave asked.

"He wanted me to start a trust and give the money to charities like we told him to do."

"That sounds better than a regular job."

"Because it is better, but I want you to help. You don't have to decide now. Let's think about it for a while."

Dave groomed his Longhorn mustache, and a smile emerged on his stubbly face.

"Good idea. Now, let's get out of here," Dave said.

We left the campground and headed toward Chalons en Champagne. I didn't waste time figuring out why they picked me to find the last page of the *Book of Ancients* despite everything Marcus and Mary told me. I didn't know what my next steps would be, but whatever they were, I hoped it'd be a while before I had to take them.

While we pedaled along the country road with a clear sky above us, a disturbing vision of mobsters, casinos, and dreams gone awry emerged in my mind. I felt a sense that my training as a time traveler and angel fighter wasn't over and that my involvement with Turel and the last page of the *Book of Ancients* was about to become much more intimate.

The End

dorsement! After you read this story, could
about what you thought of it in the Review
you!

WH HAPPENS NEXT?

To get what lies in store for John Harrod, read the first chapter of the second part of The John Harrod Trilogy, *Vengeance in Vegas,* on the next page.

VENGEANCE IN S

PART TWO OF THE JOHN HARR OGY

FIRST CHAPTER

Thank you for your interest in my book, *Divine E*
you please take a moment to leave a few words
section on this book's Amazon.com page? Thank

ANDREW J. WEIS

CHAPTER 1

WHY DID GOD hate me? Was He pissed off at something I did in my life? Was I not religious enough? Was it because I never prayed or went to church on a regular basis? I asked myself those kinds of questions over the last seven years. After Dave and I had returned from our bike trip to France, where the powers of creation drafted me for their divine agenda, my life was no longer my own.

Human beings had no protection against the powers of a real angel, whether it was good or evil, so it didn't come as a surprise that I got help. The angels in Hali called it divine endorsement. Cool stuff, but the novelty wore off for me a couple years ago. Opening time windows any time I wanted became as easy as drinking a glass of water, essential but not exciting.

The time travel ability was purely utilitarian. There was no way they'd ever let me use it to have fun or even fall in love again. That was the hardest part since the angels served up Mary, my one-day fiancé, to a sniper back in World War One. I never forgave them for that, and those selfish bastards never apologized.

Going to different times also grew old, but I made the best of them. I loved being in the 1930s. On this occasion, while I sat behind the wheel of a sparkling new black 1934 Duesenberg Phaeton with its cream leather interior, I listened to the gentle spring rain as it pelted the car's canvas roof with soft wet thuds. I looked through the windshield, mesmerized, as the water drops bounced off the sleek hood that stretched several elegant feet in front of me.

I looked over myself in my black suit, black raincoat, fedora, and felt utter disgust. My best friend, Dave, a transplant from the cattle fields of Dumas, Texas, sat quietly on the passenger side while he checked his forty-five caliber revolver, a souvenir from our trip to World War One. Then, with a sudden flick of his wrist, flipped the cylinder closed with a metallic clink. He adjusted his fedora, took a breath, and looked toward the theater.

I turned and faced the shuttered Noble Theater across the street from us. The Noble was an unfortunate casualty of the silent-era that tapped out thanks to talkies, and then robbed of second chances by the Great Depression. We got out of the car then leaped over puddles to the broad shelter of the Noble's dark marquee.

Faded newspapers covered the windows and masked the inside from curious outsiders. Dave grabbed the theater's tarnished brass door handle and pulled the door open.

We stood in the musty lobby in quiet reverence. I imagined this place in its heyday with crowds packed in every weekend night to see the latest Hollywood offered. We viewed what once was impressive architecture with intricate plaster moldings while the rain rattled outside. I loved these old theaters even after the glamor had worn off.

We stepped toward a graceful marble staircase with moldy, carpeted treads. Gold-leafed crown moldings and celestial paintings on the ceiling reflected the faint glimmers of streetlight that reached through the two-story façade's stained glass lobby windows.

We climbed the marble staircase up two flights to an office where a dim light cast a sepia-like glow through its frosted glass door. I've been in situations like this many times over the past several years, but this time I felt unusually confident. Dave kept a close hand on his gun as we cautiously approached the office door. Thanks to the leaky roof, our footsteps squished on the wet carpet and made a stealthy approach impossible. I pushed the door aside until it bumped against the wall. I peered into the room and found three men looking back at us.

Two Italian-looking, brutish bodyguards arose slowly from their chairs and clasped their hands in the rotted office. Wallpaper and paint peeled off the walls and the swampy stink of wet wood did nothing to lighten the mood of the place.

The leader, a fat cat whom a tipster told me went by the name of Scalia, lit a cigar while he sat behind the desk. He was older, plumpish, maybe fifty or sixty, bald, with a few strands of hair combed over. Whoever he was, confidence ran through his veins like fresh oil through a hot engine.

Dave stepped beside me, cracked open his black raincoat, and hooked it behind his holster like an Old West gunslinger. He exposed the forty-five caliber revolver strapped around his waist, prepared for any action those thugs wished to dish out.

I carefully stepped to the window. My gun, still buckled in its holster, stayed nonthreatening. I split the oak window slats with my fingers then peered outside. The sound of a raucous truck engine caught my ear then I watched as it splashed the Duesenberg. Between the inclement weather and dim lighting, I ruled out the possibility of another sniper attack.

The bodyguards went for their guns, but Dave drew his gun faster and covered them.

"Easy, boys," I said in a soft, determined lilt. "Are you Scalia?"

The man behind the desk nodded then eyed me keenly. He reached for a match that rested in a dish beside an art deco antelope lamp beside a shallow, empty wooden paper bin.

"Ready?" Scalia asked in a husky voice.

"I ain't here to sing you a love song," I said.

"Sit down, wise ass."

Under the shadow of my fedora, I scanned the room. I cautiously sat in front of Scalia's oak desk, its shellac finish flaked off and veneer pulled away from the edges. Dave stood beside me with a clear shot at everyone.

"Enough with the delays," Scalia said. "If you got the goods, then I got the green and a free pass through turnaround in case you do something stupid. Either way, you're covered."

Scalia set a briefcase packed with thousand-dollar bills onto the table.

"Turnaround can't do anything for me," I said.

"Maybe not, but I'm sure the money will. Let's see it." Scalia leaned forward on the table.

I hesitated at first but knew I had to show him eventually. I checked the bodyguards who remained as stiff as concrete pillars. I pulled up my coat sleeve and showed Scalia the marking. He squinted through a cloud of cigar smoke for a closer look. There it was, the seven-pointed star tattooed on my wrist. It was exactly like the one I first saw when I was in World War One.

"He's the goods," Scalia said.

The bodyguards whipped out their guns, but Dave shot them dead. Then, a blinding flash of light burst from Scalia's chest. His appearance instantaneously morphed from human into that of the fallen angel Turel, my declared enemy, who then let out a horrific screech. Turel crouched into an attack stance while his leathery wings stretched wide. He retracted his wings then revealed a long, glowing dagger.

I tackled him then gripped his throat, determined to end him fast. Turel's crimson eyes burned with rage as he rolled me across the floor to free himself. He then flung me off him, and I slammed against the wall. Dave approached for a closer shot when Turel swung his wing wide and beheaded Dave.

"Dave!" I shouted as his head tumbled to the floor and his body crumpled down against the wall.

The rippling waves of a time window suddenly appeared. Turel dashed into it then closed it. I looked at Dave's lifeless body with his gun still in his grip, and then a wave of anger washed over me. I tapped my divine endorsement abilities, opened my own time window, and raced after Turel. Residuals left from closing time windows yielded determinations about the time and place the window led to, and I got good at reading them.

I dashed out of the time window and dove onto Turel. We tumbled onto the sandy, dusty road of a rustic town in the Old West. I still wasn't sure how divine endorsement allowed me to change my clothes to match the era. Maybe I imagined the clothing and the ability took care of the rest. My clothes spontaneously changed from a 1930s gangster suit to 1870s Western wear. Town folk screamed and ran for safety while a mounted cowboy tried to regain control of his startled horse.

I wrangled my way around Turel and snapped one of his wings. He shrieked and flipped me over his shoulder. I rolled away and scrambled onto all fours. Turel charged at me with his dagger. I opened another time window then rolled into it. Turel dove in after me.

My clothes again changed into a bizarre 1970s style with bell-bottom pants with a matching polyester print shirt. I grabbed Turel, spun him around, and threw him into a bank of slot machines in a casino somewhere. Panicked casino patrons stampeded out of our way, shocked at the unusual fight that played out in front of them. Turel backhanded me, and then hit me with a roundhouse kick, which knocked me onto a craps table.

I felt a rage deep inside of me, an unstoppable kick his ass ten ways to Sunday rage. Turel charged me as I scampered off the table. Turel dove at me. I caught him then body-slammed him to the floor. I finally had him. I gripped his neck and was about to give it a quick twist when an attractive woman standing beside a roulette wheel caught the corner of my eye. She had a look of terror in her eyes as she slowly approached me.

"John, watch out," Mary, the one-time love of my life, said. Turel then plunged his dagger into my chest.

Everyone in the casino stood still as mannequins, including Mary. I took a breath then looked at her as her likeness faded away.

"Thanks, Mary. Sometimes a guy can't get screwed enough," I said.

I looked at the dagger shoved in up to the handle then shook my head as the knife faded away. Next came the part of the training that I hated the most, the evaluation.

The casino setting dissolved away. The surroundings then returned to those of the training room in Hali, my home away from home. I sat there on the floor surrounded by the golden shimmer of angelic walls while three squat evaluator angels looked down at me from their high table shaking their heads.

"Hey, try it in my shoes, pal," I said, disgusted with myself with yet another failed session under my belt. I hated the evaluators since they only spoke when I screwed up. They never encouraged me.

Ellis, an Archangel-class Protector angel, charged with preparing me for my duty to stop Turel from getting the last page of the *Book of Ancients*, approached from the other side of the room. Despite never seeing the outside of Hali, I grew accustomed to coming here, even though to me the familiar training room was nothing more than a huge, fancy room with a divine flair. Ellis told me in earlier sessions that Hali was an angelic world, not a planet nor a star, but an existence in Heaven where selected angels became Protectors.

Newly arrived candidates who survived training started out as Guardians. Over time, they'd climb the ranks to Watchers, Archangels, and finally Powers. I never set foot outside the training room, which sucked because I wanted to know what Heaven looked like outside the unfriendly confines of the Hali Training Center. Ellis said that maybe I could see it after I died. However, his offer didn't seem sincere.

I've been coming to Hali for seven years. However, I quit counting the sessions after a hundred. By using time windows, Ellis used his divine endorsement power to pull me from Earth and train me for days on end. When the training session ended, he'd send me home at the same moment he took me. Sometimes it felt weird, as though I lived extra days. Recently, I showed problems with concentration as well as adversarial reading. As a result, I made one bumbling mistake after another.

Sometimes I thought Ellis enjoyed watching me fail. He was hard to figure out. Maybe he didn't like his job much, but from my experience with angels, none of them seemed thrilled about my usual crushing defeats. How many angelical body bags would I end up in before they realized they got the wrong guy to do their dirty work?

"You made several mistakes," Ellis said then crossed his arms. I stayed on the floor and sat cross-legged. The more I trained with angels, the less Hali impressed me.

"Yeah? What'd I do wrong this time?" I asked with attitude.

"You trusted Scalia too quickly," Ellis said with a shot of frustration and a dash of temper.

"I didn't see any reason to wait. Dave and I had everyone covered. Did I do anything right?"

"You've mastered the use of time windows. You can place yourself where you choose far better than any other Interceptor had before you. Your spontaneous clothing choice was perfect for all periods, so there was no wasted time in blending in."

"That's a plus."

"Now, what if he killed you for real?"

I cupped my hands together then spread them apart as I made an explosion sound.

"Exactly," Ellis said with conviction. "No turnaround for locals, not even for out-of-timers like you."

"Don't I get some kind of special consideration? You guys forced me into this crap, remember?"

"We know, but you're also human. When you go to other time periods, you'll be an out-of-time local yet still vulnerable to pain and death as any other human."

"Who are locals?"

"They're people within their own time period."

"Why can't people go through turnaround?"

"Turnaround was made for angels only. Archangels can put humans through turnaround with approval, but that has never happened. If an angel's human form dies, the angel can return to humanity but with severe memory problems. This serves as an important safety measure, a sort of time out, if you prefer."

Ellis walked toward a holographic image of a podium-like pedestal that once supported the *Book of Ancients.* I got off the floor and stood beside him. Strange hieroglyphic-like symbols surrounded the pedestal rim. Then, I touched one, a seven-pointed star.

"I've been trying to kill Turel in this fantasy land for years but can't seal the deal. If I can't kill him here, how can I kill him for real?" I asked.

"Try not to focus so hard on killing him," Ellis said. "Concentrate on getting the last page at the handoff. The page itself affords some protection while you possess it, so Turel won't be able to kill you as easily if you didn't have it. If you succeed in getting the last page, Turel will have no choice but to wait for you until the Redemption Moon."

"How do I do that?" I asked.

"By properly dealing with distraction, like your friend Dave's death for starters."

"Throwing in Mary was a cheap shot, by the way," I said.

I never won a fight in a training session. I tried all kinds of tactics, but they all ended with me dying in some unique fashion.

"You can't let the closest people in your life, living or dead, distract you," Ellis said then clasped his hands.

"Thank God this isn't complicated," I said.

"Ending the sarcasm as well as appreciating the gravity of your situation will help," Ellis said in a loud, impatient voice.

Ellis's brow squeezed tightly. He turned to the podium then bowed his head respectfully.

"Only one page remains," Ellis said under his breath.

"What does the last page look like?" I asked.

"In an angel's possession, the page is in a divine form no man can hold. It has to appear in physical form for them to pass it on to you. There have been other Interceptors, many more handoff attempts, but no success."

Over time, I understood why the angels used me for their purpose. I only hoped they wouldn't lose sight of that. Maybe there was a special reward after all this was over that showed some appreciation for my trouble and sacrifice. My life wasn't mine anymore, and they owed me big time.

"I don't like those odds," I said. "So you guys chose me to be the last one to succeed? I hope you know what you're doing because I sure as hell don't."

"You're our last hope, John, but be forewarned. Evil likes to play," Ellis said. "Somewhere along the way, they might send a woman into your life so be careful. Don't be too trusting of anyone, not even your closest associates."

"Thanks, I'll try to remember that."

"That's enough for today. We'll try again soon. Continue with your weight training to maintain your strength. Despite your life setbacks, we're happy that you've progressed as well as you have even after Mary's passing. It's in everyone's interest that you be as strong as possible, physically and mentally."

"Yeah, all right," I said with an exhausted sigh.

I opened a time window then left Hali for home, a trip that lasted all but a blip of time. The time window was paper-thin, so whatever distance I traveled between Hali, Chicago, or other times was undetectable to me.

The sun shined bright as the Cubs hosted another team ready to destroy them. I wasn't up for going back to my apartment, so I went to Sluggers for a couple of beers and to gather my thoughts.

While I watched the game on an overhead television mounted above the bar, Dave entered, sat on the stool next to me, and smiled.

"Did you have a bad day at school?" Dave asked.

"I can't nail this thing down," I said then gulped my beer. "Every time I'm ready to pop the bastard, I get screwed."

"It can't be that bad. They're doing this to prepare you, you know?"

"I've been training with them for over seven years. Hit me with the shit, already."

I took several swigs from my beer bottle then dragged over a cheap, faux wood bowl of pretzels.

"I know what you mean," Dave said. "On a side subject, did you find the Florida pictures? I want to show Rita."

"I found them. Man, I can't believe you're getting married."

Dave smiled as he patted my shoulder.

"You'll find someone," Dave said.

"Yeah," I said. "Maybe."

I paid the bartender, and then we left for my Wrigleyville apartment.

We walked past Wrigley Field, and as we came underneath the CTA elevated tracks, a passing train squealed to an eardrum-bursting stop.

"So what are you doing in training now?" Dave asked.

"Lots of time travel. I tell you, it ain't any vacation either. I always die. I've been shot, stabbed, meat-hooked, crushed, drowned, and otherwise done in by industrial tools you never knew existed. They even had a fake you. Turel cut your head off last time."

"Classic," Dave said as he chuckled.

"It's so annoying. They always ask to see a seven-pointed star."

"Do you have one?"

"There I do. Here I don't."

I removed my apartment key from my pocket then used my shoulder to push through the vestibule door of my apartment building.

"Can you at least tell if they're good or bad angels?" Dave asked.

"They got good angels doing bad things and bad angels doing good things. They trip me up pretty good so I can't tell who's on my side," I said.

"Sounds like a lop-sided playing field. It's like they're setting you up to fail."

"No doubt the deck's stacked against me."

"So how are you going beat the house?"

"Cheat, I guess. I don't know how, but there has to be a way to beat that house."

We entered my apartment. The pungent smell of rotting food or a dead mouse made me cringe. I tossed my keys on the kitchen counter where they slid into a small stack of junk mail and a tall pile of *Chicago Tribune* newspapers.

Dave paused in the living room and stared at the mess. It didn't matter to the angels if my apartment looked as though a sloppy hoarder lived here or that I didn't think much of refuse disposal. All aspects of my life went down the crapper after Mary died anyway. I handled the occasional foul odor problem scientifically by opening a window. I looked down at the baseboard and saw a small rat, dead, stuck in a glue trap, the lucky little spud. I picked up the trap with the deceased then tossed it in the garbage can beside the refrigerator.

Dave grimaced as he pulled the red drawstrings of the white plastic bag and knotted it. I took over, pulled out the bag from the white plastic garbage can, and set it beside the front door.

"John, I'm not one to tell people how to spend their lives, but you can't live like this, buddy," Dave said.

I didn't feel offended or insulted. I just didn't see the point in keeping a clean house since the angels could pull me into action at any time.

"Maybe I'll straighten things out later today," I said.

I went to the coffee table to retrieve a small cardboard box. I loved Dave, and we had some great experiences. We spent a couple summers working in Florida on a lawn maintenance crew but only thought to take pictures on a couple of occasions. Thank goodness, I kept those pictures safe. It was the end of an era for us when he proposed to his girlfriend and moved out.

"Are you still seeing Margot?" Dave asked. "You haven't mentioned her lately."

"No, that didn't end well," I said. "I've been in a romance coma since Mary died. Maybe there's no room for a woman in my life with this angel nightmare going on. I'll never find anyone like her again anyway, so why bother looking?"

"You never know. Besides, time changes everything."

I went to get a couple beers from the fridge when a time window suddenly opened and startled me. An Italian-looking guy with silver hair, gold necklaces, and wearing a dark blue running suit emerged. He angrily punched Dave who stumbled against the wall then fell to the floor. Before I knew it, the intruder slugged me then pushed me against the kitchen counter where I spun off it and crashed on the garbage bag.

An explosion of terrible pain seared through my eyes as the intruder pounced onto my back. The air rushed out of my lungs as his weight pinned me fast to the floor.

"What the hell's going on?" I strained to say.

"We've been tracking your ass for years, pal, and now it's time to pay up," the intruder said, his hot breath inches from my ear. I didn't recognize his voice, but the familiar clicking sound of a cocking gun hammer sent a racing chill down my spine.

MORE INFORMATION

To purchase *Vengeance in Vegas* or any other books by Andrew J. Weis, go to www.Amazon.com.

For more information on *Vengeance in Vegas*, go to www.AJWeis.com.

ABOUT THE AUTHOR

While writing unique time travel adventures with an angelic flair, Andrew works in information technology for a Fortune 500 insurance company. To prepare for this book, Andrew flew in a Stearman biplane during a presentation of the Chicago Air show. This experience enabled him to get a feel for what it was like to fly in an open cockpit airplane and imagine what those first aerial fighters experienced. A distant relative of Andrew's served with the U.S. Cavalry during World War I and suffered a service-ending injury when a horse threw him off his mount. These personal experiences inspired Andrew's interest in the war and to use it in a new way with *Divine Endorsement.* He's competed in rifle matches and achieved sharpshooter status. While exploring interests in time travel, genealogy, and little known religious writings, Andrew has applied these interests and life experiences in creating time travel adventures with angelic influence, notably The Hali Nonology. He lives in Arlington Heights, IL.